# THE FIGURES OF BEAUTY

**ALSO BY DAVID MACFARLANE**

Summer Gone

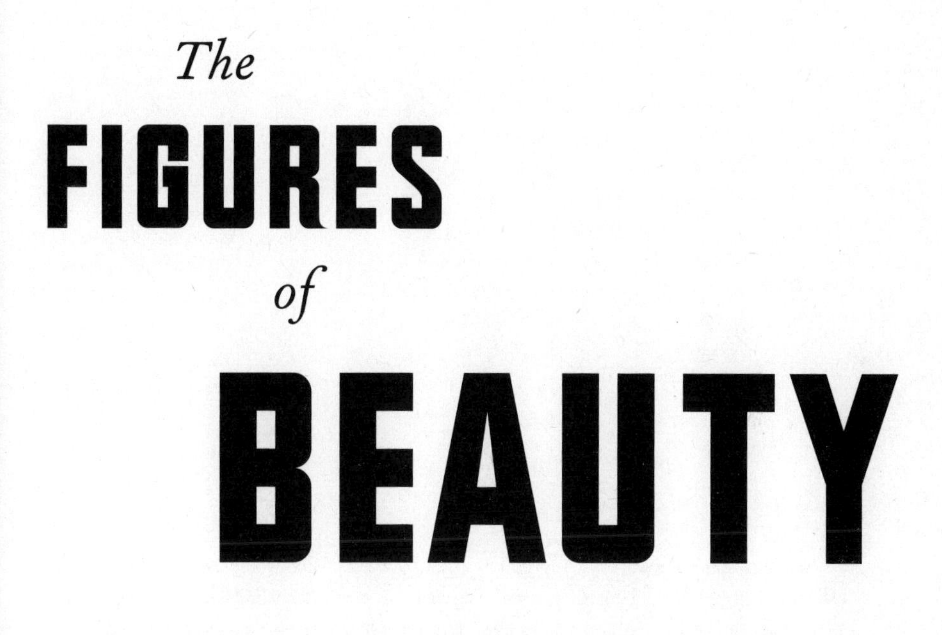

# *The* FIGURES *of* BEAUTY

A NOVEL

DAVID MACFARLANE

HARPER
*An Imprint of* HarperCollins*Publishers*
www.harpercollins.com

HarperCollins books may be purchased for educational, business, or sales promotional use. For information, please e-mail the Special Markets Department at SPsales@harpercollins.com.

Published in Canada in 2013 by HarperCollins Publishers.

FIRST U.S. EDITION PUBLISHED 2014

Library of Congress Cataloging-in-Publication Data has been applied for.

ISBN 978-0-06-230719-4

14 15 16 17 18 OV/RRD 10 9 8 7 6 5 4 3 2 1

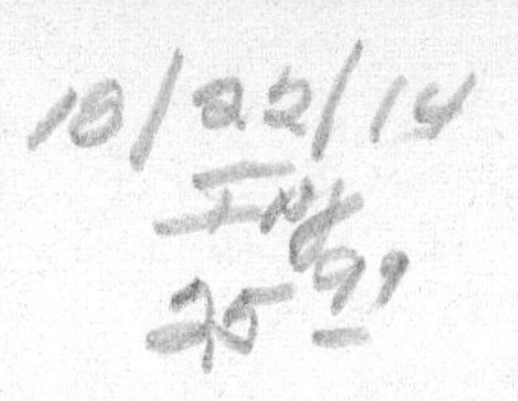

*To Janice, Caroline, and Blake*

*Prologue*

# THE STONE

*The sculptor's work actually begins before the carving—*
*it begins with the choice of the marble block.*

—RUDOLF WITTKOWER, *SCULPTURE*

## Pietrabella, May 2013

Conversation was slow, as it often is on such occasions. But eventually a subject brought things to life. It was the sideboard. Everyone had something to say about the walnut sideboard.

They'd all grown up with it. It was as familiar to them as a relative. It came from Milan. Or maybe it didn't. Some were sure it could command a good price, although some were just as certain it wouldn't. It was inherited from either a great-aunt whose maiden name nobody could now remember or one of their great-grandmothers, although which one and where she had lived was the subject of dispute. Their parents would have known.

It was heavy and dark and ugly—not out of place, exactly, but certainly unlike anything else in the scoured interior of that bright, modest home. When, as a young girl, I visited the Taglianis, I found the grimace of the upper drawers quite menacing.

The house had always been uncluttered and orderly and cleanly swept. It always smelled polished. But it had possessed its own spirit. For many years it had been a cheerful, busy place, and for a few moments it was that brightness that returned.

Suddenly everyone was telling the stories that clung, however inaccurately, to the walnut sideboard. There were some arguments about the great-aunt's second husband. Some stories had to do with a Bugatti he had to sell to cover his gambling debts. Some concerned a grandmother's deafness. She had an ear trumpet. For a few moments the house came back to life.

There was even laughter. The wine helped, I suppose.

And then, just as suddenly, it stopped. The day's glum presence returned. Until my mother spoke the room had fallen back to awkward silences.

The living room clock clicked above us like a muffled metronome. The kneeling figure of Mary on its face, the starburst of heavenly rays, and the spread wings of the white dove at eleven o'clock had always fascinated me as a child.

My mother did not share this enthusiasm. She was half-turned, regarding the clock and its dangling electrical cord with the distaste she reserves for the disasters of the modern age. Her arm was resting with the tentative weight of much the same disapproval on the highly varnished curlicues of a mustard-coloured settee. Her hair is silver now but as thick and wild as it was when she was young.

"You see," my mother announced.

This was in the childhood home of my best friend. We'd been invited back with the family. Clara's father had been lonely and miserable since the passing of his wife four years earlier. He had been sick for almost as long.

My mother hardly knew anyone there. But she addressed everyone in the room with a full voice. "You see," she repeated, just to make sure everyone was paying attention to what she was about to say. "Death makes us happy."

There were about a dozen people in the living room, most of whom were Clara's older siblings, or the spouses of her older siblings, or the grown children of her older siblings. We had just come from the cemetery where, despite Mr. Tagliani's ninety-four years, and despite the fact that his suffering, finally, was over, there had been a lot of crying. Some of the ladies were still becoming overcome with grief from time to time in the house, reaching for the linen handkerchiefs in their smart purses. My mother, whose name is Anna Di Castello, has a talent for the unpredictable.

She speaks with the confidence of someone stating the obvious. She is impatient with explication, believing it to be a diminishment of any statement it claims to support. Nothing irritates her more than a request to supply the meaning of something she has said or made or done. "It is what it is" is her usual response.

In this case, however, the speechlessness that greeted my mother suggested—even to her—that some elaboration was required.

"Stories are hidden in objects," she explained to the silent room. She looked down at the calluses on her own rough palms as if to indicate that she could provide proof of this theory if necessary. "They are hidden like figures are hidden in stone. The dead leave stories for us to find because they know that telling them will cheer us up."

The clock went *tick, tick, tick.*

My husband and our two sons had come to the funeral but not to the house after. They wouldn't have known anyone other than Clara and Paolo, her husband. The gap in age between Clara and the rest of her family was sufficiently great that she had always seemed to be like me—an only child.

I grew up in an apartment in a house just a few doors down Via Maddalena from Clara. My mother, who has always been stubbornly independent, raised me on her own. Anna Di Castello never knew her own parents, or her grandparents, or her aunts or her uncles, or her cousins. In the absence of much in the way of tangible family history, and in honour of her belief in artistic beauty, she named me Teresa after her favourite piece of baroque sculpture.

In fact, the baroque is not her favourite period. Michelangelo is the sculptor she most admires. But Michelangelo's most beautiful female figures presented difficulties when it came to choosing a name for me. My mother is even less keen on the Vatican than she is on electric clocks and mustard-coloured settees. If forced to choose, however—and this was a line of inquiry I liked to explore with her when I was a little girl—it might be Michelangelo's *Pietà* in St. Peter's that is her favourite piece of sculpture. But she wasn't about to be the mother of a Maria.

A word people use frequently for my mother is "bohemian." It's a description she doesn't like very much but does little to discourage.

Just as often, and usually by the same people, she is described as a "free spirit." She dislikes this term particularly because it seems to have so little to do with her work or with raising a child. She was always a good parent—devoted, in her idiosyncratic way, to making sure that I knew that I was loved. She never sided very openly with school authorities, but she insisted that my education was important. Somehow, there was always money for clothes and books and for school excursions to Florence or Rome. Even so, there was one thing she made clear: a mother is what she is, but her work is what she does.

If she's free, she says, she's free to go to bed with aching arms. And if she is spirited, it's because without spirit she would have stopped years ago putting up with cuts on her fingers and with fists she could only painfully unclench. There's nothing easy about what my mother does. In her view, she is the least flighty person she knows. It's for professional reasons that she does not bother very much with the distinction between reality and imagination. She is a sculptor.

She lives by herself in a rented farmhouse in the hills between the town of Pietrabella and the village of Castello, and she spends her days there carving stone.

When my mother is beginning a piece of sculpture—wearing out her arms and scraping her hands with the glances of her battered old mallet off her point chisel—she hovers. She looks as if she is asking questions of the stone as she moves around it. She addresses the marble from this perspective and from that. She says she is looking for the planes and curves that lie between the various angles of her first strokes. These connections aren't always obvious. But my mother doesn't think much is.

Her work is abstract—at least that's how anyone other than my mother would describe it. She doesn't see much difference between her sources and what she does with them. Her sculpture is drawn from the valleys and the sky and the mountains of the place where she has lived all her life. I once read that the singer Joni Mitchell sometimes tunes her guitar to the ambient sounds of birds, and the wind in trees, and the falling water of stony brooks, and I remember thinking that's exactly the way my mother finds the rhythms she looks for in stone. Her work, to my eye, is very good, but—for reasons that have a lot to do with her prickly relationships with gallery owners—her celebrity, like her modest success, has remained local. I'm not so sure this isn't her preference.

She doesn't have much money—a condition that has never perturbed her. The pleasures she most enjoys have never had much to do with the precarious state of her economy. We usually ate inexpensively, but my mother has always cooked with the enthusiasm of someone who loves to eat well. She loves music too—all the more because she never has any money to spend on it. Music was always playing in our apartment, and as a little girl I thought that her badly scratched records were part of her taste for odd, repeated composition. There was a Dizzy Gillespie album that lasted forever, it seemed—until my mother noticed that the same eight bars of "Salt Peanuts" were skipping. On one of her favourite records, the stutter of "I remember you well I remember you well" seemed the vocal momentum Leonard Cohen needed to reach the refrain of "Chelsea Hotel." My mother always sang along, skips and all.

My mother had many lovers over the years, but she never married. She plans on dying, she says, covered in marble dust with a mallet and a chisel in her hands.

With her carelessly abundant hair, her full dark smock, her loosely woven sweater, her bracelets, and her coils of fringed scarves, my mother was an unlikely presence to find addressing that conventional family in that conventional living room on that conventionally mournful afternoon.

But none of Clara's relatives disagreed. Nobody appeared shocked by what my mother said. Some of those present were puzzled. People often are by my mother. But there were—slowly, eventually—a few nodding heads. "Yes," one of Clara's brothers conceded. "Death is what makes us glad to be alive."

And he was right. That was all she meant.

I walked her home later. As if to prove the point she had made at the Taglianis', she was in a cheerful mood. She still strides through the half-hour walk to her house with the energy of a hiker. And as we made our way through the olive grove, and the long grasses, and the patchwork of little fields that lead up through the hills above the town of Pietrabella, she stopped several times to take in the terraces of vines and the slopes of long, velvet shadow.

"Such beauty," she exclaimed at one point. And then, as if she were more irritated than pleased with her own intensity of feeling, she whisked the scene away and continued walking. "It can be too much sometimes."

At the edge of the field that surrounds her house, at a place in the corner of the property, just beyond the overgrown hedge that protects my mother's near-total privacy from the occasional wandering dog and even more occasional passing tractor, there is a marble statue. Nobody knows who carved it. Nobody knows how old it is. By the time you get back to the early twentieth century its provenance already begins to get murky. It had been left to my mother by my father when he died. That wasn't exactly the plan. But that's what happened.

Intermittently, the marble figure is a fountain, but that seems to depend on the mysteries of the water table and the runoff from the hills. Sometimes the low, faraway gurgle of approaching water can be heard from the depths of old tile pipes long before any water actually reaches the poised, waiting figure. It is a three-quarter life-size, partially clad woman bending forward to pour water from the jug she is carrying.

My mother stopped, stared at it intently, and then walked toward it. It was about twenty metres off the path that led directly to her house. This was a detour she often made. She would have been no more attentive had she just encountered the piece in the Bargello.

"There," she said to me. "Look."

The figure's upper body is naked. My mother pointed to the crook of elbow and forearm, and then, with a sweep of her hand, she showed me how the folds of the long skirt echoed the same angle, and how this resonance draws the viewer's eye into the mass of the piece as a whole. As my mother pointed out, you can actually feel the shifting of the figure's weight as she kneels to pour. You can actually sense the tipping volume of liquid inside the jug. The statue is carved with such skill you can sense the immediate past and the immediate future in the poise of the figure's present. You can see motion in its stillness.

My mother had shown me this before. But her repetition seemed to have nothing to do with forgetfulness. It was more a kind of genuflection—one I suspect she made to an anonymous, ancient sculptor every time she came through her gate.

But uncharacteristically, and for the second time that afternoon, she seemed to feel further explanation was necessary. She had something to say that she wanted to make sure I understood.

"Do you think that ever happened?" she asked. "Do you think it matters whether there was a moment long ago when a young woman's arm and her garment were aligned so perfectly?"

Her hand moved back and forth as if she were polishing the air. Her bracelets jangled.

"She is beautiful," my mother continued, "because her beauty does not only echo with what was. The carving rhymes with the space around it. Now. Do you see?"

She raised her hands as in a priest's blessing, although the simile is not one she'd welcome. "Her beauty rhymes with this," she said. And I could see that by "this" she meant what Clara's older brother had explained so plainly at the Tagliani house. She meant the present. Not even the improbable coincidence of love ever surprised my mother more than the amazing luck of being alive.

"It doesn't matter what really happened," she said to me that day. "Tell the stories anyway. That's all we ever do."

*Part One*

# THE POINT CHISEL

*The sculptor mentally visualizes a complex form from all round itself: he knows while he looks at one side what the other side is like . . .*

—Henry Moore

# CHAPTER ONE

## The Morrow Quarry, August 1922

THE ACCIDENT OCCURRED during the half-hour allotted to the workers for their midday meal. Until that time, the day had been routine.

The quarry's foreign name was accommodated by the Italian workers, but only to a point. The owner was Welsh. But his name was usually pronounced as if it were French and spelled "Moreau."

The rain had ended by the late morning. Now it was hot—although hot in the puzzling way that summer days can be at this altitude and in this part of Italy. The mountain quarries of the Carrara region are not far from the border of Liguria and Tuscany, and the air at this height has a fine sharpness to it, a quality that can sometimes confuse clarity and temperature. From the Morrow quarry, the workers could often see for miles up the northwestern coast toward Cinque Terre or to the south, past the distant hillside village of Castello and the town of Pietrabella and all the way down the seaside to Viareggio.

They could see the large, bald bluff of stone that Michelangelo had imagined carving into a colossus as a beacon for ships. They could look to the southwest, out over the flat blue of the Mediterranean toward the distant island of Corsica. The views were detailed, crisp in a way most often associated not with the haze of summer but with the brightness of a very cold day.

There was the rhythmic grate of long-saws, each operated by two men, working back and forth through blocks of stone. There was the hum of the cable cutting its way slowly through the steep extruded slope of the mountain. Long, narrow water troughs cooled the half-kilometre loop of wire.

There was the ringing of hammers, the clang of iron tools, the turning of wooden wheels on the quarry floor. There was singsong shouting to men working high on the rigged lattice of scaffolding, to men bent over saw beds, to men coiling lengths of thick rope and checking cables and pulleys.

There was the occasional scattered cascade of cliffside debris. And it was this last sound—the clatter of falling rock—that carried through the valleys and delivered to those who heard it the greatest alarm.

Just before the accident, five workers had hoisted a quarter-ton block of marble onto a wooden sled with rope, straps, and pulley. Of the crew, three were from the same family—a father and his two sons. They lowered the stone, adjusted it, squared it. They secured it with heavy wooden wedges.

A third son had started in the quarry only a few days earlier. He was too young to work with the crew. His job was to bring tools and carry rope and fetch water for the thirsty men.

The stone could stay at the head of the trestle while the crew had their lunch. The tackle was locked, the leather belts were cinched. The block sat poised on the sled at the same angle as the slope up which young Lino Cavatore was climbing.

The boy was carrying a bucket. The handle was cutting into his fingers. But he remained intent on keeping the shifting weight of the water level. He did not want to spill a drop. The wooden track was very steep.

# CHAPTER TWO

Castello, August 1944

THERE'D BEEN REPORTS of Germans in the hills above Pietrabella. But the sergeant, who was about as level-headed as anyone could want a sergeant to be, wasn't all that worked up about it. His men figured this was an example of his intuition about these things. But that was wishful thinking. It was just that his thoughts resembled uncomplicated equations. And quite a while ago he'd noticed that the ratio of Germans in the hills to Italian kids who wanted cigarettes was pretty much one to one.

"What the hell," he said when the order came down. "It's a good day for a hike."

Had there been a photograph it would have shown the fourteen of them in a stretched-out, staggered line, walking up a stone-scrabbled path that was about the width of a hay wagon. There would be something about the light in the picture and something about the weary posture of the soldiers that would convey the afternoon heat. Their fatigues were about the same colour as the dirt. They had their guns over their shoulders. Their helmets had netting.

The recon troop was heading across a wide, unfolding valley toward one of the villages in the hills above them. They were out of the 371st U.S. Infantry and currently engaged in the comings and goings along the northwest sector of the Gothic Line. It was a nasty business. Everybody wished the Germans would just get the hell on with their retreating.

The first sign of trouble was the silence. In groups of three and four they'd clanked across the open stretch of land between the cover of an olive grove and the village wall. Most of them had been in Italy since Sicily. And by now, huddled at the base of the old stone wall and just to the right of the only gate that led up into the few narrow streets and the one square of Castello, they all knew what an Italian village sounded like. And it wasn't this.

They were all listening for something, anything, from inside.

That's probably why they all heard it. Although it might have been a quirk of acoustics. Because a sound that was so hushed it almost wasn't a sound at all echoed from ancient surface to ancient surface and found its way to them. And what they all heard was the sharp intake of the breath of a baby about to cry.

They went carefully to the first few doors, staying close to the stone houses while spreading out down the cobbled street. But their search became less cautious the more it became apparent the place was abandoned.

They kicked doors in. They went room to room. "All clear," they shouted back to the street.

When one of the soldiers found the baby, he lifted it from the marble vat in the kitchen and said, "What the fuck?"

Somebody found an earthenware jug on a shelf. It was identified as goat's milk by a private who had been raised on a farm in Minnesota. He thought it wasn't that sour. They found some bread to soak. They brought another blanket from another room. It was kind of a miracle. But even finding a baby would not prove to be their most vivid recollection of the day.

The bodies were piled around the perimeter of Castello's central square. That's why nobody in the patrol fully grasped what had happened until they reached the end of the narrow street that led them into it. Even then it took a while to sink in.

"Christ almighty," said the sergeant.

There were so many bodies in so circumscribed a space they did not seem like people. Depending on where in the States each of the soldiers was from, he'd remember the population of Castello looking something like the last ridges of snow at the edge of a field, or mounds of beach kelp, or spills of coal on a foundry floor.

The Americans were standing pretty much where the German machine guns must have been positioned. The G.I.s could see the radius of the spray.

Women and children, all of them. Except for a few old men.

And except for the figure hanging from a branch of a tree in the centre of the square. He was suspended above a few charred, still-smoking pieces of wood. His feet were burned to stumps. He might have been in his thirties. It was hard to say.

"I seen this near Salerno," the sergeant told nobody in particular. "They build a pile of firewood, then they stand the poor bastard on top of it with the noose around his neck. He kicks himself free when he can't stand the flames anymore."

One of the soldiers was holding the baby in the crook of his arm. He was amazed by the force of her sucking. He could feel the swallows through his combat jacket. He was thinking exactly these words: I shall never see anything as strange as this for as long as I live.

Because it wasn't just the baby. And it wasn't just the corpses. And it wasn't just the body hanging from a branch of an old tree in the centre of the square. It's amazing what you can get used to seeing in a war.

It was the goats. They were the strangest thing.

There were about a dozen of them. They must have come into the square after the Germans had left. They must have come through the same gate in the wall and down the same cobbled street as the Americans. And now, there they were: unperturbed by the clattering arrival of the recon patrol in the square. The bells made only the softest and most occasional tinkle. It was as if they were grazing on the slopes of a peaceful hill. They were milling slowly around the taut rope, and the black stumps of feet, and the remains of a fire. It was as if they were waiting for something to move.

# CHAPTER THREE

Paris, May 1968

TROOPS WERE CORDONING OFF parts of the city. The police were securing other parts. The students were in control of other parts still.

All this made for a lot of unusual noise. But Oliver Hughson didn't know what usual was in Paris. He'd never been there before. He assumed the constant sirens were somehow characteristic of the pale, enormous place. He was twenty years old. He was going to travel in Europe for the summer.

Late that afternoon he set out for a walk from the Louvre in what he took to be the approximate direction of his hotel. It wasn't, as things turned out. It wasn't anything like the direction he thought he was headed in.

The rushing convoys of police and military vehicles through the streets were noted by Oliver as he walked, but noted in the same way the immense city was noted. Something was going on. He was aware of that. But because of his eccentric, almost random route through the streets of Paris he never actually laid eyes on how big that something was.

Everything was new to him. Everything was strange. Even the air, he thought, was different from any air he'd known. Smoke came from somewhere in a city that was so big he couldn't imagine from how far it could be drifting. The echoes of amplified voices and roiling crowds were coming from a distance he could not guess. It all seemed grey: part exhaust, part running gutters, part the littered proclamations of the strike, part the long-settled drift of black tobacco.

Oliver had attended to his banking earlier that day at the Société Générale at Place de l'Opéra, signing the required forms, providing the appropriate documentation. He had protested in not very competent French—and to no avail anyway—when he was informed of how long it would take for the Grace P. Barton Memorial Travel Bursary to be made available for his withdrawal. He would have to manage for three business days on the cash he had in his wallet.

He walked for the rest of the afternoon. He stopped in a café for a sandwich and a glass of red wine. And then he started walking again. All evening he had it in mind that he would soon come to a wide boulevard with windows full of suitcases and cheap shoes and with a café on the corner of a narrow, whitewashed street that had a sign somewhere near the middle. His hotel had been recommended in the copy of *Europe on Five Dollars a Day* that his parents had given to him.

But it was very late when he decided to make his way along the cobbled banks of the Seine. He was beginning to think that he would soon feel tired. But he liked the idea of walking along the river late on a moonlit night. It seemed the kind of thing a young traveller did in Paris.

This would prove to be a problem.

"You were on your way back to your room?" Inspector Levy asked. He looked at Oliver searchingly for a moment and then glanced down at the papers on his desk.

Oliver could see his own handwriting on the form on the top of the papers, with the name and address of the hotel at which he was staying. Inspector Levy was considering all routes by which one might walk from the Louvre to the Rue de Saussure. Following the river wasn't one of them. He gave the wan, insincere smile that Parisians reserve for the stupidities of tourists. "You were lost, Monsieur?"

The Seine had been black and smooth that night, only wrinkled here and there with the reflection of yellow lights from the embankment. Traffic had droned in the distance.

Occasionally, a little wave had slapped the dark stone wall below. Oliver's loosely fitting desert boots had slopped along the wet bricks. And this is what happened.

Oliver approached the narrow bridge that crosses from the Avenue de New York on the Right Bank to the Quai Branly on the Left. He stepped out of the soft light of the moon. Then he walked directly into a pair of dangling shoes.

The face, a young man's, was swollen black. His lank, blond hair was long but, except for the sideburns, not stylishly so. He wore a work shirt, rolled jeans, no socks, and hard-soled black shoes. Oliver let out a little yelp that he hadn't heard come from inside himself before.

Inspector Levy had eyes deeply encircled with weariness. Oliver had never encountered a sadder, more tired gaze. Two fingers of the inspector's left hand were yellow. He smoked unfiltered Gauloises throughout the interview.

Levy sat behind a neatly ordered desk. The photographs the attending constables had taken of the hanging body were already in front of him. The darkroom was the most efficient department in the station. Sometimes he thought: the only efficient. To his left was an old typewriter. The walls of his office were a dirty beige, and his tall windows opened onto the courtyard of the prefecture. It was almost four in the morning. The night was chilly and damp. The city's lights, caught by the night clouds, kept the sky a solid, unmoving grey.

The decor had the intended unsettling effect on those the inspector was required to interview. There was a row of six different gauges of shotgun shells lined up across the top of a metal cabinet. And there was a poster for a Goya exhibition at the Orangerie. It was of Saturn. Eating his son.

Inspector Levy passed Oliver the large black and white photographs. They gleamed like movie stills. The policeman watched Oliver carefully as he looked at them. He rested his chin thoughtfully between his thumb and forefinger.

Oliver passed the pictures back.

"Your forearms, please, Monsieur."

Oliver looked blankly at the inspector.

"Please. Will you roll your sleeves?"

Oliver did as requested and rotated his bare forearms for inspection. Levy leaned forward, disappointed with the absence of information on Oliver's unmarked arms. He nodded.

"The body . . ." he said. He switched momentarily to French, as if to make sure there was no confusion. "*Le pendu* . . . showed signs of addiction."

"Oh," Oliver said.

Inspector Levy was beginning to think there was nothing to this. Nothing, that is, beyond the obvious: a tourist stumbles on a suicide. There are many in Paris.

Tourists.

Suicides.

Still, it was a little strange.

"It is curious," the inspector said, "that of all the people in all of this city who might have made this discovery . . . It is curious that the body of this unfortunate young man should be found by another American of about the same age."

"Canadian," Oliver corrected.

Inspector Levy seemed unimpressed with the distinction. "North American," he conceded. "Even so. Two young men. From towns less than two hundred kilometres apart."

"There's a border," Oliver said. "Between them."

The inspector shrugged. "Still. A little strange, don't you think?"

Oliver remained silent.

"And the knot. It would not have been easy to tie, don't you think? Alone."

"I don't know," said Oliver.

The inspector butted a cigarette into a well-occupied ashtray. He stared at Oliver with an expression weighted with his professional obligation to disbelieve all protestations of innocence. He considered the facts. And, as he had done so many times before, he considered possible interpretations.

Monsieur Oliver Hughson had been nowhere near his hotel. What was he doing by himself, by the river, so late?

They fished bodies out of the river almost every night. Hangings were less common but by no means rare. Was Monsieur Hughson there to assist a friend? To fulfill a pact? To abet a lover? Or was there no connection to the deceased and was Monsieur Oliver Hughson there to commit suicide himself? Or—as had to be considered in May 1968—was he a revolutionary intent on an act of insurrection that had been foiled by an unanticipated encounter with a dead junkie hanging from the struts of a footbridge?

All were possibilities. What believable story could be spun from them?

Or was Monsieur Oliver Hughson just an idiot tourist? In which case no story was necessary.

This was more likely, Levy decided. Still, tourists tended not to stay up all night, by themselves. It had been well after midnight when Monsieur Oliver Hughson called the police. But why call the police if you are planning to kill yourself. Or someone else? Or blow up the Pont de l'Alma? Which hardly seemed like the kind of bridge anyone would bother blowing up.

Inspector Levy had a headache. He was very tired.

He was saddened by his inability to piece together anything unusual that might, in an unexpected and brilliant way, connect the facts at hand. From a policing point of view, improbability was far from satisfactory. It bothered him.

But there it was: a coincidence. And the more Inspector Levy stared at Oliver the more he seemed to regret a universe in which things just happened, for no reason. But that's the way things were in May in 1968 in Paris.

"Everything I have told you is true," Oliver said.

Levy considered this. It was an odd thing for the young man to say. Unless, of course, it was true. Then it was not so odd. He closed his eyes. He massaged his brow.

"You are under no official obligation," the inspector finally said. This, he knew, was nothing more than the procedural representation of indecision. He put down his hands. He opened his eyes. "But you may be asked to come back to the prefecture for further questions."

Oliver had been raised to be helpful when he could be.

"That's fine," he said. "I can't get my money out of the bank for three days, anyway." He even decided to risk a small joke. "And the Louvre probably deserves more than an afternoon."

Levy would later wonder if his departure from customary procedure was the result of his being on the brink of some kind of collapse. It was possible. He was exhausted. Every policeman in Paris was.

Or perhaps he was acting intuitively but responsibly. It may have been that with the city about to burn to the ground, he didn't want to waste anyone's time.

He was tired—tired of barricades, tired of megaphones, tired of crowds, tired of television crews and reporters, and very tired of Danny the Red.

He was tired of it all. But he was not so tired that he did not notice something revealing in Oliver's open expression. He was not so exhausted that he could not see something entirely innocent in the way Oliver Hughson said, "That's fine."

Levy prided himself as an investigator. Some aspects of the job he liked better than others, but he had no doubt that his greatest talent was his skill as an interviewer. He was observant. He noted the smallest flickers of expression.

Inspector Levy had long ago stumbled on a truth that, while not universal, was universal enough for police work. He had discovered that somewhere in a guilty suspect's story there is something that isn't a half-truth, or a shaded perception, or an uncertainty of memory.

Levy had a knack for seeing the slight clenching of jaw, blushing of cheeks, or flitting of gaze that revealed that he was getting close to the part of a story a suspect least wanted to discuss—the part that is entirely made up.

There was something in the young man's flat, uncomplicated acceptance of Levy's request to make himself available for further questioning that struck the inspector as material. He knew at that moment that Oliver was not lying.

But Inspector Levy also knew that however convinced he was of Oliver's innocence, his belief was based on nothing but instinct. This would not be something he could pass on to those who would read his typed report after he went home later that morning. Reports contained facts, not hunches. There was the business of the knot. There were the curious coincidences of age and geography. What was a young man doing by the river at that hour, alone?

The officer receiving the file in a few hours' time would not be likely to inherit Levy's certainty.

This was going to be nothing but trouble. Inspector Levy could see that. Useless, unnecessary trouble.

He made a decision. Possibly, it was rash.

He stood and walked abruptly around his desk to Oliver. "Monsieur," he said, "I am going to give you some advice. And I advise that you take it."

The gravity in the inspector's voice made Oliver suddenly anxious.

"There are many deaths in Paris every night."

Oliver turned in his chair and stared with alarm at the surprisingly short, surprisingly slight man. Inspector Levy smelled so strongly of tobacco it was as if what he had been inhaling for the past forty years was seeping from the pores of his skin that night.

"Some of these deaths are suspicious," Levy said. "Most are not."

Oliver was looking into a pair of sallow eyes, wondering where this was going.

"And this death . . ." The inspector gestured back toward his desk and the several black and white photographs. "This death might seem suspicious. To many. It might seem suspicious that in all of Paris it is a living American who finds a dead one."

"Canadian," Oliver said.

Levy ignored this. Such a distinction was immaterial in view of what he was about to say.

"But this death is not suspicious. I can see that. It is only sad. Sad because whatever troubles the young man was facing, he might have been able to overcome them. He might have gone on to live a life that now is not a possibility. Who knows? Young people don't always see things clearly."

It was Inspector Levy's voice that Oliver found confusing. The inspector's stiff, brisk steps from behind his desk had seemed to indicate that the interview was nearing its end. But his mournful tone wasn't that of someone telling Oliver he was free.

This could become complicated. This was the thought that was weaving its way through the dull pulse of Inspector Levy's headache. His colleagues would be thorough. There were too many uncertainties here for them not to be.

But his forgetting to ask the young man to make himself available for further questioning would not be seen by anyone as a very consequential slip-up. Because that's what the inspector had decided to say. He knew that the uncoupling of bureaucratic procedure was often mistaken for its conclusion. Nobody would take much notice. Everybody was tired. It's not as if they didn't have enough to worry about.

"So my advice to you is this: Leave. Leave Paris. At once. You have your passport?"

Oliver did. He had needed his passport to open his bank account earlier that day.

"Leave the way young travellers leave," Levy said. "It's perfectly natural. You've had your visit to the Louvre. You've walked through our famous streets. And now it is time for you to move on. As young people do on summer vacations. To London. To Copenhagen. To Rome. To Barcelona. Leave in the early morning. Leave before the traffic is terrible again. Leave before the students start their demonstrations again."

The inspector brought his face closer. It felt to Oliver that he was being given an unusually candid view of the inner workings of a Parisian police station. "Leave before the morning shift," the inspector whispered.

Oliver stared.

"I am not joking," Inspector Levy said. "Believe me. This is a strange time to be in Paris. We cannot count on things making sense anymore."

Oliver realized he was being dismissed.

"Do not wait even a few hours," the inspector said. "Things will be much better for you if you take me at my word."

And so Oliver did.

He got back to his hotel. He repacked his knapsack. He left.

The hitchhiking was terrible. It took forever. But he found his way, eventually, to a town near the border of Tuscany and Liguria called Pietrabella.

# CHAPTER FOUR

Cathcart, Ontario, June 2009

THERE WAS SOMETHING about the militant swing of the young woman's arms that led Oliver Hughson to believe she had been hurrying in his direction well before she came into view. She was wearing a print dress. She was striding fiercely up through the garden. Her quick steps seemed as if they were the last of a determined journey. He had no idea who she was.

It was a hot day. He was barefoot, vacuuming the pool. It was well into the afternoon. Oliver was wearing the kind of loosely fitting, muddy-brown madras swim-trunks that men in their sixties tend, for some reason, to wear. He had already replenished his drink.

Her hair had a halo in sunshine. It was the henna she used. It wasn't orange, exactly, but the name of no other colour that Oliver could think of came closer to describing it.

She marched resolutely toward the pool. She strode up the stone steps from the garden without hesitation. He guessed her age to be thirty—an underestimation, he would later learn, of exactly ten years.

Oliver placed his plastic tumbler down on a patio table. The ice cubes had already melted to noiseless wafers.

She stopped abruptly at the top of the stairs. She stood at the opening of the hedge, her right hand resting on the gate. She was taking everything in.

"*Dio,*" she exclaimed.

The pool was a surprise. The pool was a surprise for everyone, the first time they saw it.

But she was not going to be distracted—not even by green water, and marble statues, and flagstones, and a stone bathing pavilion, and a graceful, antique fountain that looked, she happened to know, exactly like a swimming pool that had once been on the terraced grounds of a villa in the northwest corner of Tuscany in the hills between the town of Pietrabella and the village of Castello. She had only recently studied photographs in an archive in Lucca.

Because that wasn't why she was here. Because now she was walking toward him.

Had Oliver been given time to make several dozen guesses, and had he been given a lot of hints, he might eventually have been able to figure out who she was. Her eyes were very much her mother's. So was her penchant for drama. She could have warned him.

"I believe I am your daughter," she said.

He was looking into the pretty face of a woman he'd never seen in his life. He'd never considered the possibility of her existence.

"My name is Teresa."

"My daughter?" Oliver's voice rose precipitously.

She said nothing. A good ten seconds passed in silence.

"Teresa?" he eventually squeaked, mostly because he couldn't think of what else to say.

He groped for his plastic tumbler.

He took two fast, large gulps. He paused momentarily, and then took a third. He'd always liked the combined effect of gin, tonic, and hot sun, and it was good to know that not even his present state could entirely withstand its warming, happy way.

He wondered: Was there a response that could appropriately address this surprising young woman's announcement? He concluded there wasn't. He had no idea what to say. But it was slowly becoming clear to him that the orange-haired, impish-looking figure—now waiting for him to speak—could not have been more miraculous had she been hovering above him.

He considered things.

"Well," he said, finally. He looked into the blank air and took a deep breath. "It certainly is a lovely day."

The cicadas were buzzing. The water from the fountain at the end of the pool went *splash, splash, splash.*

# *Part Two*

# THE FLAT CHISEL

*And clenching your fist for the ones like us*
*who are oppressed by the figures of beauty . . .*
—Leonard Cohen, "Chelsea Hotel #2"

*Delivered by Hand*
CATHCART, ONTARIO. APRIL 2010.

I am writing this in the hope that you won't start anything with it. Although there is an argument in favour, I admit. You are my daughter—a woman who has come to know her father belatedly, mostly through letters. Almost a year's worth, so far. So using one might be forgiven. But I don't advise it. Your mother would not be thrilled.

Furthermore. Beyond reading it, beyond remembering some of what it contains, and beyond filing it among the childhood drawings, school essays, and old photographs that families never know what to do with, I would not encourage any further use of something you will receive after my death. Such a document will involve my lawyers—as you are, by now, aware—and that would get things off to a misleading start. I have nothing to reveal to you. It's not that kind of letter.

It was my solicitor—the handsomely bespoke Robert Mulberry (LLD)—who suggested this addendum. He "strongly advised" that I compose a note "of a personal nature" to be included in the estate-related material you have now received. "The swallows will return to Capistrano before lawyers anticipate everything," he cautioned.

Robert works at an old Cathcart firm. In fact, he is the grandson of one of the original partners. But his slight build, livid eyeglass frames, and fashionably tight suits do not immediately suggest the wisdom of the ages. If I didn't know he was a lawyer I'd guess he was eighteen. But then, I think everyone under forty is eighteen. Nonetheless, it was Robert's experience—so he said, with no hint of irony—that had taught him the benefits of including a personal statement in the hefty package of legalese that has now been delivered by someone's hand to yours.

"It is often necessary to explain . . ." I remember Robert pausing as he searched for a word. He rested back with some distaste into an enormous leather desk chair. Judging by its inelegant size, he'd had nothing to do with choosing it. "Nuance" was the word he was looking for.

There is one disbursement from the estate that will precede my death. Your mother will receive one statue from the swimming pool. I am bringing it when I come to visit you and your family in Italy in a few weeks' time. I am planning to present it to her myself. As gestures go, this is a little over the top. I admit that. But Anna did say it would take a miracle. And anyway, I find I like the idea. Perhaps your enthusiasm for drama doesn't come exclusively from your mother.

I'm not quite sure why my giving the statue to your mother feels like the right thing to do. But it does—despite what the cost of shipment will be. I've made some initial inquiry. And believe me: you don't know how densely crystalline a substance marble is until you learn the extortionate charges of air-freighting a three-quarter life-size female figure across the Atlantic.

Otherwise, you are my sole heir, and when Robert first made his suggestion that I write you a letter "of a more personal nature," I couldn't see that there was any need to say anything more than what is already in probate. There isn't any nuance involved. I suppose I could tell you why I've decided to sell my house and the old pool in Cathcart, but that would mean I'd have to understand my reasoning—which, to be perfectly frank, I don't. Not entirely. All I can say is that selling my property, like giving your mother that statue, feels like the right thing to do.

A friend came by a few days ago to discuss my plans. He was very concerned, he said. He is one of those people who take a certain irritating pleasure in being concerned. And partway through our conversation, I realized that what concerned him most was my sanity. Or my lack of it—as his overly gentle kindness made clear was his best guess. I think I managed to convince him that I am not having a nervous breakdown. But he was not greatly comforted.

"It just seems such a bizarre thing to do," he said.

I suppose it does. But I've decided that it's time for me to be unencumbered. It's time for me to be what your mother always thought I should have been when I was young: unreasonable.

I can't see why, after I visit you in Italy, I can't travel wherever curiosity or happenstance takes me. For as long as I care to. I missed most of the world the only other time in my life I set out on such a journey. There's no shortage of places I haven't seen.

And anyway: Why should wandering around the continent of Europe remain the prerogative of youth? I can afford to travel now, for one thing. For years, if I want. I have time. It's not as if I have to get back to anything important.

Getting old is not the strangest thing about age. It can be unsettling. But what is really strange is getting used to the idea of getting old. That's a shift, let me tell you. That's a new perspective.

Twice during the summer I was with your mother I woke from the same dream. It was of my father vacuuming the swimming pool. It was night, which is an odd time to be vacuuming a pool. And for some reason, I was in the water, watching him. He was poling hand over hand, drawing the head of the vacuum slowly across the bottom. The sadness the dream left in its wake seemed out of all proportion to what little I could remember happening in it.

Anna understood this to mean that I would not be happy back in Cathcart. For a long time I thought she was right. But now I am beginning to think the dream was even sadder.

There are retirement homes in Cathcart. I'm not ready for one—not for a long while yet. But they aren't going to go away. They can wait for me to get old enough to come back. That's my plan, anyway. Beyond that, I don't have a lot to say on the subject. Certainly not a letter's worth. And anyway, I'm going to break off here.

It's odd. However carefully I rake in the fall, there are always wet leaves to be dealt with when the snow disappears.

Robert Mulberry is fond of quaint, cautionary aphorism—a stratagem that he uses, I'm sure, to appear older to his clients than he is. It was Robert who negotiated, on my behalf, with NewCorp Development Ltd., the eventual purchaser of my Cathcart property. When, finally, it appeared that they would agree to both our hefty asking price and our unusual conditions of sale, he looked up from their offer and said to me, "Well. I think we can start counting our chickens." And when we met a few weeks later to discuss my estate planning, and when I said I didn't think a letter such as this was necessary, Robert looked at me with the sad expression those who plan ahead reserve for those who don't.

His gaze fell with what I took to be concern on the miniature marble replica of Michelangelo's *David* that I had just given to him. I guessed that the lengthening pause was his search for an old-fashioned commonplace.

I'd prepared a few words of thanks before handing Robert the statue that morning. While he had listened, obviously pleased, I pointed out that while *David* remains one of the most popular reproductions of Carrara's long-established souvenir industry, this model came from an earlier period. It had been carved by someone who obviously respected the beauty being copied.

"This," so I'd explained to Robert as I passed the little statue carefully into his hands, "was created by a nameless artisan among the legions of nameless artisans in the region. But this was carved with skill and pride. It comes from a tradition established before memento became cheap."

Robert had placed the six-inch *David* amid the files on his desk. I could see that he had been touched by my little speech, and by the gift—which may have been why I felt so chastened by the expression that crossed his face when I told him that I wasn't sure a letter to you would be necessary.

"There's many a slip between cup and lip," he finally said. I took this to mean I shouldn't assume what I'm assuming.

My expectation is that these documents will be handed to you years from now, and that the new and unknown chapter of my life on which I am now embarking will, by then, be old and known. The question that occupies me—Will your mother so much as give me the time of day when I see her again?—will be long resolved. Time will have passed.

You'll probably hear from an official calling you from Cathcart—from an institution of assisted living called something like Meadow Vale or Pine Croft. You'll be told that I shall be greatly missed by my friends at bingo night. Although such a prediction is impossible, I'll predict anyway: the estate will sustain itself however long I live. As you see, I have made the necessary arrangements.

But Robert Mulberry is professionally obligated to consider calamity. "Hope for fair skies, plan for storms," he advised. And so, I agreed that I would think about what I'd like to say to you now—under these unusual circumstances. Unusual for me, that is. It's so bright, I am going to have to go down to the house in a moment to get my sunglasses. The weather this April has been unseasonably warm in Cathcart. I'm writing this up at the pool.

By the look of it, the cover won't last another winter. But that's not my problem. Not anymore.

I have pulled out an old chaise from the bathing pavilion and opened it near the deep end. There are no leaves on the maple trees yet.

I've brought a clipboard and some paper up from the house. Quaintly old-tech, I know, but, as you know, I prefer to handwrite my letters to you. I opened a bottle of Prosecco and mixed up some frozen grapefruit juice in the late morning. And I've been sitting here for a few hours a day, for the better part of the week.

I recline, slipping backward and forward in time like a lazy, ancient god. And young Robert Mulberry was quite right. Doing this did help me sort a few things out. Eventually I realized what it is I want to ask you to do for me.

Clouds will continue to pass over the hillside. Swirls of wind will continue to flicker across flagstone. For some reason, I find it particularly difficult to think that office girls will continue to skip across busy streets in their high heels when I am not around to see them. Nobody likes to be left out of what is going to happen. And so, I'm hoping that some faint ghost of who I was might in some way continue too. I'm hoping you might find a way to bring a spirit back to life.

For a little while. Every now and then.

I want to be remembered.

That's all.

Don't worry. It's not as if everything depends on you. There will probably be a small notice in the back pages of the Cathcart *Chronicle* about my career as a print journalist. I was a recognized byline, locally speaking. And I was reasonably popular in the newsroom—which may have something to do with the fact that I never actually worked in it. I dropped in now and then to show the flag. Most of my work was done from home.

The crew at Cable 93 will remember that my Sunday-afternoon art-appreciation program, *For Art's Sake,* had its loyal viewers—dozens of them. I'd like to think that I'll be remembered as an informative television host. But what the crew might recall most fondly is that I was a good deal more relaxed than my fellows. That's because other hosts were younger and under the impression that their cooking or home repair shows would lead to more high-profile network positions. Usually it takes three or four seasons for them to realize their mistake. They can get grumpy.

My easy going professional nature was due largely to the inheritance I received from my adoptive father, Archibald Hughson. I didn't need my job to lead anywhere. In fact, I didn't need the job—which is a useful advantage when it comes to employment.

People are inclined to like people with money so long as the people with money are reasonably understated about demonstrating they have it. I always arrived for tapings with cookies, muffins, and lattes for everyone. I remembered birthdays and Christmas presents. It's the little things that stick with people.

There might be a few women in the Cathcart area who will remember some adventure of the heart with me that sadly didn't go anywhere beyond being briefly thrilling. My neighbours will recall that I kept my front lawn raked in autumn and my sidewalk shovelled in winter. When the summers became very hot, I slipped notes through their doors inviting them to make use of my pool.

So. There will be plenty of others who will remember the longest and by far the most obvious period of my life. But my request to you is more specific. What I want to ask you to do is remember a particular time—because if you don't, soon enough nobody will. It's the time when I set out to see the world and ended up finding your mother instead. Because who knows? It might happen again. It's not impossible.

It was only four months—four months that began the year before you were born. Other than my memories and what your mother cares to divulge, there is no documentation of that summer—as you have already discovered. But that shouldn't matter. Historical evidence isn't so important in this instance. Anna didn't really approve of accuracy.

Your mother thought literal truth was fine. So far as it went. But she thought it left out a lot.

"Michelangelo's sculpture, for one thing," she said. "Look at the *David.* Look at his hands."

We were sitting at the outdoor table, in front of the house she rented from a local farmer. It was after our dinner. Anna was telling me one of the stories she liked to tell. It was set in her idea of America in the years just after the Second World War. It was a crass, under-lit, improbable country—more like a cheap, black and white detective movie than reality. But no matter what I said to the contrary, this was her notion of the place from which I'd come.

It wasn't unusual that a discussion that seemed to have nothing to do with Renaissance sculpture should end up being about one of Michelangelo's great works. No conversation with

Anna ever orbited very far away from the idea of stone. She loved its mass, and its hollows, and the way the Tuscan light sculpted it with shadow. She had the beauty of marble in her core. She'd been born into it.

Marble was as secure in Anna's universe as her certainty that she would always live in the hills somewhere in the vicinity of the Carrara quarries. It was impossible to imagine her anywhere else—which didn't stop her that evening, after our dinner, from sounding as if she'd been away for years, pounding the gritty streets of America, investigating a well-known local story of a young man from the region who'd gone away to get up to no good.

Gianni was handsome as the devil. And clever with a hammer and chisel. He could be a charmer. The ladies went for him. But he had a bad temper and a selfish heart, and he wanted more than he would ever be able to get by carving stone. So he pursued other options. He went to North America as an apprentice in a marble workshop. It was owned by a distant cousin of his mother.

"And then," Anna said with great drama, "Gianni became Johnny."

She exaggerated the shift of pronunciation—as if properly to emphasize the evils of postwar emigration. Things went wrong pretty quickly for Johnny. It came as no great surprise to me that there was an icy villainess. She had hair like an angel.

"Did she look like Veronica Lake?" I asked.

"Quite a bit," answered Anna.

In the story Anna liked to tell there was an old house outside a town near the border where the smugglers met. And there was the connivance of transporting heroin in the skilfully concealed cavities of ornamental statuary. They used an old trick that carvers used to hide breaks in stone.

There was a gun on the kitchen table. There were headlights slashing through the shadows of the drive. This was in the days when sedans were as big as boxcars and still had running boards. There was a body in the trunk.

All this appealed to Anna's enthusiasm for film noir.

But I made the mistake at the table that evening of saying she wasn't being reasonable. I'm not sure why I felt it necessary to make this point. Anna seldom was. I must have been in a particularly small and literal frame of mind. But Anna had a habit of passing from fact to conjecture to invention in our conversations without so much as pausing to acknowledge their borders.

"Was Angel the kind of dame a man would kill for?" I asked.

Anna's English wasn't good enough for her always to spot sarcasm. "She was," she said solemnly.

There was something about the certainty in Anna's voice that provoked me. I told her that she couldn't really know if there was any truth to what she was saying. She didn't really know anything about a handsome, young drug smuggler, or even if there had ever been one. It was already a dimming local legend—one that persisted in the collective memory of the marble studios of Pietrabella and the quarries of Carrara largely because there were so few facts about it to forget.

"Look at *David*'s hands," she repeated softly, and there was something in the quiet of her voice that made me realize that I'd lost whatever argument I thought we were having. So I did what Anna told me to do. I tried to picture *David*'s hands.

"They're all wrong," she said. Anna spoke with her customary confidence. "He carved them out of scale. Crazy out of scale. They are not reasonable. Do you see that? But the piece is true."

So. As you see. Remembering my time in Italy on my behalf need not be an exercise in accuracy. That would run counter to the spirit of the summer I was with your mother. And it is the spirit of that summer that is what I want you to think about every now and then. That's all.

And that is why I am suggesting that you make no literal use of what Robert Mulberry has advised me to write. The presence of Herkimer, Mulberry, Cannon, and Flatt can't help but make things sound more Dickensian than they are. Although, here again, you'd have reasons for ignoring my advice. After all, you are the daughter of two orphans—both of whom have beginnings more suited to fiction than biography.

The circumstances of your mother's survival as a newborn are well known—at least in the Pietrabella region they are. Mine are not known at all—not anywhere. What facts there are reside almost entirely with me—and with what you may remember of what I told you when you came to Cathcart last summer. How much your mother will care to recall is anyone's guess. This letter will be a chance for me to set a few things straight.

I'm wondering if I will go down to the house to get another drink.

I'm thinking I should.

Invent is what people who know something of their backgrounds do. It is not a privilege of the abandoned. Those of us who know next to nothing about our past are stuck with the comparatively dull task of writing down facts. Such as: Archibald Hughson noticed a cardboard box beside his swimming pool on a June morning in 1948.

As much as it was his age, it was Archie's proper, old-fashioned manner—and his loose grey flannels, short-sleeved dress shirt, balding head, and rimless spectacles—that made him look more like a grandfather than a soon-to-be new parent. He hurried across the poolside flagstones.

The urgency in his voice was unmistakable. His wife came running.

"Oh my shattered nerves," she said when she saw what the box contained.

Somewhere there must be a police file that indicates that the complainant walked up through his garden early on that June morning and reported sensing an unusual quiet by his swimming pool. He quickened his step as a result. The gentleman reported that he noticed the cardboard box the moment he stepped through the gate at the top of the stone steps.

And Archibald Hughson might have remained an auxiliary detail in a manila folder stored in a crammed metal filing cabinet in a police station. Even in those simpler days, finding a baby did not bestow advantage when it came to adopting it. Authorities and agencies stepped in then, as now.

"Well, I'm not sure, really," Archie said to one of the three policemen who responded to his phone call. "The birds were silent for one thing. They're usually quite boisterous at this time of year."

The burly cops stood, amazed, looking down at the contents of the box, as practically useless as wise men.

"The blue jays can make a terrible to-do," added Winifred Hughson.

But in this case the Hughsons' stature in the community overcame what red tape there was—in part because the couple felt obligated to overcome it. Winifred and Archie suspected that the swimming pool had not been randomly selected by whoever had carried me there in the middle of the night. The pool was not an obvious place to find nor a particularly easy place to get to. And this, they felt, established some connection between the owners of the pool and the baby left beside it. In the blink of an eye—bureaucratically speaking—they became my parents.

Archie was a high school geography teacher. He and his wife lived in a pleasant, tree-lined neighbourhood. Cathcart, in those days, was neither small enough to look like a town nor big enough to feel like a city. All the same, Archie liked to preserve a few verbal souvenirs of his youth. He had grown up in the country.

That morning, so he used to say, was a break-your-back-hot, strawberry summer morning. The sky was so still it was almost white. The cicadas were already buzzing despite the early hour. If you didn't know better you'd think it was the air that was vibrating. And the sun, just coming above the Hughsons' next-door neighbour's roof, was turning the pool's surrounding red maples the same filigree that he recalled seeing on the windbreak during his summers working as a picker on the strawberry flats out near Cayuga.

It was unusually quiet. But the cardboard box was not still—so Archie could see as he approached it.

"Oh, you were a kicker," Mrs. Hughson always said to me at this point in the story. Her pride in this fact could have been no more evident had she carried me for nine months.

The carton had been placed with a precision that Archie found inexplicable. It was sitting in a shaft of sunlight, at the spot where his gaze always fell when he first came through the gate. It was the spot where everyone's gaze fell. Somehow, the box had been left in the night exactly where it was most likely to be seen immediately in the morning. It was right beside the statue.

It may have been the splashing water of the fountain that

made the half-naked figure at the deep end of the pool the centre of everything. Or it may have been the graceful beauty of her form. Either her bent arm was carved with particular skill or the crook of her elbow just happened to catch the sun at the perfect angle in the early morning. It was hard to know.

There was an ocean of sky and there were continents of trees surrounding the pool, but the centre of that world was always that statue. There was the play of light on the surface of the green water. There was the movement of that reflected light on the facade of the old stone bathing pavilion at the shallow end. And there were a dozen other smaller marble statues around the water and in the hedgerow. But it was always the bending female at the deep end that people first saw. And it was there, on the marble flagstone, beside the figure pouring her water jug, that Archie spotted the cardboard box.

Aylmer. Grade A. Archie always said *tamatas.*

And that—the weather, the time of day, and the brand of canned tomatoes—are all I know for certain of my origins. This was an ignorance your mother found perverse.

The story from which I'd come was likely very ordinary and very sad. Those were details enough for me. But not for Anna. She believed in fate. That's why she believed in a devil named Johnny and a dame with hair like an angel. At least, that's what she said. Their story was true, so far as she was concerned. Like *David*'s hands.

"America," she said, "is what everybody dreamed. In those days."

The more I said I didn't want to know the story of my origins, the more Anna decided she knew what it was. She took pleasure in her attempts at an American accent when she told it.

Angel moved to the window. She watched the car coming in the darkness. The light through the venetian blinds made her hair look as white as her skin. Its smooth gleam was parted on her left, and its wave covered her right eye.

Good, she thought. That bastard Johnny's here.

Your mother thought a love story should have a dramatic beginning.

The Hughsons named me Oliver. They were readers of Dickens. Obviously. It was less predictable that your mother was too. Being Italian and being a fan of so English a writer were not characteristics I'd imagined coexisting until I met Anna. But I was not very worldly. I'd never met anyone like your mother.

It was a discovery I made the first morning I woke up in her rented farmhouse in the hills outside of Pietrabella. This was early in the summer of 1968. Your mother was twenty-four. I was twenty.

There were a few well-thumbed paperbacks under the ashtray beside her mattress on the floor. The one on top was a good deal thicker than the Dashiell Hammett below it. She reached across me. I wasn't sure if she wanted to read a few pages of *Bleak House* or if she was going to kiss me. Neither, as it turned out. She clapped a hand over my mouth and shook her head solemnly in a way that conveyed my need for toothpaste. She was always direct about things.

She didn't want the book, either. She wanted to retrieve a half-smoked joint from the ashtray before making coffee—although your mother never used the word "joint." She favoured a mixture of blond Lebanese hashish and black French tobacco. I'm sure she still does. And she favoured the Briticism, which, with her Italian accent, was further exoticized to "spleef."

Your mother had little patience for the niceties that I was brought up to believe were good manners. And etiquette was something in which I had placed a great deal of stock when I was young. Being an adopted child was sufficiently strange in Cathcart in the 1950s, and even at a young age I could see that strangeness was no advantage. As a boy, I instinctively cast what weight I could against my circumstances by being extremely respectful of convention.

This was something that your mother saw as a challenge. She took it upon herself to educate me in quite a few things that summer. Drumming out my middle-class instinct for small talk was one of them.

I came by it honestly enough—Winifred and Archie Hughson commented on the humidity, and the quality of August peaches, and the milkman's friendly nature as avidly as they spoke of anything. But the first time I engaged in conversational pleasantry with Anna, she cut me off. "Talk to me about something I do not already know," she said. From that day on, whenever I said something that she took to be meaningless chatter she made fun of me with her replies.

"That's what I told to Michelangelo when I met him on the path coming up from the town," Anna might answer. "This is exactly what I said." Her English became elaborately, preciously polite. "Lovely day. Isn't it?"

I'd learned that it was usually good, and always easier, to go along with what Anna wanted to do. So I followed her lead. "And what was Michelangelo doing on the road?" I asked.

"He was on his way to the convent to do some work for the abbess. There is a carved figure in her fountain that needs repair."

But the thing to know about Anna is that her stories had a wider intention than just making fun of me. She believed in the presence of great art more literally than anyone I've ever known. Beauty was a spirit that she took to be as real as the wind. It was her religion, really. The sculptures of Bernini, Brancusi, and Michelangelo—her big three—were not artifacts for her.

She was stubborn on this point. When she was still in school she was suspended for two days. She had refused to acknowledge to the sisters that her answer to a question about Michelangelo was frivolous.

When did the greatest of Renaissance sculptors live?

"Now," she said.

In her way, Anna was always meeting Michelangelo on the path.

I'd reply, "And is his nose as bent as people say?"

Anna nodded gravely. "Michelangelo's nose is very bent."

"And how was he?"

"Michelangelo was in a very bad mood. He was cheated by a marble agent. And he does not think the abbess appreciates his assistance."

So this was how it started. It started because Anna would not talk about the weather. Or the traffic. She felt it was a slippery slope. Next we'd be talking about something we'd read in the paper that day—and at that point, Anna believed, the population of the local bourgeoisie would have increased by two.

It grew from there. It was a game we played. Anna's oblique responses to my perfectly obvious remarks became the beginnings of the stories we told to one another that summer. It was one of the ways we passed our time.

Anna came by possessions easily. Sculptors she knew in Pietrabella often left her things when they went back to Antwerp, or Frankfurt, or Pittsburgh, or Sheffield. It was understood that these would be given back to them when they returned—but often their return to Italy was not as immediate as they had imagined it would be. In many cases, their return never happened at all. They got caught up in other things. Anna's Cinquecento and an equally rusted bicycle had come to her this way.

One departing sculptor left a record player and a radio. But this made no difference to our domestic activities. The farmhouse had no electricity. We sat, surrounded by the hills and valleys, at her outdoor table, smoking spliffs and drinking cheap Prosecco and grapefruit juice in the day, black rooster Chianti at night, and ignoring what your mother regarded as the irritating constraints of time.

The Germans retreated through those hills in '44, backing off the Gothic Line, with the pincers of American, British, and Canadian tanks closing in on them from the south. As you well know, this history is connected to your mother's own story. And it was only natural, given her background, that she should include the Second World War in the tales we spun. "I think the artillery is getting closer, don't you?" This was the kind of thing she said in response to some banal comment made by me about distant thunder or the blasting from the marble quarries in the mountains above us.

Were I to mention something about potholes, she might say, "Charles Dickens passed me on the road today. He was on a donkey."

Dickens spent a few days in the Carrara area during a trip to Italy in the summer of 1846, and your mother was immensely proud of this minor biographical detail. She liked getting stoned and reading a few pages about Oliver Twist, or David Copperfield, or *Jarndyce v. Jarndyce*—slowly, because her understanding of written English was painstaking even when she didn't smoke a spliff, and her appreciation of it all the greater when she did. Dickens was a presence for your mother in the same way Michelangelo was.

"Signor Dickens," she would say, "was on his way back from his tour of the quarries when I saw him. At first I thought it was a statue of a man on a donkey because they were so covered in marble dust."

Your mother liked Dickens because she felt she recognized a kindred spirit. She loved the way the fates of his heroes and heroines disappeared in the thickets of the past and then resurfaced, in unexpected clearings. This made sense to her. It's why she also liked Mickey Spillane and Raymond Chandler. And it was the same with stone: Anna worked with the no-nonsense toughness of a hard-boiled detective. She was always finding connections she refused to believe were coincidences.

I was not so inclined to put the same faith in the universe. But I never succeeded in changing Anna's mind. As she pointed out more than once: I wasn't a sculptor.

As well, there was a weakness on my side of the debate that I found distracting. You must not take this as a boast because, believe me, there was nowhere to go but up, but I was becoming a more confident and a more generous lover that summer. Thanks to your mother. And while those summer lessons were unfolding, I sometimes wondered: if I'd previously understood so little about making love, perhaps I was equally underinformed about fate.

Teachers always take inordinate pride in a local history. I knew everything there was to know about the colonialists who settled Cathcart by the third or fourth year their dates were pounded into our heads at elementary school. I'm sure the same enthusiasms prevail in Italy. You probably have no memory of a time when you did not know that marble is quarried near Pietrabella.

In the summer of 1968 I had come to a place that was all about the famous stone.

With its trappings of tombs, palatial lintels, and crumbled ruins, marble has never seemed new. Even in the Renaissance, the popularity of white Carrara marble had a good deal to do with its automatic allusion to antiquity—an allusion that was never on very solid ground, as a matter of fact. The artists and the great patrons of the quattrocento either didn't know or chose to overlook the fact that it had been weather, not noble refinement of taste, that had washed away the gaudy colours with which the ancient Greeks painted their heroic stone figures.

"Marble has been carved for centuries in Pietrabella's famous workshops." This must surely have been a caption on one of your annual projects for a history or geography class when you were little.

I could have helped. I could have told you that it was Elisa Baciocchi, the princess of Lucca and grand duchess of Tuscany, who, in the first decade of the nineteenth century, saw the possibilities of the souvenir industry. She established the Académie des Beaux-Arts in Carrara—an initiative designed to make the region an exporter of finished sculpture as well as raw stone. Dozens of new studio workshops established in the bustling streets of Carrara were the result.

Elisa's intention was too commercial to be strictly artistic—but she was one of those great benefactors of the arts whose generosity depends on misunderstanding. These were reproductions, after all. Not art. But the idea of reproduction was not yet ubiquitous, and mediocrity was not part of the princess's thinking. Beautifully carved Venetian lions in the public gardens of provincial towns, surprisingly detailed Bernini paperweights on the desks of actuaries, quarter-size *Cupid and Psyche*s beneath the palm fronds of hotel foyers, devotedly transposed *David*s beside Royal Doulton figurines on mantelpieces, and marble busts of her brother in antique stores everywhere owed their existence to Napoleon's youngest and most culturally ambitious sister.

A sad thought—your being little. It's an odd regret to have—with so many others from which to choose—but I am very sorry to have never helped you glue *National Geographic* photographs of mountain peaks, and quarry workers, and dusty-white artisans to bristol board for a grade school assignment. I would have liked that.

When I was with your mother she spent her days—as I'm sure she spends them now—working marble with her battered wooden mallet and her chisels, her points, her punches, her drills and rasps, her sandpapers and emery. And with her tanned, strong arms. I loved watching her work. She was always at the side of the farmhouse, in her shorts and construction boots. She could work for hours without saying a word. She never gave any warning when she was about to speak.

Anna was pushing the back of her wrist across the sweaty white dust on her brow when she said that she didn't think our meeting was an accident. She said that she believed it was marble that brought us together. She thought the evidence was indisputable.

But I couldn't see it. Not at first, anyway. Marble seemed to have nothing to do with what had happened to us.

When you place your hand on Carrara marble—whether a piece of sculpture or a bathroom tile—there is always something sepulchral in the sensation. Its cold beauty seems to belong to the same realm of time as the distant stars.

Anna's warm skin and dark, rosemary-scented hair were the very opposite of marble. Or that's how I thought of her. If there were *memento mori* carved into the frame of those four summer months—skeletons and skulls and Grim Reapers in the overgrown hedge that surrounded the property on which the farmhouse stood—I didn't see them. I've never been further from death. Anna brought something to me that I was simultaneously young enough and old enough to enjoy most completely. But white stone is not the medium I'd choose were I ever to describe what that something was.

On the surface, there were no signs that I had ended up with your mother in the hills outside Pietrabella by anything but accident. But your mother isn't all that interested in what's on the surface of anything. She is a sculptor. Which is an unusual thing to be, really—since every other art I can think of is accumulative in some way. Even writing this letter is an addition of memories. But carving marble is the opposite. It's all about finding what lies beneath the surface. It's about taking away what is there in order to find what isn't.

Anna and I were lying in bed. We were talking.

There were other things we did in bed, of course. And while it's probably wise for me to avoid their description, my discretion should not be mistaken for our restraint. We spent a lot of our time doing exactly what you'd expect us to be doing that summer. But for some reason, I cannot picture anything as precisely as I can picture the two of us lounging in bed afterward and talking.

I had just told Anna of a childhood memory. It involved the church in Cathcart to which I was taken, every Sunday, by Winifred and Archie Hughson when I was young.

Your mother was not exactly riveted. As you well know, she has little patience with organized religion, and no patience at all with the formal trappings of Christianity. Fury at the circumstances of her birth had set her against the notion of a single, benevolent god from a surprisingly young age. A few nuns and priests had attempted to claim her as a kind of miracle when she was little, but they retreated quickly enough from her fearsome tantrums. Even as a girl, Anna made it clear that this was not a battle she was prepared to lose.

She was not, therefore, well disposed to a story of anything that happened to me in a church. But this was not because she wasn't interested in my childhood memories. Usually, she encouraged me to tell her about the neighbourhood in Cathcart where I'd grown up and the hillside trails where I played guns with my best friend when we were boys. She wanted to know all about Winifred and Archibald Hughson. She was interested in how they came to own the old Barton pool.

She also listened, amazed, when I told her about Cathcart as it pertained to the subject of food.

"No," she gasped, when I informed her of tinned spaghetti. "This is not possible. And what do you drink with such horrible a dinner?"

"Milk," I replied.

I'm not certain that she was only pretending to gag. Anna enjoyed being horrified by America.

But listening to my memories of church was not what your mother had in mind. Not at that time of night.

It was late. We'd come inside the farmhouse. We'd undressed quickly.

Those nights in the hills had their own perfume. I know that sounds improbably romantic, but it is true. Drying hay and dewy wildflowers were the most immediate additions to a breeze that, coming from the sea and across the patchwork of gardens and little farms on the coastal flats, flowed up into the hills like a slowing wave. Those evenings—all purple sky and fireflies—were so gradual in their fading, it seemed as if the light would never really go. But it was never a disappointment when finally it did. "A big amazement of stars" is what your mother called our view over the valley. Crickets were pretty much the only sound.

The bedroom window was always open, and when it was late, it was as if the darkness that drifted over us was a quilt of scent. And as the sky above the farmhouse turned from inky blue to black, the perfume shifted its tone—the warm floral notes of summer began to slip away. Night air fell from the mountains.

It was cool as satin. Under the duvet, your mother pulled herself closer. She smoothed her left leg over mine while I spoke.

"This does not seem so interesting," she said very softly into my ear.

I was getting a little sleepy with the story myself—but that may have been a factor. Had I lulled myself into some kind of trance? Was I remembering things more completely, the way dreams sometimes allow?

With your mother nestling in against me, I came to a memory I hadn't visited for a long time: the cold, smooth marble floor of Montrose United Church. This was where I had to lie—uncomfortably, on my stomach—during the Thursday night rehearsals for a Christmas pageant called *The Wayward Lamb.* This occurred during the chilly late autumn and the cold early winter of 1958. And what I remembered about those rehearsals was not only Miriam Goldblum—not only her rich, black hair and the way her choir gown folded over the pale chancel stone when she knelt beside me. What

I remembered was not just her perfume and the way she smoothed my hair off my brow. What I most clearly recall about those rehearsals was that I was flushed with embarrassment throughout all of them.

I told Anna what had happened. This caught her attention.

"There," she said. Her lips moved against the side of my neck as she spoke. "You see." I could feel her smile. Her hand slid slowly across me.

When I closed my eyes, I pictured Anna's hair as the shadows in a forest. I'm sure it was the rosemary infusion she made herself and used to wash her hair that inspired this association. And Anna had a way of touching me that always made me close my eyes. She pressed her hips into my side. "You are obsessed, aren't you?" she said.

Because Anna could usually count on my co-operation, there were not many moments when she wasn't capable of my immediate seduction. She didn't much like doing dishes, and so, despite my instinct for order and good housekeeping, they often didn't get done. When she was tired of our stories, she was quite adept at getting me to stop.

"You see," she whispered. "You can't deny it."

"Deny what?"

"The thing you have. For marble. I knew always that you did."

Anna made it sound as if we'd been discussing the subject for years.

"You have always been obsessed," she insisted. "Haven't you?"

"Me?"

"Totally obsessed."

"I hardly know anything about marble."

"This is true. But you do not need to. What you need to do is remember what you just told me. About what happened when you were the shepherd boy. In the Christmas play. When you became . . . on the marble floor. When you had to lie on your stomach . . ."

Her voice and her hand paused together.

"When I became excited?"

Anna lifted her head and looked at me. She narrowed her eyes suspiciously. She viewed my English the way a customs officer observes travellers. She wondered what contraband of meaning I was trying to smuggle past her.

"That was not the word you used," she said.

But she decided it would do. She closed her hand around me. "What was her name? The one with the black hair and the red lips . . ."

"Miriam."

"And the long black gown . . ."

"Miriam Goldblum."

"Exactly. You have been waiting there all your life, haven't you, little shepherd boy?"

I closed my eyes again.

"Pushing against that marble floor. That very exciting marble floor."

We both had to laugh at this.

But Anna raised her head from my chest. "Am I right?"

"You are," I replied. And only partly because it was the easiest thing to say.

Marble was what everyone in Pietrabella talked about anyway. How busy were the quarries? How enormous were the lobbies of the towers in New York? How much marble flooring would be required by the shopping mall in Hong Kong? Which workshop won the commission for the square in Berlin? How big is the running shoe magnate's mansion on Lake Geneva and how much bevelled panelling will it need? The subject of marble was like a smoke that seeped through everything in that town. It's not surprising that it drifted through our stories.

Much of our information came from what Anna picked up from the artisans in local workshops where she acquired the stone for her own pieces: lore of Michelangelo's time in the area, and tales of accidents in the quarries, and stories of the local marble merchants such as the Welshman, Julian Morrow, whose grand villa once stood, more or less, where Anna's rented farmhouse stands now.

There were the facts and figures of the marble industry that Anna had acquired at various odd, and usually brief, jobs she'd taken around town. She especially liked to cite them when she thought a flight of aesthetic theory needed to be brought back down to earth—especially when the person doing the flying (me) had never so much as carved a bar of Ivory soap.

"Marble," so Anna might say during some discourse of mine on Mannerism or Neoplatonic theory, "was quarried by Roman soldiers. This was a few kilometres southwest of Carrara. At the outpost of Luni."

Shipping marble from Luni to Rome by sea, as dangerous as it was, proved to be far more cost-effective than moving it overland. More than a thousand years later—so Anna explained—this was still the case. Very little of the marble in the great buildings of Milan, for instance, came from the Carrara region, simply because it cost so much to bring stone the relatively short distance overland from the Apuans. In Roman times, stone from Luni was shipped to Ostia and then barged up the Tiber.

My course selection at university was weighted heavily toward the arts—an academic direction that, naturally, had nothing to do with actually creating art. This, so far as Anna was concerned, left me—as it left most of the gallery owners, journalists, critics, and cultural theorists she enjoyed ignoring—distinctly unqualified. For almost anything.

It's unlikely that the Romans initially settled in Luni because of marble. It's more likely that it was a strategically advantageous position that provided access to the Po Valley to the east. Its port was a useful point of transit for trade on the Mediterranean. With the mountains on one flank and the sea on the other, Luni oversaw almost all overland traffic between Rome and the north.

But marble was there. The Apuans had long used it as a building material—and its presence became increasingly important as Rome became increasingly grand. In the second and first centuries BC, Luni gradually eclipsed the Greek quarries of Paros as the chief supplier of marble for Rome.

To this day I cannot see the white stone of an office foyer or the backsplash of someone's fancy new kitchen without remembering being interrupted by Anna when she'd had enough of my undergraduate aesthetics. "Listen to me," she would say. "I will tell you about stone." There was nothing like the history of extraction methods or the annual tonnages for the region of Carrara to get my feet back on the ground.

The Allied advance, and the German retreat, and the bravery of the mountain partisans figured largely, of course, in Anna's stories—as did the miraculous circumstances of her own survival. But the barest of her own biographical facts were so sad, they always obscured everything else about her background: her father had been killed in a hillside skirmish with German troops less than a week after her mother had been gunned down, along with most of the population of her village, in Castello's central square. But you already know these stories well. Most people in Pietrabella do.

My Italian memories are not so famous. Nobody knows them—except your mother. And now you. That's because they have no broader history. Most of them are only memories of my discovery of pleasure. Which does not mean I think of them as trivial. In fact, the older I get, the more important they become. But they come to me as sudden, occasional sensations, over almost as soon as they begin.

The stories your mother and I concocted as we watched the fireflies in the thick dusk are the best way for me to recollect the pace of those few months. They are the best way to remember the day-to-dayness of being in love with Anna. For the truth is: they were lovely days. Time never passed the same way again.

I added my own information to hers—a little reluctantly, at first, but she insisted that I contribute to the stories we told. She always thought they were parts of the same history anyway. Arbitrary distinctions—such as the division between the past and the present—were not of much interest to her. They ran counter to her sculptural instincts. If there was no obvious link between a baby abandoned in 1948 in North America and the Italian Renaissance, Anna would figure one out. So, at her request, I told her about growing up in Cathcart. I told her that the path from Pietrabella to her farmhouse reminded me of the trails along the wooded, limestone ridge behind the Hughsons' house where I played as a child.

Anna found ways—some almost plausible, I admit—to weave our stories together. I was never sure whether this construct was a metaphor, or whether she thought it was close to the truth. In either case, it expressed the same view: she believed the universe had conspired to bring the two of us together.

I am someone who has been described—usually by disappointed women—as unemotional. But the truth is I am too emotional.

As a child, flushes of happiness would pass through me like shocks—often during recess in the green washroom of the school I attended.

Actually, there was no green in it. The floor was a blue-grey composite stone and the walls were brown tile. The copper pipes were luscious with condensation, and the full-length porcelain urinals marble-like in dignity. They were white as icebergs.

But somehow the basement air was green. It was like being deep in an ancient sea. The water fountains, the wooden toilet stalls, and the smell of the janitor's Dustbane created a sub-aquatic effect—clean, cool, dripping, spacious. I would not have been surprised by drifting jellyfish.

Recess was a relief from the blank, thick air of the class-rooms above. Don't read too much into this, but peeing into a urinal the size of a sarcophagus caused a rush of pleasure—a pleasure I couldn't always manage to conceal. The little seizures of joy that overtook me made me shiver—often with disastrous impact on my aim. I contain sadness no more successfully.

At the end of the summer of 1968 I hid from your mother my decision to leave her until almost the last possible moment. This was because I was selfish and cowardly. But it was also because I have no capacity for unhappiness. I couldn't imagine being with Anna when we were not happy. So I made our period of being miserable together as brief as possible. And as awful. She did not take the news at all well.

Later that night, after my telling Anna I would be leaving, I came back to her farmhouse alone, returning from a party of foreign artists in town. Anna and I had gone to the party together—in glum silence. She was furious. But once we arrived, her mood appeared to change. Ridding herself of me seemed part of this transformation. But perhaps less important a part than I might think—or so the coldness of her eyes conveyed the few times our gazes met through the crowd in the smoky, noisy studio. She laughed, and she danced, and she sang "Bella Ciao." She was dancing quite a lot with a young sculptor from Rotterdam. And it must have been close to midnight when I realized they were both no longer there.

I walked back, alone. And the moment of my arrival at the farmhouse coincided with her climax. One of them, anyway. Anna could wake the dead sometimes.

I've always wondered: When Anna was in the Dutchman's arms, with her back arching off her bed, did she somehow know that I was standing on the path? And was what I heard in the thick, otherwise quiet darkness not at all what I thought it was? Was she wailing some Tuscan *maledizione* through the bedroom window at my humiliated silhouette?

If so, the curse would have been a particularly pointed one. Knowing Anna. My guess is it would have been something like: *You shall live your little life in the same little house in the same little provincial North American town in which you grew up. You shall never leave the place where they eat canned spaghetti and drink milk, and you shall never again find a love like the one you have just abandoned.*

Because that's what happened. Unexpectedly, unpredictably, that's exactly what happened. Here I am. Although being a single, reasonably attractive heterosexual who had the words "culture critic" under his byline in the Cathcart *Chronicle* was not always so heavy a burden. You'd be surprised how many women, single and otherwise, are interested in the arts.

Some affairs lasted longer than others. There was one that danced for years around the subject of marriage. But one of the anxieties I've always had about dating is that sooner or later it's bound to involve a couch, a bowl of potato chips, and an old tear-jerker on a movie channel. *Goodbye, Mr. Chips* was the most embarrassing.

I am neurotically susceptible to pathos—which isn't surprising, really. I can't manage sadness because my life began with it. At least, that's my guess. There's not much chance that the history that immediately precedes the abandoning of a baby beside a swimming pool in a town in southern Ontario in 1948 is going to be anything but sad. There would have been a girl. And a boy. There would have been nothing more mysterious or glamorous than a moment of bad timing. And so I always steered clear of any investigation of my own origins—even when, as your exasperated mother used to say, "All the connections are staring you in the face, you *stupido*."

Your mother's interest in my background might seem a writer's impulse more than a sculptor's. But I always thought it was the process of carving marble that informed her—about this as about most things.

Once when I was watching Anna work I asked her what she was doing. My question was actually quite specific: I hadn't previously seen the wooden-handled, claw-toothed chisel she was using. But she took my question to be more general and thus more stupid. "What do you think I'm doing?" she said. "I'm looking for the fucking figure in the fucking stone." She enjoyed demonstrating her command of colloquial English.

Anna believed that the last buff of emery on a piece of Carrara marble was predicted by the first stroke of her point chisel. The intersection where the plane of a question and the plane of an answer meet—despite the countless opportunities for them to miss one another entirely—is where your mother puts her faith.

Your mother believed in the same perfect beauty that

Michelangelo did—the one that he was always trying so furiously to find. It's the frequent subject of his poems: the sculptor, chisel in hand, his face and his hair and his arms white with the dust of his impossible quest.

Anna thought love was much the same kind of search. It was surprising, really.

My upbringing could hardly have been more North American and more middle class. Before I arrived in Pietrabella, I knew about macaroni, and I knew about spaghetti, and I thought that olive oil was something that was kept in a small vial in the bathroom in the event of stomach disorders. Still, somehow, Anna and I answered each other's question. We could lie together for an hour after, our lips hardly touching, our hands hardly moving, doing nothing but looking at one another.

The mistake I made was not recognizing how rare such coincidence is. I was wrong to think I would ever love anyone as much again. But Anna knew. She did not think things happened by accident. Whereas the only thing I could claim as a birthright was the certainty that they did . . .

# CHAPTER FIVE

My father's letter was delivered to me by the Italian appointees of his Cathcart attorneys, much sooner than he had ever imagined. On the envelope, in the fine, black ink he always used, were written the words: "To my daughter. Delivered by hand."

He had imagined that the letter would become an artifact—something that closed a period of his life that he expected to be obscured in importance by the years to follow. But, as things turned out, there were no following years.

It is a strange story—not complicated, exactly, but without the benefit of familiar pattern. And it was my mother who suggested that I use parts of my father's letters to tell it. This was contrary to his wishes, but being contradicted by my mother is not an uncommon experience for those who have anything to do with her.

When I asked my mother for her advice on the matter, she was silent for a good thirty seconds before answering. We had just come from the Taglianis' house after Mr. Tagliani's funeral. My husband and our two sons had gone to the seaside for the afternoon, with their soccer ball, and the picnic I'd packed for them, and the towels and sunscreen I made sure they didn't forget.

When my mother is asked by tourists or by some newcomers in the Café David in Pietrabella why she loves stone as much as she does, her answer surprises them. "Because I can move around it," she says. "That's what space is for."

When she works—as she does every day—she has her hammer in her left hand, a chisel in her right. Her hair is tied up. Its colour is no longer changed very much by marble dust.

My mother works outside as much as possible. She enjoys the play of sunshine on stone as much as she enjoys anything. Rather than by the wristwatches she always loses and the clocks she forgets to wind, this is how she usually keeps track of time. The way light is dispersed across the surface of a rough block of marble accords with her non-sequential sense of things. This is how she marks the progress of her working days. She circles her chosen stone the way a god might circle the void that is going to become creation. "There are many beginnings," she says. "The trick is choosing the ones that lead to the same ending."

But my father's request had been troubling me. "How do I remember something I didn't know?" I asked her.

Her long pauses are characteristic. They are the deep caverns of possibility down which anyone who speaks with her eventually tumbles. When she answers a question she has a way of waiting for as long as it takes for everyone to dismiss all preconceptions of what her answer might be. People often find this unsettling. It is like speaking to a mad person. Not that my mother is crazy. It's just that there is no point in even trying to guess what she might say.

She might well have considered my father's request frivolous. I'd only known him for a year. And it was entirely possible that my mother thought that distance and brevity were the only pertinent realities of the relationship. She is the least sentimental person I know. But it was just as possible that she might decide that my father had asked the one thing that he should have asked.

What I had not anticipated—predictably—was what my mother said. "Nobody remembers anything. They only ever remember what they make up."

There was another lengthy pause. I knew not to interrupt it.

"It's what I said to him always," she continued. "But your father wasn't so bright. I told him always to let what he knows stay close to what he imagines. That's how to be alive." Her tone was matter-of-fact, as if passing on some advice to me about cooking or how to remove a wine stain from a blouse. "But he didn't think he knew how."

She regarded me closely, to see if I'd got her point. She is always a little impatient when she sees I haven't.

"You should write it."

I shot her a look of surprise—a response that seemed equally to surprise her. "Well," she said, looking down at her own hands, "you're not going to carve it, are you."

"Carve what?"

"What he wants you to dream up. What he was finally starting to dream in his letter."

Irritation is never a good debating tactic with my mother. But it's the one I usually end up using. For once my mother ignored my sharpness. She brushed objections away with the same gesture that sweeps the ashes of what she is smoking from her work shirt.

"I don't care what he said. He doesn't want to be remembered. He wants to be part of who you are—the way you might look, or talk, or move, or maybe even write. He wants you to be a little bit like him. Because you're alive. Not because he's dead. That's all. He wants to be heard a little in your voice. He wants a little of who he was then to be a little of who you are. Now."

My mother almost never cries. But sometimes her voice becomes briefly, almost imperceptibly, shaky.

"That's all we want," my mother told me. "That's all the past ever is."

# CHAPTER SIX

IT WAS LATE in the muggy August of 1922 that Julian Morrow—not yet Sir Julian—noticed a couple in the old part of the town. They were on the bridge of the Via Carriona, inspecting a marble statue. Visitors, obviously.

Morrow stopped. He smoothed his moustache and beard with his left hand as if moulding thoughtfulness into his face.

He was wearing a comfortable suit of the palest yellow—the light, rumpled linen a far better choice for the weather than the houndstooth jacket of the gentleman he was considering. It was already hot.

Julian Morrow drew a handkerchief from his breast pocket. He patted his brow. He adjusted a soft-brimmed Borsalino. It was a favourite of his summer hats. He was about to start over the street but his crossing was interrupted by two heavy carriages pulled by yoked oxen.

It was unusual to see tourists. Carrara was off the beaten

track. A correspondent for an English travel journal had recently complained: "Thanks to a surfeit of marble, there is not the shadow of anything that can be called 'society' in Carrara." This, so far as Julian Morrow was concerned, was not a bad thing.

The wagons each had a single canvas strap holding rough blocks of stone in place on their wooden flatbeds. An old woman and a few hungry-looking dogs hurried out of the way.

Morrow's calculations were these: The couple was English, possibly American. Of some means, judging by the cut and quality of their clothes. He guessed that they were in Carrara because the wife—younger, very pretty—had an interest in art or history or something of that nature that the husband, Baedeker in hand, was accommodating.

This presented promise. But what is important to know about Julian Morrow is that his calculations were so coincident with his own pleasure that he hardly thought of them as calculations. It was what he most enjoyed about this place: business was part of the same pleasure he took in the temperature, in the light, in the mountain air on his freshly shaved cheeks. It was a delight resplendent and swift, like water slipping over stone.

There had been some morning rain in Carrara.

He looked down at the toes of his own shoes, poised at the curb. They were the darkened brown of a saddle. They were well worn but well looked after. They were made of excellent leather. The runoff from the morning shower was clear in the marble gutter.

JULIAN MORROW WAS SOMEONE who was good to know—certainly that was the reputation he fostered. He invited people to visit him. That these people might prove to be customers and clients was not beside the point. It was just not an objective

Morrow was inclined to make very obvious. He was too good a salesman for that. They came to see his quarries, to tour his workshops, to stay with him at his villa.

His love for the place was so obvious that it was not so much an emotion that he shared as a characteristic he was unable to hide. His girth was substantial and his shoulders were broad, but these were only part of the reason he was so often described—even by Italians—as larger than life.

He loved the industry and art of the place as much as he loved the hills and the sky. "*Buon giorno,*" he called to everyone on the sidewalk as he made his way through the clattering morning streets of Carrara. "*Buona sera,*" he called to everyone in a café when, after his *digestivo,* he stepped briskly into the early evening light of the square. He broadcast his affection effusively—exclamations at the excellence of a fish soup endeared him to the cooks who prepared it, to the waiters who served it, and to the restaurant owners, who always greeted him so warmly when he stepped through their doors.

He was the best of guides. He took his visitors to this statue, to that bridge, to a white marble baptismal font in a country church that they would never have found on their own. He took them to eat in country inns where there were no menus because there were no choices to be made. They drank the local wine. They ate whatever the kitchen had prepared. The lunches lasted for hours.

On Sundays—the only day of the week when the quarries were not worked—he took his house guests on hikes into the mountains for picnics. He pointed out the cliffside that Michelangelo had imagined carving into a colossus as a beacon for ships. He helped them discern the purple shadow of Corsica on the horizon. He gestured to the south, in the direction of Torre del Lago, the home of Giacomo Puccini.

As he set out the meal his cook had packed for the Sunday picnic, it was Morrow's custom to sing "Un Bel Dì." This was a performance, but he did not let its lack of spontaneity diminish the pleasure he took in delivering it. Pausing, with the cork half pulled from a bottle of wine, he looked west to the distant blue line of the Mediterranean. *Vedremo levarsi un fil di fumo sull'estremo confin del mare.* Morrow's speaking voice was gruff, but his singing was surprisingly musical. He transposed Butterfly's soprano with improbable respect. *E poi la nave appare.* His guests often thought they heard a catch in his voice, so moved was Julian Morrow by the aria that he had decided, seemingly on the spur of the moment, to sing.

The food was the simplest fare, but more than a few of those fortunate enough to experience an al fresco luncheon in the mountains with Julian Morrow would claim it as one of the best meals of their lives. The moist bread, the smoked sausage, the hard goat's cheese, the blood oranges, the bottles of a local white wine so young it was almost effervescent were all set out in the sharp sunlight on a rough wooden table used for the same purpose by the quarry workers. At his customary lunch spot, there was a wall of marble that rose over them. The floor of the plateau was carpeted with wild thyme. The red-roofed towns and the bone-coloured beaches were far below.

As they ate he showed his guests—"somewhere out there"—the distant sea where Percy Shelley drowned. Morrow was then often asked: Could he recite a few lines? He wondered if he could. He poured out more wine for the table. "Ah," he said. "Let me see."

"Ozymandias" was what came to mind. All fourteen lines.

His guests were charmed. Everything about Morrow was charming—his villa but one example.

His residence was a former convent in the hills above the

town of Pietrabella, and his visitors remembered it as the most pleasant of homes. Summer breezes passed through it like billowing silk.

The linens were exquisite. The soaps felt like cream. His servants were present when he wanted them to be, invisible when he did not. The stone floors were cool underfoot as his visitors passed from their toilet to their beds.

The architects and builders, municipal officials and church leaders, developers and hotel owners, aristocrats and society doyennes, landscape artists and decorators who arrived in Carrara as Julian Morrow's invited guests, left as his friends. A miniature *David,* about six inches in height and carved in white marble, arrived after their visit, with Julian Morrow's business card.

MORROW INTERNATIONAL produced chancels, vestibules, lobbies, war memorials, altars, public conveniences, mausoleums, garden ornamentation, tombstones, embassy foyers, bank counters, office building facades, boardroom panels, and the grand bathrooms of royal suites, to name but a few areas of specialization. The brand was known anywhere anyone wanted substance, dignity, formality, luxury, and (it had to be admitted, on occasion) ostentation.

"From excavation to installation" was the company's early motto. This was phrasing that wanted for dignity, so Julian Morrow felt. His wife proposed "Purveyors of Fine Italian Marble"—a suggestion he politely ignored long enough for the company to attain a level of success that required no elaboration beyond his surname.

Julian Morrow had not been born into stone. He had not grown up surrounded by marble. He was raised in a coal town in South Wales, the son of a mine company manager and a schoolteacher. As a young man he had seen opportunity in the construction trade. It was a skill he had: seeing opportunity.

Morrow was already married, with three young daughters, and his building company was already successful when he embarked on a European trip with his wife and mother-in-law. It was, by far, the longest time he had spent alone with both of them together. His wife had planned the holiday six months after her father's properly mourned death. It was in the second week of their itinerary that Morrow was unexpectedly obligated to get off the train in Carrara. For business.

Morrow made arrangements to rejoin the ladies at the Hotel Baglioni in Florence two days later. He was confident he would not be missed. He'd been having some difficulty getting a word in edgewise. He wasn't sure, exactly, what his business in Carrara would prove to be. But he'd never been happier to get off a train.

On his first day in Carrara, he stepped from a smoky café in which he had taken shelter from a passing rainstorm. As he did, he looked down at the sidewalk's curb and realized what it was made of. It was hard to tell if it was the marble itself or the shaft of sunlight on the white stone that could make something as ordinary as a gutter so beautiful.

He did not need more society—although the ceaseless conversation his wife and mother-in-law had been having since Calais made him realize that his view was not everyone's. The teas, the engagements, the babies, the illnesses, and the achievements in banking and accountancy of his many in-laws and their charming circle of friends were not great passions of his. Society had assisted him in his rise, but now that it was without this particular utility it was no longer as engrossing as it once had seemed to be.

He had been longing for something when he stopped off in Carrara. He wasn't quite sure what.

In the chill stricture of Cardiff's sea-weather, in the restraint of boiled beef and parsnips, in the muted browns and civil greys, Julian Morrow was a provident husband, an attentive father, and a successful businessman. But Carrara brought out something else in him.

He fell in love with everything: with the distant peaks and unfolding valleys, with the intimacies of narrow, sleepy streets, with the narrow runs of millstreams below the open windows of bedrooms. He loved the weather. He loved the air. He loved the pouts of acquiescence, the slow untying of sash and ribbon. He found profitable reasons to return. In less than a year he owned his first property.

Now he visited his quarries. Now he climbed to newly opened marble terraces, argued with his managers, strode through shipping yards. He inspected orders, and he joined shoulder to shoulder with his men in the high-ceilinged, arch-windowed studios when they hoisted a piece of stone to their wooden, iron-braced turntables.

He loved mornings filled with work that was so physical it could resist the chill of the mountains. He loved the noontimes subsequent with sunlight, warm as fresh bread. He loved sleeps after lunch, rich in dreams. He loved the soft country ditches and the little roadside crucifixes. He loved the dusk of cypresses, and the hoist of skirts pressed against the stone of ancient walls.

The town of Carrara was, as Morrow liked to say, an acquired taste. It had long possessed beauty that he happened to love: the beauty of work and the beauty of industry.

By the eleventh century, the population had retreated to the hillsides, away from the pestilence of the seaside marshlands. With the rise of the region's towns came the need for building material, and marble was the material close at hand. Those who first went looking for it simply followed the rivers and creeks and streams upward to the sources of the hard, smooth stone. The trail of little water-tumbled pebbles—some pure white, some misty grey—led into the foothills and up into the gorges of the mountains to vast deposits of marble. Quarrying began, and gradually, as the reputation of Carrara marble spread, the town took on its inevitable role. Pisa wanted stone. Florence wanted stone. Rome wanted stone. Carrara devoted its industry to unearthing, carving, and shipping the marble the world wanted. In 1922, that's what it still was doing.

The workshops of Carrara were always busy, the streets often jammed with wagons down from the quarries. The Carrione River ran white with commerce.

Morrow could watch an artisan at work and lose all track of time. It was an idiosyncrasy of his. He loved the noise. He loved the dust. He was far from indifferent to art, but he knew that the real domain of his soul lay in transaction. His visits to Carrara became so extended, the distinction between home and away began to blur. He'd been in Italy for almost two months by the muggy August day in 1922 when he encountered the couple on the cobbles of the Via Carriona bridge.

THEY WERE STUDYING A STATUE. It was made of local marble, as almost everything is in Carrara. But the statue was much older than any other monument they had yet seen in the town.

The man was tall, pallid, with a grey moustache. He was consulting his Baedeker, apparently without success.

The woman's auburn hair was not entirely concealed by a wide-brimmed hat and the wrap of a pale silk scarf tied under her chin. Her coat and dress were full length and cut for walking.

One of her boots had an elevated sole, Morrow noted, and both were laced in a tight criss-cross that made him think of corsets. He often did.

When the woman stepped back to take a longer view of the statue, he could see that she had a pronounced limp.

"Damn useless book," Morrow heard the man say. Morrow took the accent to be American—an error, as he was soon to learn. Grace and Argue Barton were from Cathcart, Ontario—a place with which Morrow was not, he would later have to admit to them, familiar.

He was curious, though. The gentleman gave the appearance of understated affluence. And the woman . . . well, Julian Morrow was inclined, always, to be curious about a beautiful woman.

As the weather cleared, it was becoming apparent that it was the haze of industry that was drifting across the distant peaks, not parting clouds. The sun caught the skein of marble dust.

Glorious, Julian Morrow always thought when he saw this.

He stepped across the wet cobbles. He guessed he would soon make some money. He had an instinct for these things.

# CHAPTER SEVEN

My father, Oliver Hughson, died on a flight from Toronto to Milan in late April 2010. He was sixty-two years old at the time. But this is not—as Paolo, the too-handsome husband of my best friend, Clara, told me—so very unusual. This is not what is strange.

Paolo is a commercial pilot—an occupation that gives him greater expertise in more subjects than most men imagine they have. Which is saying something. The best kind of tires, the most reliable automobiles, the cause of my father's death—these are all subjects to which Paolo provides the answer, whether or not anyone asks him a question.

Normally, this would make me uncomfortable. Good looks and an assertive personality are not as good a combination as a lot of men think they are. On my own, I would probably not be comfortably belted into Paolo's silver Mercedes once a week. But my best friend loves Paolo, and he loves my best friend, and that changes everything. He often picks Clara and me up after our weekly African dancing class in Casatori.

The beat of the hand drums is usually still with me as we return to Pietrabella. I always feel radiant after dancing. Clara says it's the same with her. The ride is so smooth it feels like we are gliding over the Autostrada.

Clara and I have known each other since we were girls. We are very close in age. We played on the terraces of vines and fruit trees that were the steep front gardens of our street.

There is a long climb of stone steps from the pavement to the front doors of the homes on Via Maddalena. The backs of the houses look up to the rooks' nests, and garlands of capers, and the crumbling turrets of the old town wall. Clara's parents, Mr. and Mrs. Tagliani, owned a neat little box of a house up from where my mother and I lived. The Taglianis' home was built in the late 1950s.

We rented our apartment. It is the second floor of a big, three-storey family home that is by far the oldest on the street. At one time the house must have been alone, just outside the old town wall—a primacy that suited my mother's aesthetic dignity. When we moved from the countryside, my mother was drawn to Via Maddalena because she could see that its steepness meant that however much Pietrabella was expanding to its north, to its south, and to its west, our street would always remain on the eastern outskirts of the municipality. Where the houses stopped, the hills began. And where the hills stopped, the mountains started.

My mother's coolness toward the "new houses on the street"—which is to say all the homes except the one in which we lived—might have been aristocratic disdain for the bourgeoisie were she in any way aristocratic. But the upper classes were as objectionable to my mother as postwar architecture. Her politics meander from anarchism to communism to socialism to liberalism. The practical outcome of this is that she can, and often does, argue with everyone about everything.

My mother puts "sculptor" in the space reserved for "Occupation" on the very few government forms she ever reluctantly fills in. But this isn't her complete job history: She had a daughter to raise and so she could not afford to be entirely impractical, however naturally she was that way inclined. My mother never resented the responsibilities of parenting. She just kept them in perspective.

Over the years she worked sometimes as an artist's model. Her English is good, if idiosyncratic, and she was hired sometimes by marble merchants to act as a guide for visiting clients. But she was always clear: these were temporary measures. Her own stone sculpture has always been her most constant employment.

As a result, we never had any money. We were frequently in arrears on our monthly payments to the family that lived, in ever-expanding generations, above the wide wooden beams and below the cool marble floors of our apartment. But my mother can be very charming when it comes to the bills she owes and funds she doesn't have. She is almost seventy now, and she has always been a good-looking woman She still has the posture of a teenager, still works stone, still poses on occasion for artists in town. Her hair is silver but still a thick tangle. Her smile is disarming—as is her disinclination to offer her creditors anything that sounds like circumstantial excuse. Her position is sweetly unapologetic: She is a sculptor. What do they expect?

The fact that we were the only tenants on Via Maddalena, and not homeowners, did not mean to my mother that we were in any way inferior to our neighbours. Quite the contrary. I was brought up to believe that living in a hovel would be only slightly worse than sleeping in a room with dropped ceilings and sliding, vinyl-clad windows. The less said about aluminum doors and white wrought-iron railings, the better.

I returned to live in Pietrabella in 1999, the year I turned thirty, but it was neither nostalgia, nor my significant birthday, nor any sense of millennial significance that motivated my husband and me. It was a practical decision. The boys were one and three at the time. I had to find a decently paying job. We had to find an affordable place to live, with a good school, somewhere within a thirty-minute drive of the community college that had offered Enrico a not-very-decently-paying job as a teaching assistant.

Clara emailed me about a position at the Agency of Regional Tourism. She had already been working there for eighteen months. She had returned to Pietrabella two years before, because her mother was not well, and because her handsome husband didn't mind driving in his diesel-fuelled, four-door car with its excellent sound system and wonderful suspension to and from airports as far away as Milan and even Rome.

My mother does not believe in coincidence. She thinks that fate, not chance, has governed her life. Her ego is healthy in this regard. She was dismissive of all the excitement about the millennium. "Media bullshit" was her summation. But when I called to tell her that we would probably be moving to the vicinity of Pietrabella, she took this as a cosmic sign that it was time for her life to change too. I wonder sometimes if my mother doesn't secretly believe that the purpose of other lives is to provide auguries for hers.

She learned that the German couple who had been holiday tenants in the same hillside farmhouse that she had rented many years before had decided to give the place up. Or rather, the husband had decided after tragedy befell them. His wife had been killed in a highway accident. My mother decided this was not happenstance.

My mother moved back up into the hills, and Via Maddalena 19 became my home address once again. Enrico and I and the boys settled into the flat in which I grew up, although the absence of her battered copies of *The Stones of Rimini* and *The Maltese Falcon;* the coffee-stained, disc-ringed covers of her old Leonard Cohen and Miles Davis LPs; her marble dust; her overflowing ashtrays; and her various works in progress make it seem quite a different place to me. Only the views from the high casement windows are the same—views that I discovered my father remembered very well.

# CHAPTER EIGHT

JULIAN MORROW STEPPED across the curbside stream. His linen suit was the colour of butter. Despite his size, he moved with a surprising lightness of step.

When Morrow introduced himself to the couple he had spotted across the bridge of Via Carriona on that muggy morning in the summer of 1922, he spoke with confident, startling volume. Speaking quietly, being unobtrusive were beyond him. His English, Welsh accent notwithstanding, allayed the couple's fears that they were being accosted by an unscrupulous local.

The man to whom Morrow addressed himself was pale in a way that seemed a result of too much time in offices, not ill health. His eyes were younger than his grey moustache suggested. As was he, actually. The difference in age of the couple was more apparent at a distance than close at hand.

Their romance had its beginnings on the day the publisher of the Cathcart *Chronicle* found himself at the newsroom's entrance at the same moment as the paper's young and, so he had noticed, quite pretty art critic. She had a bad leg of some sort, but it did nothing to diminish her good looks.

He held the door for her. At a loss for conversation—as he generally was with his staff—he complimented her on a review she had written of a sculpture exhibition at the provincial gallery.

His awkward attempt at small talk revealed that he had not seen the exhibit and had no intention of doing so. This, Grace announced, was "absolutely ridiculous." She would take him to the gallery herself the following week if he were free. Her tone was playful and not at all impolite. But she made it clear that she wasn't joking. This impressed him. Very much.

He shook Morrow's extended hand.

"Barton," the gentleman said. "Argue Barton." And then he turned with the measured slowness of a man still new to acknowledging his great good fortune. "My wife."

Morrow bowed, his hat held by his spread left hand against his lapels.

The three of them spoke. And as they did, Morrow admired the woman. He was careful not to be obvious.

He had no designs, of course—and not because she was married. This had not always been an impediment. But Morrow liked to say that he was good at his job because of two skills he had acquired over the years: one was reading stone, the other, reading people. He didn't doubt that he was reading the couple accurately, and his assessment only made the pleasure he was taking in a morning in Carrara all the more keen. He was, he was the first to admit, a sentimentalist.

He was of the view that what is often described as "love at first sight" is, more accurately, the realization of two people that they are soon going to be in love. In Morrow's view, love took a little longer in life than it did in popular song—an opinion that made him more of a romantic than most men, not less. The prospect of love, he believed, is so exciting it can be mistaken for love itself.

Morrow knew he was witnessing this very process. He could see that their affection for one another was on the brink of becoming something deeper.

He admired her lively smile. Admiring women was something Morrow could not help doing.

When Grace Barton was amused there were those who couldn't escape the suspicion that she was amused at them. There was something a little dangerous in her intelligence. When she smiled her teeth were very white, set off, as they were, against her tanned skin. Only the built-up sole of her left boot and the shortened, tilted rhythm of her step prevented people from immediately assuming she was a runner, or a tennis player, or a champion golfer. There was something about Gracc Barton that brought to mind a beautiful pony.

He found the confidence in her mouth and eyes simultaneously attractive and disconcerting—a lack of equilibrium that he enjoyed. Her slender face was of so established a character that any change—fewer freckles, for example—was impossible to imagine.

Julian Morrow felt no threat. He could see that her pleasure—pleasure in the appearance of sunlight on the bone-coloured walls as the weather cleared, in the diminishing rattle of wooden wheels on stone as the quarry wagon became more distant on Via Carriona, in the Welshman in the Borsalino on the old stone bridge—was a pleasure general in nature. It coincided with his own.

Morrow imagined that prior to her engagement to Argue Barton, more than a few of Grace's suitors had made the mistake of assuming she'd think herself lucky to have them. Their vain misjudgment was probably because of her bad leg. Or because her slender good looks were more sharp and boyish than what was in fashion. Or because her lively, assertive face obviously could not accommodate the wide-eyed blankness of acquiescence that was equally in mode.

She'd been underestimated by the handsome young fellows who had called upon her. Morrow guessed that Barton, with the wariness older men bring to younger women, did not make the same mistake.

*Cathcart*. Morrow let the name echo in the business corridors of his brain while he chatted with great enthusiasm about the name of the river, about the dogs in the cobbled street, about the statue they were inspecting. *Cathcart*. Morrow ran the name through his memory of contracts and commissions. He concluded that to his knowledge he had no business in a place called Cathcart. And his knowledge of these matters was extensive.

He owned several marble workshops in town, each employing a dozen or so skilled artisans. He owned several quarries, each providing work for hundreds of men. There were office lobbies in New York and Chicago, mansions in Tuxedo Park and Baltimore, public facilities in Shepherd's Bush and Leicester Square, all built with his stone. Furniture outlets in England and the United States were stocked with his mantels, his sconces, his balustrades, his dresser-tops, his ornamental replicas of famous sculptures. There were even a few reputable shops in London and New York that carried his recently manufactured "antiques."

Did Cathcart have no churches, no town squares, no cemeteries, no need for memorials to the dead of Ypres, or Amiens, or Vimy Ridge, or the Somme? Were there no train stations, no public washrooms, no office lobbies, no pools, or private gardens? Morrow thought that probably there were. And that, perhaps, there could be more.

"I am in newspapers," Argue Barton said.

Morrow noted the plural. He could see that the man, though dressed for touring, frequented an excellent haberdashery. He had noticed the label on the foulard. The shop was in Paris, around the corner from the George-V. Morrow's firm had supplied the marble for the hotel's bathrooms. He shopped at the same store himself. He was familiar with its prices.

They stood at a niche in the old town wall. "The marble statue dates from the late Roman Empire," Morrow explained.

The Bartons were pleased to find so genial a source of information. "What fun," Grace said to her husband, putting her arm through his and tilting her head in attention to their guide.

It was only in retrospect that they realized that this was a turning point in their honeymoon. Had they never encountered Julian Morrow they would likely have said that their European trip had been most pleasant—and they would have been perfectly sincere. Delightful was what it ended up becoming. Morrow's guess that they were somewhere between falling and being in love proved to be exactly right.

The Romans, Morrow continued, were skilled at choosing the finest and most durable stone. "There are medieval cathedrals," he said to Grace and Argue Barton, "much younger than this piece. A thousand years younger, in fact. And the stone of their construction has deteriorated far beyond what you see here."

The statue was worn by time and by weather, but its principal figure was clear. It was a young man. "Poised to leap into a deep chasm," Morrow explained to his new friends. "To demonstrate his willingness to sacrifice himself—his strength, his beauty, his youth. For Rome, you see."

"Rather a waste," said Grace. Her abrupt tone and the brief flash of anger that crossed her face revealed what Morrow took to be strong views on the Great War. But this avenue of conversation was interrupted by the approach of an old man to where they were standing on the bridge. His stubbled face was thin and deeply wrinkled. He had a cane.

It was the old man's habit to stop anyone he passed on the Ponte delle Lacrime to tell them about the dangerous road, and the dangerous work, and about the mournful sound of the horn that announced an accident in the quarries.

"Ca-vay," Julian Morrow translated for the Bartons. "The quarries." He gave the old man a few coins, then waved him away.

The compulsion to transform something fleeting into something permanent is among the most ancient of human instincts. So Julian Morrow said. Had his voice become any louder it would have required a stage and a hall.

"I feel I should be taking notes," said Grace.

Morrow waved off the suggestion. "I've noticed that, for reasons I cannot entirely explain, the clear air of the region makes for a clear memory. Notes will not be necessary. You shall see."

Morrow was working up a speech for the Arts and Letters Club in Pontypool to be delivered at a luncheon lecture several months hence. It was already partly written. But with the judicious use of thoughtful pauses, Julian Morrow was able to give the Bartons the impression that his thoughts were taking form before their very eyes.

"Our awareness of transience," Morrow continued, "jostles constantly against the hope that our stories will last. Possibly the urge to create is nothing more than the wish to contradict the inevitability of death."

Grace Barton expressed some mock dismay at this sad thought—and it was the humour in her eyes that inspired him to continue full-voiced, unabated.

"We imagine that a human figure cannot simply vanish. So inglorious a disappearance seems impossible. And so from antiquity, faces and bodies, heads and torsos were memorialized in mud, in sand, in clay."

The history of sculpture, so he explained, is a history of convergence: of tools and material. Wood could not be carved without flint, just as stone could not be shaped—not finely, not reliably—until the advent of iron. As tools improved, the choice of materials became more specific to the task at hand. The need to memorialize—the urge to create tombs and portraits—became part of something else. By the time marble emerged as a lasting and surprisingly adaptable substance, by the time the tools that could work it became more sophisticated, by the time the marble quarries of Carrara began to dominate the worlds of architecture and sculpture, the motives for carving stone had become complicated. What was being immortalized by artists was not only a noble face that needed to be remembered by citizens gathered in a piazza. It was not only a parable that needed to be recalled by worshippers standing humbly in the shadows of a great cathedral. What was being caught, what artists were rescuing from the relentless stream of the temporal, was beauty itself. This is what sculptors—"from Renaissance masters," said Morrow, "to the most wild of our young modernists"—look for in their labour. "Beauty is what they hope to preserve in the myriad varieties of our marble."

Morrow let this settle in. His face was tanned. He smelled pleasantly of tobacco and shaving soap.

"They change what is ordinary—and what is more ordinary than stone?—into what is divine."

But the Bartons were puzzled.

"Myriad?" Argue asked.

"Isn't Carrara marble . . . well, Carrara marble?" his wife added. She pointed as she spoke to the white, weathered stone that told the story of the young Roman consul.

"Oh, my no," said Julian Morrow. His laughter boomed. He took some delight in its effect on his audiences.

"These mountains are like sculpture," Morrow continued. "Their surface is only the most recent exposure of an intent far beyond our capacity to understand. And we regard the evidence of eternity as we would the marks left by a chisel in an unfinished piece of stone. These are glimpses of something beyond us. Something passing from a past too distant to comprehend to future eons we cannot hope to fathom. What was the Lord thinking when he set the forces of geology into motion that created marble? What was Michelangelo thinking when, with chisel in hand, he first glimpsed the possibilities of his own genius?"

Morrow was an experienced enough public speaker to recognize long before it became a problem that he was losing the thread of where all this was going. He paused—but his confident stance seemed to insist that this was not because he'd lost whatever point he thought he was making.

He smiled at his tendency to get carried away.

"One thing, you say? Marble? No. Here, there is no single marble. There is: Statuario, Ordinario, Bianco Carrara, Bianco P, Calacatta Cremo, Arabescato Classico. The list goes on. And on. There are scores of different varieties of Carrara marble."

Julian Morrow stepped back, into the road, pleased with his rhetorical flight. "I see I have confused you entirely. Forgive me."

The Bartons protested. Oh no. They found it all fascinating.

"And the only cure for such confusion—a confusion that is entirely of my own making, I assure you—is thankfully at hand. I am a fulsome tour guide, I'm afraid. It is a weakness of mine. But I hope you will do me the honour of joining me for lunch. My villa is not far—just beyond the next valley."

He smiled, as if in apology for his effusion.

"The sky is clearing. We shall be able to eat by the pool."

"Very kind," said Argue Barton, "but . . ."

"We couldn't possibly . . ." began Grace.

"Nonsense," said Julian Morrow. "The cool mountain air falls from these hills and, in my experience, it inspires those of us lucky enough to breathe it with a healthy appetite. The noon-hour meal is one of the region's greatest delights. My cook is much sought after. I'm sure you were planning to stop at some point for luncheon . . ."

He paused. They did not disagree. In fact, the mention of food reminded them both that the bread and apricot jam served with their coffee at breakfast were slipping into the distant past.

"Very good then," said Julian Morrow. "I shall not hear otherwise."

# CHAPTER NINE

VIA MADDALENA 19 is the address at which Oliver Hughson first arrived when he hitchhiked to Pietrabella early in May of 1968. His entire European trip had thus far consisted of less than forty-eight hours in Paris and the better part of three cold, wet days on the southbound shoulders of French highways. He'd been obliged to leave Paris much more abruptly than he'd expected—a change of itinerary that left him without money and uncertain where to go.

Returning to Cathcart had not been an option. His ticket required a stay of no less than three months, no more than twelve. And the only address he had in all of Europe was that of an American he had met during his one and only visit to the Musée du Louvre.

It was a brief conversation. The man's name was Richard Christian. They met in the Italian Sculpture Gallery. They were both slowly circling Michelangelo's unfinished marble *The Dying Captive.*

Richard Christian was an American sculptor living in Pietrabella for whom my mother occasionally modelled. He had a large moustache and a pronounced Texan drawl. He was working on an ambitious tableau of marble figures at the time, and he'd gone to Paris for the specific purpose of seeing *The Dying Captive*—one of the pieces Michelangelo had intended for the tomb of Pope Julius II.

Michelangelo wanted to quarry the stone for this enormous commission in the quarries closest to the town of Carrara—in part because the marble was of such excellent quality, in part because it was convenient, in part because he was on friendly terms with Marquis Alberigo, the lord of Carrara. But Vasari recounts that while Michelangelo was in Carrara word came to him that the pope "had heard that in the mountains . . . near Seravezza, in Florentine territory, at the top of the highest mountain, Monte Altissimo, there were marbles of the same beauty and quality as those of Carrara."

This was exactly the kind of unhelpful change of plans that popes could be relied upon to make. Michelangelo suspected some other agenda was at play—some repayment of a province; some borrowing of an army.

"I've been traipsing around Italy," he wrote in a letter to Florence, "borne all kinds of disgrace, suffered every calamity, lacerated my body with cruel toil, put my own life in danger a thousand times . . ."

As you see, he was an artist.

Still, Michelangelo had learned from bitter experience that when it came to disagreements with popes, there was only one rule: the popes always won. He left Carrara. He signed the contract for the stone at a meeting in a dim, airless, second-floor room overlooking the main square of an unappealing provincial town that was a good two-day climb below the quarry from which his marble would come.

After more than ten minutes of neither Richard nor Oliver orbiting very far away from the marble figure that so held their attention, their gazes met, and Richard raised his bushy eyebrows at Oliver. This was an acknowledgment of a kindred spirit. They were two rocks around which tumbled a teeming rapid of tourists.

They encountered one another twice more in their slowly opposing circles before Richard turned to Oliver.

"Unbefuckinglievable," he said.

It wasn't clear that Richard was commenting on the greatness of what they were looking at, or the fact that nobody else in the sculpture gallery appeared to notice it. Richard spoke with a friendly, unfussy ambivalence that often allowed for more than one interpretation of what he was saying. The Texan accent helped.

Oliver had entered the long, high-ceilinged room, fully intending to breeze through it. That's what most people seemed to be doing. The tour bus driver had given everyone an hour and a half in the Louvre. But then Oliver saw *The Dying Captive.* By the time he was talking with Richard, Oliver was already rethinking his itinerary.

The $1800 for cultural improvement that Oliver Hughson had been awarded as the recipient of the Grace P. Barton Memorial Travel Bursary had been deposited, in his name, by Barton Newspapers in an account at the Société Générale near Place de l'Opéra. It was a bank of such burnished *fin de siècle* dignity, its 1940s telephones looked too modern.

Of course, this was long before computers and debit cards. And my father's comprehensive tour of the youth hostels, cheap hotels, and second-class railway cars of Europe would be just as old-fashioned as his bank. Using Paris as the hub of his continental excursions, he would return to the city as his carefully worked-out travel schedules intersected with his need to draw more funds from his account. He would pick up his mail at the American Express in Place de l'Opéra before catching the next train to Amsterdam or Vienna or Madrid. Or such was the plan.

MY MOTHER DOESN'T DISCOUNT the possibility that other lives are ruled by chance. She is sure, however, that hers is not. When she begins working a piece of stone, she says she can't explain what form she is seeking. But she also says, there is a difference between what can't be explained and what can be imagined. She is not alone in this, as she often points out. Michelangelo believed that the hard, dusty journey of carving is looking for the destination that awaits the carver's arrival.

For a sculptor immodest enough to compare her working process to Michelangelo's, my mother was always understated about its results. "Because I'm not very good" is the most common response she gives to tourists in the Café David who wonder, gingerly, why they have not heard of her. But with my mother, an admission of not being good is not necessarily a sign of being modest. Whether she judges herself in relation to her contemporaries or to the sculptor who, in her opinion, is the greatest who ever lived, is not clear.

*The Dying Captive* was not a name chosen by Michelangelo. Death is not at all what it brings to mind to anyone who stops in the Italian Sculpture Gallery and actually looks at it. The name must have been dreamed up by somebody—a priest is my mother's predictable guess—intent on deflecting attention from the solitary erotic pleasure that appears to be the figure's dreamy preoccupation.

Richard and my father spoke for only a few minutes, but that was time enough. Richard talked about a piece of sculpture he was beginning in his studio. It was going to be called *The Pope's Tomb.* It would be a dozen figures, each one mounted in a niche of a rectangular stone portico. The whole grouping was going to be about as big as a freezer—a dimension about which Richard's gallery in Houston had serious misgivings. But Richard didn't think he could make it any smaller. It was on the large size, he admitted, for a private collection. But it was small for a pope's tomb.

Richard told Oliver that he should look him up if ever he got to Italy. As it happened, Oliver had every intention of getting to Italy. He'd even planned to stop in Carrara. He was aware of a connection with the old Barton pool. Archie Hughson had spoken of it.

Richard said he was going to need male models for *The Pope's Tomb.* "Maybe I can give you some work," he said. But this was not so much an offer as a way of ending a conversation. He didn't expect to see Oliver again. Nor did Oliver expect to take Richard up on his offer.

Richard wrote his address on a scrap of paper that he dug out of a well-worn brown leather wallet: *Via Maddalena 19, Pietrabella, (Lucca), Italia.*

And that, pretty much, is everything Oliver Hughson knew about Richard Christian when, very early the next morning, Oliver left a Paris police station, returned to his hotel, packed his knapsack, and set out to find him.

THAT'S HOW IT HAPPENED. My father walked into the Italian Sculpture Gallery on a fine day in early May 1968, and *The*

*Dying Captive* obliged him to reconsider his busy, transcontinental travel plans. This was a recalibration that he considered unhurriedly in the corridors of the Louvre—a delay that caused him to miss his tour bus, or at least that caused him not to be careful about catching it. And missing the tour bus meant that he could wander Paris on his own after the Louvre closed. Which is what he did for the rest of the afternoon, and for the evening, and into the night.

As the last hours of his first day on the continent of Europe passed, Oliver's meandering return to his hotel had more to do with wishful thinking than actual navigation. Not that he minded. Paris is a good city to walk through at night—especially if you are young and have never been there before. He was pleased with his decision. He was happy to be in no hurry.

Every street was new to him and yet, in the manner of dreams and black and white films, not unfamiliar. He kept walking. And he was still walking a little before one in the morning. He was beginning to think that if he were ever going to get to bed, he would have to admit that he didn't know where he was. Even he knew his hotel was nowhere near the river.

A piece of the footbridge might have fallen loose. A cable could have been left dangling. But neither was the case. There was just enough light to make out what was there. But even before Oliver's summer abruptly changed from anything like what he'd imagined it might be, he knew without looking up what the stillness was, suspended so silently in the darkness above him. There is something unmistakable about the thin, hard smell of leather soles.

# CHAPTER TEN

THIS IS HOW THINGS had always been in the mountains. In as long ago as Michelangelo's time not much was different. This is how it looked then. And this is how it looked in the summer of 1922.

Even the sounds would have been similar. Michelangelo would have watched blocks of similar size, ready to be slowly lowered on the same kind of wooden trestle with the same great creaks of leather and rope. Except for the long loop of cutting cable—a technological advance introduced by a Belgian quarry owner to the Carrara region in the late nineteenth century—little else in the methods of extraction of stone had changed in centuries.

The stone that the Morrow crew had loaded onto the wooden sled was rough with a crust of rusty brown that a grind and a polish would remove quickly enough. The quarter-ton block was the size of a large icebox—though solid. It was without interior flaw. Or so it appeared. No one ever knew for sure.

There were tests to ascertain stone's internal consistency. The ratio of a block's weight to its dimensions was informative. There were often visible clues in the quarry wall from which a block had been cut. Sometimes just the varying sound of a hammer struck against a block could reveal the existence of a hollow flaw at the core. But the piece the crew had strapped to the sled seemed solid.

Solid. But not safe, exactly.

Like all marble, the block was so densely crystalline, its mass was dangerous. Whether revolving slowly in the traces by which it had been hoisted from the quarry floor or poised for its descent on the sled, it was intent on returning not so much to the ground as to the centre of the earth.

The trestle on which the sled would be so slowly and carefully lowered was constructed on a built-up ledge of rubble. It was lined with a system of winches, ropes, and pulleys that reached down a quarter of a mile to the quarry's loading area, to the wagon and to the sleeping driver and to the team of oxen waiting below. From there the stone would be transported down the switchback mountain roads to Carrara.

Few of the workers in the Morrow quarry had ever been to the city. The cost of such a trip was beyond them. Even though they had jobs—difficult jobs, dangerous jobs, jobs that demanded diligence and ingenuity and practical intelligence, and jobs that, for generations, had produced a good profit for the quarry owners—the workers were poor. Too poor for salt, so the saying went.

They were all from the villages that are tucked high in the folds of the surrounding hills. Few of them were ever out of sight of the white gashes that for centuries had been cut into the sides of the peaks. The villages were small places of cobbled streets and skewed walls. They were built-up levels of beamed floors and wide sills and tiled roofs and old, heavy wooden doors.

These towns would come to be known as picturesque—a notion that would have been preposterous to the people who had always lived there. They didn't see anything picturesque in the cold air, in the winter sleet, or in labours only relieved by sleep. There was nothing pretty in the flat tolling of the bells of the stone churches. For them, there was nothing quaint about the cool marble vats in which they seasoned the pork fat that the quarry workers spread on their hunks of bread on their midday break. There was no romance in the deep windows, or the peeling walls, or the slopes of vines that they knew too well ever to think of.

Everything in the village could be seen in a five-minute walk. Here, barefoot children played in the cobbled streets. Their voices carried far down the valley. Here, wooden barrow wheels rattled past the old tree at the centre of the piazza.

Here, the women smacked their wet washing on the flats beside a shallow stream just beyond the village wall. Babies cried. Old men argued. Dogs barked.

Pots clattered, pans sizzled. Knives *thunk*ed through onion on wooden counters. The voices of mothers and daughters and grandmothers came clear as the air from kitchen windows.

Past the worn marble flagstones where the town's families gathered after Mass, beyond the baptisteries and the stone crucifixes of the old churches, at the fenced and tended verges of the modest parishes where weddings and holy days were celebrated and weeping mothers and wives were never comforted, the rows of tombstones stood like crooked teeth. The names of the men who had been killed in the quarries were carved in the same white stone they had died trying to obtain.

The crew that stopped for lunch that noon hour, like all quarry workers, knew extremes of temperature that were particularly cruel. But they didn't separate work from the weather in which the work was done. They complained of neither the cold nor the heat. They might as well have complained about gravity.

None of them had spent any time in Carrara's cozy cafés, its comfortable art institute, its gale-free cathedrals, or its shaded, sheltered marble studios. Only the quarry's timekeeper was from Carrara, and the workers conjured the unfriendly ways of the town largely from the evidence of his formal, rounded accent, his official cap, and the way he stood at the open gate with his pocket watch in hand, threatening to report anyone who was even a few seconds late.

The Morrow workers had all been in the quarries from the time they were teenagers. Except for Sundays and on Christmas, they worked every day, leaving their homes each morning and walking through the woods, upward, along the secret network of damp paths that they knew well enough to follow in the dark. They carried coils of thick rope, their own heavy tools, and the oiled canvas shoulder bags that contained their carefully wrapped drinking cup, and maybe some wine, and a pouch of tobacco, and their bread and seasoned lard. Some of the younger men, having never worn a pair of shoes in their lives until the day they started work, tied their workboots together and slung them around their necks because they still found it more comfortable to be barefoot for the two-hour walk to the quarry.

As they walked to work the sky lightened—but not very much. Rising above them, through the trees, was not the brightening morning but the silhouette of the mountain range they were heading toward, the dawn still beyond it. Even though their journey was eastward, it was as if they were on their way back into a remnant of the night.

It was too early for even the most boisterous among them to whistle or sing a song. They were shadows passing through the trees. Except for the occasional clank of tools in their haversacks or a rustling of leaves against their coarse trousers, they moved in silence. They used the woods because were they to use the gravel roads, they'd be charged a toll by the company for their passage.

Gradually, the men of one village joined the men of another, and then another, along the forks of the paths they followed, until, just before the hour they were required to arrive for work, the entire force of the quarry emerged—the woods suddenly revealing dozens of men. It was like a trick. It was as if the mountainside were able to perform some ingenious sleight of hand. In old fedoras and vests and heavy, worsted pants, they appeared all at once, from out of nowhere, sliding down through bushes and bramble to the gravel at the quarry's front gates.

AMONG THEM THAT DAY WAS A BOY. It was the third day of his first week at work. Lino Cavatore had a thin face and tousled hair. He was younger than the rest—only twelve. He was working where his father and his brothers worked. And so he was very proud.

But it was true: he carried a slight hollow of sadness in his pride. But only slight. He knew you can't choose your work any more than you can choose your family. He was what the men called a *bagash*—a water boy from the village of Castello. But the Morrow quarry is not what he would have chosen. Were the choice his.

There was a gully beyond the village wall, near the stream where the women did their laundry. Good clay could be found there. As a very young boy Lino had shown a talent for moulding figures and faces. The likenesses were often remarkable. But his family had no connections with the workshops of Carrara. The studios might as well have been on the moon. Lino had no way of learning about sculpture. His father and his two older brothers worked in the quarries. As did his uncles. As did his cousins.

Men learned as they worked. This was on-the-job training that did not often allow for mistakes. In the quarries there was no apprentice system beyond the watchfulness that an older brother might keep for a younger, or a father for a son. The only position that gave a young boy an opportunity to learn something about the quarries before actually working them was that of the *bagash*, hired to fetch tools and rope, and to bring water up to the hot, thirsty men.

Shortly before noon, Lino Cavatore was hurrying through the staging area. He passed oxen and the clusters of drivers. He greeted a cousin. He said good morning to one of the foremen.

Lino's rushed intensity made people smile. There was something about how seriously he undertook his tasks in the quarry that made him seem not like a boy so much as a boy pretending to be a busy old man.

Lino's father and his brothers were in the crew that had just strapped a slab of stone to a wooden sled. Lino had looked up in time to see them hammer the wedges into place. They would soon be sitting down at their wooden table in the cool shade of a marble wall.

The water was a concession to the workers. It was a symbol of the owner's concern for their welfare—or so the owner's managers who had devised the system imagined. It came from a mountain stream. A young woman doled out the buckets to the boys who were sent down to get them.

Lino Cavatore looked up the quarter-mile of incline. His boots were still new and uncomfortable. The wire handle was already digging into his palm.

He decided to follow the slope of the sled tracks. It would be faster than the switchback path. He heard the timekeeper's bell strike noon. He started up.

# CHAPTER ELEVEN

RICHARD CHRISTIAN WAS OUR PREDECESSOR in the flat on Via Maddalena, and it was Richard who, in May of 1968, two days after he'd returned from his trip to Paris to study the Captives at the Louvre, opened his apartment door to find my father and his backpack.

It was evening. Richard and his Italian girlfriend, Elena Conti, were having a dinner for some friends—my mother among them. Such are the incestuous circulations of real estate in a provincial Italian town.

Opposite the mailboxes and the clanging iron gates that open to the front steps of each of the Via Maddalena properties, there are no houses. There are no buildings at all across the street. There is a railing there, and usually a few parked cars. And there is a litter-strewn drop to a stream that runs down from the hills and from the mountains above the hills. Via Maddalena is parallel to the stream, and like the creek, it seemed to have no ending. This was a distinction that I always felt suited the street's holy namesake—a childhood notion I wisely kept to myself.

I was not permitted to attend Mass when I was a little girl—a ban that made Sundays quite lonely for me on Via Maddalena. My mother's anti-Catholicism is an even more stubbornly held belief than her other tenets of faith: her own work; the sculpture of Michelangelo, Bernini, and Constantin Brancusi; the music of Gato Barbieri and John Coltrane; the songs of Jacques Brel and Leonard Cohen; the writing of Italo Calvino and Charles Dickens; the effect of blond Lebanese hashish rolled into black French tobacco and smoked with her first coffee of the morning.

I was envious of my friend Clara's easy acquaintance with saints' days and miracles. I was envious of her illustrated books of Bible stories and of her frothy confirmation dress. When, for a brief period, Clara was convinced she was going to become a bride of Christ, I tried secretly to steal him away from her by thinking devotedly of his curling hair and lean torso while lying under my duvet with my hand between my legs while the bells for early Mass were ringing—a pleasure I discovered long before Clara, and that I thought I could put to some divine advantage.

Otherwise, I amused myself with aimless neighbourhood wanderings on Sundays. When I did I liked to imagine that it was possible—even for someone whose mother thought the Holy Father should be in prison—to start off from our street and, by following it upward, eventually climb high enough into the heavens to see the thin, kind, world-weary face of Mary Magdalene herself.

Even today, with all the new development that has taken place in what used to be the countryside around Pietrabella, the infinite nature of Via Maddalena has not changed. It isn't interrupted by wall, or an intersection, or a mossy, old fountain as is the case with the other streets in Pietrabella. It keeps going. Up.

Via Maddalena climbs the slope above Pietrabella's central piazza. This rise, away from the coastal flats and the sea to the west and toward the white peaks of the Apuan mountains in the east, is the beginning of the rolling folds and valleys of the green foothills that travellers admire from the windows of speeding trains as they head south from Paris, or from Nice, or from Genoa, on their way to Rome. Clara and I both work at the Agency of Regional Tourism, and our job—not the easiest in the world—is to encourage people to stop in Pietrabella and its environs. But why should they? It's the question I try to answer every day at the desk of my little cubicle, across the fluorescent-lit hallway from Clara.

A few years ago our boss, Pier-Giorgio, spent a considerable percentage of our section's annual creative budget on three twenty-metre panels of mosaic tile. This horrible triptych (Pier-Giorgio's quite pretentious noun; my quite accurate adjective) was undertaken with no internal discussion whatsoever, which is typical of Pier-Giorgio. His bureaucratic tyranny is pretty much summed up by the most frequently repeated phrase in our department: what an asshole. It is a strange dynamic of our office that almost nobody who works in it agrees with the man who is in charge—most notably with his conviction that our region's tourist marketability has to do with the new discos and bars of our seaside and not with the workers, the traditions, and the rugged history of our mountains.

The murals depict the cabanas and bikini-clad women, the athletic-looking water skiers and speedboat drivers, the beachside cafés and restaurants of the waterfront that Pier-Giorgio insists we call the Riviera of Pietrabella. The triptych decorates Pietrabella's cold grey-marble train station. It is a marketing strategy that might be more effective if the express trains actually stopped in Pietrabella. Or even slowed down.

Via Maddalena is made up of not much more than twenty addresses. At its upper end, where there are no more houses, the street becomes a dirt road with ditches of long, sweet-smelling grass and red blurs of poppies. Clara and I often played here, flattening out secret hiding places that looked like big nests. Sometimes we took picnics.

Farther upward, the dirt road becomes the two flattened ruts of a tractor trail. It cuts back and forth through the olive groves that are there—one with trees so old it is said that Dante, who once passed through the area on his way to Pisa, must have seen the same ones we look at now.

When Clara and I were children, we were forbidden to play among the olive trees. The used syringes of the town's drug addicts were scattered there in such abundance they crunched under the soles of our white sandals when we disobeyed the instructions of our elders. Heroin was common in Pietrabella—so common that the owner of the largest bar on the piazza took to drilling small holes in the bowls of each of his coffee spoons. This was his protest against what he described as Italy's catastrophic shift from proud exporter of world-renowned goods to pathetic importer of crap.

Claudio Morello was a large man with a mane of silver hair and a goatee, a voice like an old-fashioned actor's, and no bashfulness whatsoever about stating views that were much out of fashion. His bold opinions singled him out—if only because nobody else thought it advantageous to be honest about the not-so-distant past. The owner of Café David was, in my mother's description, "the one person in all of Pietrabella who admits to having been a fascist during the war."

As opposed as Claudio's crazy right-wing political theories were to my mother's vague allegiance to world revolution, the two of them enjoyed a long, improbable friendship. He never called her anything but *bella,* and his booming lack of hypocrisy was something she admired. So was his ingenuity. The tiny holes drilled in each of the Café David's spoons meant they would not be stolen. They stirred the excellent cappuccinos as well as they ever did. But they were of no use to skinny, pale teenagers, crouched in their American jeans around the gnarled roots of ancient olive trees, cooking the yellowish powder from Marseilles over the flames of their lighters from Japan.

Beyond the olive grove, the tractor trail becomes a goat path that continues upward. It winds up through woods and pasture, over old stone bridges and millstreams, past olive presses and abandoned farmhouses, all the way to the hillside village of Castello—the place where my mother, under the circumstances of a terrible war, was born.

# CHAPTER TWELVE

LUNCH BEGAN AT NOON. The timekeeper's handbell was the signal. But the foremen on the rock face could decide not to acknowledge it. When men were in the middle of a job that could not be interrupted—hoisting a block of stone to the sled or lowering the sled down the mountain with rope-creaking, winch-stuttering care—they had to continue. They got no extra time when the same bell rang exactly a half-hour later.

Experienced workers were adept at watching the sun and timing their tasks. Usually, when the timekeeper closed his watch, slipped it back into his vest pocket, and reached for the varnished wooden handle of the single brass bell, they were ready to stop. And on that day in the summer of 1922, the crew in the Morrow quarry had timed their work well.

They had secured the straps around the stone and had hammered the wedges into place only a few minutes before the lunch break began. The block could wait.

They sat on the two long benches of a bare wooden table. It was covered with a rigged-up canopy of scrap tin.

The crews who were working other parts of the quarry rested, in pairs or groups of four or five, on whatever conveniently flat slabs of stone or planks of lumber they could find. If the weather was bad, a few might be allowed into the foreman's shed—a smoky place that smelled of herring and wet wool. But on good days, by custom, those who were working closest to the old wooden table took it, without argument.

It was sheltered by a wall of marble, a section of the quarry that was as high as a church. It had not been worked for so long that the steel cables strung along its cliff were broken and dangling and rusted brown. The wall leaned over the little plateau just enough to provide some shade at noon to the table and some protection from the mountain winds.

The workers spoke loudly, as if calling out over a roar that only they could hear. They unwrapped their packets of thick slices of crusty white bread and pork fat. Before eating, they refolded the cloth and coiled the string, packing them back in their lunch sacks with careful frugality.

There was a bottle of young wine. Each of the men produced, from their sacks, a squat, sturdy, carefully wrapped cup.

There were ways to do things. These were men who snorted their nostrils clear while they worked, and who could, without embarrassment, squat to shit at the edge of a steep scree, well in sight of other men. But they would never think of drinking wine from a bottle.

Far below, the road was visible. It belonged to the company. It was maintained by a few old men who had once worked in the quarry, and who now spent their days smoothing the ruts and raking over the gravel where the teams of oxen and the loaded wagons had thinned the sharp corners. The heavy wagons came slowly, carefully down the switchback, grinding ruts into the turns.

Every morning the timekeeper opened the gates. He wore a cap like a police guard's and a blue serge jacket. He had come from Carrara, sound asleep, on the first wagon of the day. He would return, in much the same condition, on the last. He had soft white hands.

The workers nodded to him with the deference they used with any representative of their impossibly rich employer. The stories were extravagant.

The quarry owner was said to be wealthier than the duke of Milan. When he entertained in his villa the chandeliers were lit with a hundred candles and the quail were basted in the richest butter, and there were more potatoes than anyone could eat and the wine was so fine it was the colour of old velvet. His mistresses wore silk. They used soaps made of lavender oil and the rendered fat of songbirds. Their hot, foaming baths were scented with the finest French perfume. He had three, the owner did—a blonde, a brunette, and a redhead—each of whom had an ass as smooth as an angel's and who knew every secret of love. Puccini had been a guest at his table. Such were the stories.

The timekeeper had the power to report anyone who was late. He exercised some discretion in this—not to be kind to those workers who rushed apologetically through the gate ten or fifteen seconds after six o'clock in the morning, but to reinforce their sense of obligation to him. As a result, he was always to be addressed as sir and always to be treated with the greatest respect—so any new workers were told when they first approached the entrance to the quarry. The timekeeper had once held an important job at the owner's villa, the older men explained in loud voices to the younger as they passed through the gate. The timekeeper, who always smelled strongly of witch hazel, nodded solemnly back, pleased by the wide eyes and the nervous greetings of the new men. And then, out of earshot, the older men added: an important job, emptying chamber pots. And then, a few steps farther on: before he was sent to the mountains for fucking a goat.

THE QUARRIES WERE TOUGH PLACES—the kind of working environment that is almost beyond comprehension now. Perhaps the only useful contemporary comparison would be battle. If a worker was not strong enough or careful enough or experienced enough, he might not be lucky enough either. Unseen faults could widen, slowly, for centuries before the instant they gave way. Accidents were in the nature of things.

It was during a block's downward passage that the worst accidents on the mountain occurred. Timbers slipped, cables broke, wedges gave way, winches were torn from their wooden pylons. Gravity—the force that the workers spent their days trying to contain—was suddenly cut free.

Men would shout and come running. Confusion would erupt. Work would stop, briefly. And eventually—once order had been restored, once the men were back to work, once the long cables were humming—the low, mournful call of something that sounded like a hunting horn would echo across the valleys.

In Roman times, and for centuries thereafter, marble was quarried by drilling holes at the stone's natural faults. Wooden jambs were hammered into these fissures, and then kept soaked. As the wood expanded, the chosen marble sections—massive cubes of stone, sometimes as big as the shed of an olive press—would break away from the mountain wall.

In later centuries a quicker but much more wasteful method of extrusion was introduced: blasting, first with gunpowder, and later with dynamite. During his 1846 stopover in the Carrara region Charles Dickens heard the "melancholy warning bugle."

The horn that Charles Dickens had identified was called the *buccina.* It was the warning of a coming explosion. But as dynamite became less commonly used, the *buccina* took on another function. A longer, even more mournful note was the signal of a quarryman's injury or death. This was a common enough occurrence. But it was a sound that Julian Morrow never got used to.

The echoes from the cliff walls and through the valleys made it difficult for anyone at any distance to know from which quarry the sound came. Once the signal was heard, the women and children of the mountain villages could only wait until the end of the day to learn if the accident had been their father's, or their husband's, or their son's. It was later, usually during one of his regular meetings with his quarry managers, that Morrow would learn the details.

THE WEATHER WAS EXTREME. In the winter there were frozen ropes and there were winches that had to be cracked free of ice with hammers in the morning. There were cliffs of ice that formed so transparently on the edges of the high marble walls, they were all but invisible against the white stone until they gave way. There might be a shout. There might be a useless scrabbling of boots.

Springs in the quarries were wet and cold. The flooding of the transport roads was not uncommon.

And then there were the summers. By the time the crew sat down at the wooden table, that August day in 1922, they were so wet with their own sweat it looked as if they had fallen into a river.

One of the men rose from one of the benches at the table.

His tight, wrinkled face had been carved by the weather. His lips were cracked.

He walked with the balanced, measured gait typical of an experienced quarry worker. He crossed the little plateau. It was fifteen or twenty yards of trampled grass and thyme surrounded by a fringe of wild sage.

He moved directly to the lip of the mountain. There was no slowing down as he approached the cliff, and no vestige of momentum the instant he stopped at its brink. The man's view was from a height so great it could have been from the window of a plane. He kept his centre of gravity firmly behind the toes of his old leather workboots. He leaned forward.

In the quarries the weather of one season is never entirely obliterated by the extremes of another. On the coldest day the harsh glare of sunshine does not warm workers so much as remind them of the ferocity of the summer. And that August, when the walls of the Morrow quarry were like the sides of an oven, it was winter that came briefly to the man's mind as he looked down. As he stood at the edge of the mountain, he felt a cascade of cold. It fell from the marble overhang above.

He leaned into nothing. His hands were at his sides.

Far below, a tiny blue timekeeper opened a miniature gate for a little wagon loaded with pebbles of marble.

There was the sandy ribbon of road. There were the distant valleys. There were the faraway marshes and plains. There were the beaches of the seaside. The day seemed bright as ice. He leaned farther out.

Now he could see his son. Lino was toiling up the incline with the bucket. He was already more than three-quarters of the way. The sleeves of the boy's shirt were rolled, and his face and hair were protected from the sun by the peak of a battered cap.

His wife had given him four sons. Three now worked with

him in the quarries. The youngest, Italo, would not. His legs were bad. He would be a burden.

This thought passed through the man quickly. As tenderness always did. There was nothing to be done. Italo could help the women. He could herd the goats.

Carefully, still keeping his weight centred behind the lip of stone, he watched Lino's climb. He could see the boy's care and steady determination. This pleased him. Then the man turned back. He crossed the wide ledge to the table.

"Winter's coming," he said to his two oldest sons, as he hoisted a leg over the bench.

Winter! They laughed in the heat. One of the lads handed him a cup of wine. And that was the end of them all.

LINO CAVATORE COULD SEE the last few trestles. He could see, poised above him, the block of white stone, strapped and tilted on the wooden sled.

Then he heard something. Or rather, he felt it—a deep, rumbling in the back of his head. It came up inside him, through the soles of his uncomfortable new boots.

It was easy to get confused in the quarries. They were places of constant change. Their permanence was illusory. The men worked hard: their industry was as relentless as it was underpaid, and with little more than saws and ropes and pulleys they transformed everything around them. And then, without pause, they transformed it again. Walls that looked as if they could never move vanished. And so, as the boy stepped past the marble block that was strapped to the tilted wooden sled, he thought, for a moment, that he had somehow made a wrong turn.

As he moved onto the flat of the grass, he could not understand how he could have made such an error.

Then he stopped and slowly, without noticing any relief, put down the bucket. There, lying against an outcrop of rock: his brother's hammer, its shaft whittled, as he had shown him, to fit his grip. And there, against the winch, at the top of the incline: his father's coil of rope. But everything else was different.

There was no wooden table scarred with initials. No rigged-up tin roof. No benches. There was no overhang of stone.

The thought formed very clearly. It was entirely calm and entirely unsentimental. He realized that his brother would not be much help. He felt himself tightening—as if bracing for everything he knew would follow. I will have to look after our mother, the boy said to himself. It will be up to me.

On the ledge there was only stillness—a roughly piled tomb of it. There was no shade there anymore.

# CHAPTER THIRTEEN

IT IS A GOOD HOUR'S CLIMB from Pietrabella to Castello, and it is in the rugged, in-between area, about halfway from the town to the village, that my mother rents her little farmhouse. It's where, in 1968, she spent the only time she ever spent with my father. It was a summer he could never forget and a summer that my mother, with typical stubbornness, would not for a very long time admit to me that she could remember.

The surrounding land had once been the grounds of an ancient convent. Before that, it was said to have been the site of an even more ancient temple and a sacred spring.

The convent had commandeered the property in much the same way that Christian holidays took over the dates of pagan celebrations. But in this case the church's triumph was not as eternal as was hoped. At the same time that Napoleon's sister Princess Elisa Baciocchi was inventing the industry of souvenirs, ornamental statuary, and marble replicas, she also embarked on a campaign to reduce the region's redundant religious institutions.

This early example of downsizing made many people uneasy. Cost-cutting efficiency was not obviously God's will—not if the preceding four or five centuries of cathedrals, tombs, monasteries, frescoes, and lavish iconography were anything to go by. But in the case of the convent in the hills above Pietrabella, Princess Elisa and the forces of practicality did not need to intercede very strenuously. Time took care of things.

The convent's hard, narrow beds, its long, unadorned tables, its cold stone hallways, and its cushion-less kneeling benches had been unused for decades by the time the old place was converted to a villa. The place became the residence of Julian Morrow, and its refurbishment had followed only one criterion. It was exactly what he wanted.

He built a spring-fed pool that he could see from his breakfast table. This view, of cypresses and stone figures and the cascading hills beyond them, was softened with moist haze when he took his coffee on summer mornings. At that hour the pool, its terrace of hedgerow and statuary, and its surrounding gardens were brushed with soft angles of sunlight. It was a landscape that never failed to remind him that he wasn't in Wales.

The only reason I can even guess at the physical dimensions of the convent is that we know, to some extent, what Morrow's villa used to look like. The pool, the gardens, and the statues were documented in considerable detail in the 1920s by a local photographer. This is the kind of thing that is only of interest to historians, however. As my boss, Pier-Giorgio, who is not one, frequently makes clear.

Giovanni Belli made the marble quarries and the work of the region's artisans his most recurrent photographic subject. His black and white images are quite magnificent, but he never became very well known. This, in part, had to do with the fact that he never had to. His family had owned quarries in the area for centuries. He loved marble, but as a young man he concluded that the family business was manned with a sufficient number of his siblings to allow him to pursue a related love. He'd been given a camera as a boy.

Before I travelled to Cathcart to meet my father, Clara and I tried to convince Pier-Giorgio that we should produce a travel brochure for the lobbies of hotels and *pensiones* in the Carrara region, to be entitled "Michelangelo's Mountains." We wanted to use Belli's black and white pictures as its illustrations. It was our idea that the old photographs, most of which are preserved in an archive in Lucca, would appeal to a certain nostalgia that was then in fashion. We also thought that the local lore about Michelangelo's trails and his quarries could be put to good, eco-tourism use. We were not without our marketing rationale.

What made the photographs of Giovanni Belli the perfect choice of illustration for our brochure were not only their historical value and compositional grandeur. Belli's name is associated not only with photography but with his efforts to prove that Michelangelo left some evidence, somewhere, of the time he spent in the area. It was, in the region at least, a famous obsession.

Belli's knowledge of Michelangelo was considerable, and by no means unsophisticated, but the premise of his belief was unshakeably simple. He didn't think the great sculptor could go that long without doing what he most loved: carving stone.

Clara and I envisioned our brochure bringing throngs of hikers, all of them wearing expensive, Italian-made boots and carrying several credit cards. We pictured taxi drivers and waiters and shopkeepers kept busy catering to tours that came from far and wide to follow Giovanni Belli's beautifully documented quest for Michelangelo.

But we were not successful in our proposal. "I'm sorry to have to inform you," Pier-Giorgio wrote, "that we live in the twenty-first century. Not the Renaissance."

As you see: what an asshole.

Julian Morrow's villa can be seen in the background of many of Belli's pictures. Because his studies of the pieces of sculpture in the terraced gardens were so various and so detailed, the building is visible in a useful variety of angles. And this is all we know of what the old convent might have looked like. Morrow's residence—along with its pool, its statues, its fountains, and its hedged, terraced gardens—was destroyed by Allied artillery in 1944. A modest farmhouse was built in its place in the early 1950s.

It is a pretty spot. But the isolated, rustic characteristics that had appealed to my mother when she was in her twenties proved to be inconvenient when I was born. My mother concluded that life with a baby was easier with reliable running water and electricity. We moved into town, to the flat at Via Maddalena 19, in the summer of 1969. I was only a few months old.

MY MOTHER WAS A SINGLE PARENT, which was not at all common in Pietrabella even in the 1970s. And often when she was away, or busy, or just not there, I had dinner and then slept at Clara's—a home that was so orderly it seemed to me wondrously the opposite of our messy, unvacuumed flat.

These were the kind of minor points of parenting at which my mother did not always excel. But she was good at the major ones, and her occasional absences seemed demonstrations of her faith in me as much as anything. I was quite proud of being big enough to make my own plans now and then.

My mother's belief that a tidy house is the sign of a wasted life was not one shared by her neighbours. The citizens of Pietrabella are, for the most part, respectable, hard-working people—and the Taglianis were exactly that. The white marble of their kitchen floor was as spotless as a glacier. The old walnut sideboard gleamed with lemon oil.

"Bourgeois to their souls" is my mother's description. Her assessment is unkind but not inaccurate. Pietrabella is a conventional place—except for one idiosyncrasy.

The town's dependence on the region's principal industry has left its otherwise conservative population with a deep respect for artists and artisans. Sculptors are treated by the population the way holy beggars might have been treated by a community of believers. "Your mother has her own way" was as close to criticism as Mrs. Tagliani ever came when, with no sign of my mother or of dinner, I wandered up the street to Clara's parents' house with my school books. I was always made welcome.

In the bedtime stories that Clara's father told us, the path that began with our street continued its slow, sleepy zigzag up, beyond the walls and the bell tower of Castello, beyond the cobbled central piazza where a white marble tablet of forty-three names commemorates the terrible massacre that occurred there in 1944.

It went up through the higher fields and forests, and up to the clear cool pools and waterfalls and the lush beds of watercress and the plateaus of alpine grass. It went up past gorges and craggy outcrops of rock. It went up beyond scree and bluff. It continued all the way to the mountaintops and to the cold and glistening marble quarries where the great artist Michelangelo Buonarroti had climbed so long ago to find his beautiful white stone. And then, as Clara's and my eyes closed so that we could better picture the heights Mr. Tagliani's low, monotonous voice was describing, this meandering trail continued toward the sky.

Up into the snowy peaks, and up into the clear blue, and up into the lofts of white clouds where, if we followed the gently twisting path, we might find angels who could sometimes come to the aid of little girls with troublesome monkeys—so long as the girls remembered to bring the angels chestnuts, which were very difficult to obtain in the bright and holy realm of Heaven.

I loved the feel of the cool, tightly made sheets. Even in the shadows, I admired the vacant windowsills and the crucifix hung bravely alone and off-centre on the white wall. Clara's father, a kind, tired man who worked as a clerk for a shipping company in Viareggio, sat in the dark in a wooden chair between the two beds and told us his bedtime stories. He made them up as he went.

Their purpose, of course, was to lull us to sleep. But I think Mr. Tagliani often found himself under the spell he was weaving. There were times when the low, steady drone of his voice seemed to slip into his own dreams.

"There are no troublesome monkeys in Pietrabella," Clara said. She was suddenly fully awake. Her father had just introduced this strange, unexpected element to one of his narratives.

"Hmm?"

"You said 'troublesome monkeys.'"

"Did I?"

"Pietrabella is not in Africa, Mr. Tagliani," I chimed in helpfully.

"Isn't it?" The sleepiness in Clara's father's voice left me unsure whether he was kidding us or whether he had revealed some secret too mysterious to fathom.

We had just learned in school about how the unimaginable pressures of tectonic plates had transformed limestone into marble millions upon millions of years ago. Our teacher was Signor Lambrusco, a small, huddled-up man whose stoop was thought to be the result of his daily forbearance of a famously bad-tempered wife. He told us that if we could travel faster than the speed of light we could go back in time—past Garibaldi and Verdi, past Michelangelo and da Vinci, past Dante and Boccaccio, past Jesus, past the Egyptians, past the cavemen, and past all the dim-witted dinosaurs—to an age when green and ancient tropical seas were being drained and our mountains were being formed.

Signor Lambrusco's soft face took on a dreamy expression during this lesson. His voice was usually flat and weary. But he seemed entranced by the idea of getting away from the present as completely as possible. If we could only go back through the millennia, Signor Lambrusco told us wistfully, we would be able to see how marble happened. Two hundred million years ago, he explained, the Italian coastline was beneath the Tyrrhenian Sea.

"And while it was . . ." The dramatic sweep of his arm took in everything: our school, our town, his wife. "While all this was drowned," he said to us, "deep at the bottom of the Tyrrhenian Sea, do you know what happened?"

We did not.

"Flecks of minerals, bits of vegetation, and fragments of coral drifted down. Down through the warm depths. This accumulation was laid in beds of silt on the ocean floor over unimaginably long stretches of time. And these beds, in turn, were buried by millions upon millions of years of further deposits. And this mass was pressed into the layers of the calcium carbonate that eventually became . . ."

Signor Lambrusco paused to see if anyone could fill in the blank. Nobody could—an eruption of the kind of silence that usually infuriated him. But he continued, pleasantly lost in the eons upon eons that had preceded, among other things, his marriage. For once he was untroubled by our ignorance.

"Limestone," he announced. "And layers of undersea limestone is what these strata would have remained, had the earth's tectonic plates not begun their heaving and grinding thirty million years ago."

The pressure and the heat were intense in their effect. "The limestone seabed buckled upward, and took the form of a coastal mountain range. The Apuans," he said, in case we'd missed the point. "But something else happened. Something even more astonishing than a seabed turning into a mountain range."

Did we know what that something was?

"Metamorphosis," he said. "The limestone was recrystallized by this incomprehensible force into deposits of an entirely new stone."

He crossed to the window of our classroom and looked upward, to the east. "Marble," he said. "The marble of Carrara. As you see. Michelangelo's mountains."

These were the same peaks that Mr. Tagliani described in the meandering bedtime stories that he told to Clara and me—mountains that looked white in the distance, as if, even in summer, they were crested with snow, as if they were the cold ramparts of the kingdom of Heaven.

Lying in the fresh, tightly made sheets of the spare bed in Clara's room, I wondered about Mr. Tagliani's troublesome monkeys as I fell asleep. I thought about poor, beleaguered Signor Lambrusco. And I wondered whether my best friend's father was dreaming of continents that had not yet drifted apart. I wondered if his stories came from a time not yet transformed into the order we now believe it possesses.

# CHAPTER FOURTEEN

From far away in the quarries there was the sound of a mournful horn—so faint, only someone who had heard it before would pick it out from the general bustle of the town of Carrara. The low, extended note was softened and confused by the unfolding of the valleys through which it passed. It seemed not to come from a single source, but more generally from the sky.

Julian Morrow noticed it that summer morning. As always, he worried that it might be the signal of an accident. It often was. And he worried that it might be coming from one of his quarries. It sometimes did. He had not accommodated himself to the gruff acceptance of injury and death that the managers of his quarries took to be natural. But as some small comfort—not entirely convincing, he had to admit—Morrow reminded himself that the greatest beauty is never without its sadness.

This was a theme on which he could expand. Often he did.

He had a gift for describing things vividly to the attentive audiences of his speeches. He could make people see views they'd never even imagined.

It amazed him that in those community halls and Masonic temples, those library meeting rooms and church basements he could make people see: a quarry worker, his boots perched on an uncertainty of rubble, his head bent over the track he was repairing.

The worker might have heard what sounded like thunder. He might have felt the shuddering in the ground. He might have looked up to see, for his last second, a snapped line flailing in the blue air. He might have had time to understand the meaning of the scattering timber and the flash of runaway white mass.

In the past fifteen years Morrow had spent many months in Carrara. The rest of the time he attended to family life and ran his business in a chilly, frequently gloomy Welsh city that remained, officially, his place of residence. He addressed the subjects of danger and sadness and beauty in his speeches on the marble quarries of Carrara—most recently, only a few months previous, before a luncheon audience at the Cardiff Geographical Society.

Morrow had been quick to realize that these speeches—to professional associations, to toastmasters clubs, to ladies' auxiliaries and educational societies—were the best kind of advertising. Free, for one thing. Convincing, for another. He cast himself in the role of the adventurous explorer, and his audiences seemed not to notice that his motivation was more overtly commercial than Livingstone's or Shackleton's.

Julian Morrow owned several quarries in the Carrara region. The use of the word "several" was his. This is not because he was modest about the number. It's because the number was always under negotiation.

He once admitted to one of his several Italian mistresses that he was "unappeasable in appetite"—but only because her

English wasn't good enough for this admission of faithlessness to upset her. When he wasn't acquiring he was divesting. And he divested in order to do more acquiring.

He had a craggy face that could never have been described as handsome. His nose was long and his eyes had the small, unwavering attention of bullet holes. But it was his energy that obtained, not his features. His enthusiasm gave people the impression that he was attractive. And parts of him were. He had the legs of a teenager.

Julian Morrow's approach to the complexities of commerce was to control as many of them as possible. His workers took his stone from the walls of his quarries so that it could be carved in his workshops and transported on his ships to wherever a need for Carrara marble was felt keenly enough to make the labour of his excavators, his drivers, his artisans, his finishers, his shippers, his distributors, and his installers worth his while.

The breeches, boots, and hacking jacket were elements of costume he put to good use. When he delivered one of his speeches, he leaned a walking stick against the podium. And he usually read a passage from the journal Charles Dickens kept during a trip to Italy in 1846 by way of setting the scene.

"'But the road,'" Morrow intoned, "'down which the marble comes, however immense the blocks!'"

The use to which Morrow put Charles Dickens went beyond borrowing the great author's descriptive powers. The name commanded deep respect, particularly among the audiences of luncheon speeches in provincial British towns. That Charles Dickens had written about Carrara lent capital to Morrow's own musings on marble and on beauty. As well, quoting Dickens meant that Morrow didn't have to rein in his fondness for dramatic proclamation.

"'Conceive a channel of water . . .'" Morrow's left hand

meandered in the air before the rapt attention of his audiences as if describing the course of a river. "'A channel of water running over a rocky bed, beset with great heaps of stone of all shapes and sizes, winding down the middle of this valley; and *that* being the road—because it was the road five hundred years ago!'"

Morrow always paused here, to let any grammatical confusion dissipate and to let this remarkable notion settle in. For it was true: the quarries Charles Dickens visited in 1846 were not very different from the ones Michelangelo had known.

In the latter half of the thirteenth century, local demand for marble, as well as the requirements of Pisa and Florence, reopened several dormant quarries of Carrara. Marble's associations with the traditions of the ancient Romans and the Greeks made it a medium sufficiently serious to embody the most lofty aspirations.

This sense of marble's spiritual and heroic characteristics only increased as the Renaissance unfolded. In the mid-1500s, in his *Lives of the Artists,* Giorgio Vasari compared Michelangelo's *David* to the grand statuary of Rome, much of which had been quarried in the Greek colonies of Naxos, Paros, Aphrodysias, Dokimeion, and Marmara. The source of marble changed, but Vasari thought the same spirit prevailed.

Morrow continued. He knew the Dickens quotation by heart.

"'Imagine the clumsy carts of five hundred years ago, being used to this hour, and drawn, as they used to be, five hundred years ago, by oxen, whose ancestors were worn to death five hundred years ago, as their unhappy descendants are now, in twelve months, by the suffering and agony of this cruel work!'"

Morrow was a stirring public speaker. This was because, unlike many, his speeches had a purpose. He was a salesman.

"'Two pair, four pair, ten pair, twenty pair, to one block, according to its size; down it must come, this way. In their struggling from stone to stone, with their enormous loads behind them, they die frequently upon the spot; and not they alone; for their passionate drivers, sometimes tumbling down in their energy, are crushed to death beneath the wheels.'

"The quarries so vividly described by Mr. Dickens are built in terraces," he told the Cardiff Geographical Society, his large hands gripping the sides of a podium. "It is possible to conceive of them as abstractions—vast sculptures of geometric form and volume. But I am too old-fashioned for Mr. Brancusi's modern art, I'm afraid."

Morrow waited for the inevitable grumble of chuckles.

"And so I see them as ornamental gardens carved directly into the mountainside—great terraced landscapes of stone, extraordinary in their beauty. But the quarries are dangerous places, and for that reason, all the more beautiful. For beauty without sadness," he said, his voice building toward his conclusion, "is mere prettiness. And pretty is the one thing that the quarries of Carrara refuse to be."

Applause was enthusiastic, always.

# CHAPTER FIFTEEN

After my father's death in April 2010, and after I contacted his lawyers in Cathcart, a package was subsequently delivered to me through the agency of an associated Italian law firm. It contained details of my father's estate, his will, and a letter that he had written—all to be handed to me by his legal representatives. He had been thorough in his preparations—though the absence of confusion did nothing to speed up any of the Italian agencies involved. We were still engaged with phone calls and faxes and meetings with lawyers by the time I decided I'd better get back to the weekly routine of African dancing in Casatori before I went completely crazy.

Casatori is fifteen kilometres up the coast, and this was the first class I'd attended after my father's death. It had been a stressful period. There are many complexities that arise when someone arrives dead in a country that isn't the one in which he has lived.

On the way home Paolo looked at me intently in the back seat. He switched the rear-view mirror back and forth between night vision and day a few times, as if selecting the best lens for his close-up. This is something Paolo often does when he drives us back. Smouldering intensity is pretty much Paolo's default expression whenever he's looking at a woman when Clara isn't looking at him. I've come to realize it doesn't mean anything, really.

Usually, on the way back, Clara looks to her right, out to the sea and the sunset as we head south on the Autostrada, back to Pietrabella. She loves this view. But on this occasion, even though his wife was paying him no attention, Paolo wasn't trying to be Marcello Mastroianni. He was only trying to convey sympathy with his movie-star eyes.

He said, "I am sorry. But I must tell you. This is not something that is uncommon."

Paolo says most people are anxious about flying to begin with, and probably they are out of condition, and maybe they had to run half a kilometre through a terminal with their luggage because they were caught in traffic on their way to the airport. This happens.

"This is modern life," said Paolo.

Then they have to sit still. For hours. They can't stretch their legs, which is usually the problem. There are always too many seats in what is always too narrow a fuselage.

It was odd, I thought, that someone who had spent so tiny a fraction of his lifetime on airplanes should die on one.

My father suffered, but not very much, from a genetic disorder that affected his feet and his calves. As he grew older his feet grew smaller. They turned in on themselves. His lower legs became slightly withered in relation to the rest of his body. The condition could be crippling, although in my father's instance, it manifested itself mostly in his difficulty finding decent shoes. Occasionally, he lost his balance.

The disorder's chief irritant—at least in my father's case—was the uncertainty that it stirred up around it. When he was in his late forties, its symptoms appeared to advance. But just as abruptly, and just as mysteriously, they retreated. Nothing changed until the year before he left for Italy.

That was when he noticed a numbness in his feet, as if they were always cold. His balance abandoned him at unexpected moments. He took a bad fall up at the pool.

It's possible that this condition was a contributing factor to the catastrophe that shuddered through him somewhere high in the blackness above the North Atlantic. Or maybe not. But even if there was no actual physical connection to the blood clot that killed him, his problematic feet had a lot to do with why he was flying in the first place. He'd thought that the fall at the pool was a warning.

His doctor in Cathcart had not been a big help. "Things might stay as they are now for a long time," he said. "Or they could get worse."

My father considered this. "Like getting old," he said.

"Much like," agreed the doctor.

It was only the third time in his life that my father had travelled anywhere. He had flown once before to Paris in 1968 at the age of twenty—a typical North American backpacker on a typical summer adventure. Four months later he got on a plane for the second time, flying back across the Atlantic, returning to the town where he had grown up and where he would live and work for the rest of his life. And forty-two years after that, he took a flight from Toronto to Milan, accompanied by a statue, a briefcase of papers, a suitcase, a copy of the art historian Rudolf Wittkower's last book, and a red Moleskine notebook that was still open on Oliver's tray table when the flight attendant noticed he hadn't put it in the upright position.

He had a window seat. The couple to his left reported that they had taken sleeping pills and were not aware of what had happened until the landing preparations were announced.

Oliver was bringing with him a large, heavy, wooden crate that bore a resemblance to a casket—disturbing, under the circumstances. The statue had been air-freighted at unbelievable expense, and was wheeled toward me by two baggage handlers two hours after the Toronto flight had landed. I was still standing at the Alitalia counter at Malpensa, dealing with airline officials, ambulance attendants, and the police.

The contents were described as ornamental statuary. My father had written, "*The Miracle.* Artist Unknown," on the waybill. He always used the same fine-tipped, black ink.

The flight attendant had handed me his red notebook. The crew had been very thorough about his personal belongings. They'd found his pen under the seat in front of his.

"I wake from the same old dream." This was the only entry. He must have written it somewhere before the dawn into which he was flying. "Archie is vacuuming the pool. It's night. I am watching him from the water. I don't know why the trip begins here. But it does."

"NEXT TIME YOU'RE ON AN OVERNIGHT FLIGHT," Paolo advised me, "look back at the people still in their seats when you are getting off. Particularly the older ones." He paused. His deep brown eyes searched out mine in the rear-view mirror. "They might not be asleep."

The African drumbeats stayed with us. The rhythms of our Casatori dance class mixed with the steady rhythm of the

Mercedes's smooth passage. Clara and I agree that the glow from the weekly class sometimes lasts for days. Clara particularly loves the arm windmills and the hip-shimmying of the Afro-fusion movements. That evening she announced to several of the other women in the class that after being forced to sit in an office all week, she needs to go a little crazy. Nzegwhua, our teacher, overheard this. "Sometimes you move like a crazy monkey," she said. Nzegwha's sweet, gap-toothed smile made it difficult to know if this was a criticism. Clara looked uncertain for a moment, and then decided it wasn't. She took my hand and swung it back and forth. "That's us," she said. "That's who we've always been. We are the troublesome monkeys of the Casatori Afro-fusion Beginners Class."

Now, in the front passenger seat, Clara was still staring westward, out to the darkening sea.

From the back seat I noticed for the first time that Paolo's hair is thinning at his crown. I wondered if he knew this and I concluded that he didn't. A bald spot would have been more artfully disguised had he known it was there.

I thanked him for his information. And then I closed my eyes. The hum of excellent radial tires lulled me. I was thinking about an artist's model. He was locked in his pose. I was thinking of the difficulty of stillness and I was dreaming of dancing as I fell asleep. I didn't wake until the Mercedes turned up the slope of Via Maddalena.

WHEN MY MOTHER IS CARVING STONE she says she doesn't know what form she has in mind until she finds it. "Not knowing is the point," she used to say. "It's how we are when we're born. And how we are when we die. We're not so clear on things the rest of the time."

I used to imagine that this was one of her vaguely mystical excuses for not having the patience to work things out more carefully, in advance. I am, by my nature, more organized.

The writing I do for my work at the Agency of Regional Tourism—cultural festival programs, press releases, and travel brochures—always begins with a detailed outline. Even the outlines go through several drafts, and everyone in the regional office has an opportunity to comment. I welcome criticism from my colleagues as an idea moves from proposal to outline to draft. It's comforting to know exactly what you are going to produce before you produce it. But now that I find myself thinking so much about my father, I'm not sure that my mother's approach isn't the right one.

Customarily Pier-Giorgio does not take part in the time-consuming process of refining a proposal. He is a busy man. His views are only expressed when text is nearing its final form. This reservation of judgment does nothing to make our office more efficient. But it does confirm Pier-Giorgio's position by making everyone feel as insecure as possible. His rejection of the text of "Michelangelo's Mountains" came at the very last minute. We'd already booked the printer.

But I can't say it was a waste of time.

Oliver liked "Michelangelo's Mountains." At least, he said he did. I brought it to him on the occasion of my first and only visit to Cathcart. This was in June 2009. And one of the few actual memories I have of my father doing something that didn't involve talking to me is watching him read.

We were in the bathing pavilion of his strange, old swimming pool. It was evening.

I described Michelangelo as a broad-shouldered man with mournful eyes, big ears, callused hands, and a broken nose. I noted that *scultore* was a self-description Michelangelo often added to his signature—even after he'd painted the Sistine ceiling.

In the brochure's introduction I said that the act of carving spoke to Michelangelo about more than stone. "Michelangelo's gift for uncovering the three dimensions of an object's beauty was how he believed he reached the purpose of his soul." That's what I actually wrote. And that may have been the sentence that sunk us. I don't think Pier-Giorgio read any further. He isn't big on aesthetic theory.

The figures Michelangelo had in mind already existed perfectly, so he believed, in the quarried blocks. His job was to free the forms—which meant a great deal depended on what stone was chosen. That is why he spent as much time as he did in the quarries.

As my father read "Michelangelo's Mountains" on that June evening in Cathcart, his only movement was his abrupt way of turning pages. He didn't look up once as he read. In profile, his face was more finely featured than I'd realized. I could hear crows from somewhere on the hillside. There was just enough light.

The few days I spent in Cathcart, a year's worth of my father's handwritten letters, some papers, the red notebook he had with him on his flight, an old statue, and my mother's indifference to historical accuracy are all I have to work with when it comes to remembering Oliver Hughson. This is much the way it is, I suppose, with more traditional families. Most people grow up with stories they don't know they want to remember.

The package was delivered to me, by hand, by a law clerk employed in Viareggio. The clerk sat silent and motionless. I read in specified order: first, the will; second, a twelve-page accounting of the estate; and third, my father's letter. "Don't feel bound by this in any way," he wrote.

So, naturally, I do. And I've come to think that the way my mother works stone is a useful guide to my obligation.

Nobody could have planned this. Nobody can guess at love's unlikely connections. But it is by this unpredictability that our lives find their best surprises. This is what is strange.

# CHAPTER SIXTEEN

JULIAN MORROW MET Grace and Argue Barton in the lobby of their Carrara hotel at eight o'clock in the morning. The outing had been planned the day before, during luncheon at his villa.

They had also begun, during that lunch, to talk of a landscaping plan for the grounds of Barton House in Cathcart—although Grace, for the life of her, couldn't think who had first raised the subject. It seemed to her that it must have been Argue, although when she reflected on this, the notion seemed so out of character for her husband.

It was Grace who had pointed out the similarity of terrain.

"I doubt," she said to Morrow, "that Cathcart and Tuscany are often spoken of in the same breath. But my husband's house . . ." She was looking at Argue Barton as she spoke, and when their eyes met she immediately corrected herself. "Our house," she said with a smile, "is also tucked into a wooded hillside. It has the same orientation, if I am not mistaken."

She could clearly recall Julian Morrow clapping his hands and saying, "Now there, that's a wonderful idea."

But from where, exactly, had this wonderful idea come?

"Here," Morrow had said to them after their plates had been cleared and before the almond cake and coffee was served on his villa patio. He rose from the table. "Take your wine. Let's go for a stroll."

He had walked them slowly around the perimeter of his pool. "The artisans here are so skilled," he said, "they could create exactly this . . . for you . . . in Cathcart." The sweep of his hand included the pool and the walls and the hedge and the sculpture. "And you would be hard-pressed on a summer evening to know whether you were in Ontario or Tuscany. You would not be able to tell the replication from the original."

"Ah, but we would know the statues were copies," said Grace. "And that would rather spoil it."

"Would it?" asked Morrow.

"Certainly."

"Your figures would not be so beautiful as mine?"

Grace could tell that she was being made fun of. But she was willing to play along. "No," she said, sipping the deliciously cool white wine.

"And your stone maidens would not be so lovely?"

"I fear they would not."

"And the fountain? It would trickle inauthentically, I take it, into the pool."

"I'm sure it would. Wouldn't it, darling?"

Her husband, not attuned to the exchange, nodded.

"Then tell me," said Julian Morrow. "How 'antique' do you think my ancient pool is?"

Neither Grace nor her husband were willing to hazard a guess.

Morrow was immensely pleased with this. "Some of these

figures are old. Quite old, actually. But some of these statues . . . some of these ancient statues are statues that I had made. I say *made.* They were made in Carrara, here, in my workshop, by my artisans . . . all of . . . fourteen months ago. "

His laughter boomed. "Can you imagine! Fourteen months! Some of these pieces are as venerable as that."

He gestured toward the fountain.

"And I defy you to see any difference between a statue here that is four hundred years old. And one that is fourteen months. Not only do I get them confused myself, the more important fact is this: I don't care. Imagine that. I do not care. New or old, they are born of the same tradition. They are carved the same way, in the same place, by the same families of artisans. They are made of the same stone. If you believe, as I do, that it is generations of craftsmen that produce these, and not the lone talent of a carver, there is no reason to prefer the later to the earlier. No reason whatsoever."

He explained that the new statues' convincing patina was not the result of their age. The smoky skein on the white stone and the golden burnish of its surface were caused, primarily, by three months spent buried in the corner of the work yard of one of Morrow's Carrara studios. His men urinated on the carefully marked ground as often as possible. Morrow apologized to Grace for this explanation of so crude but effective a method of replicating the beauty of time.

Morrow was, by now, taking it as a given that the Barton project would proceed. He was thinking about the cost of freight. He was considering the possibility of dismantling some of the statues in his own pool when the time came and shipping them. He could replace them easily enough. It wouldn't be the first time he had sold pieces from his villa to a client.

Of course, there was a protocol to follow. Grace and Argue

would have to talk it over. This was no small undertaking. Morrow would tell them to take their time—it was, after all, a sizable financial commitment. He'd known jobs that had been years in the planning. But as they were thinking it over, he would help them picture the terraced gardens and the paths and the fountains and the pool. He would hire a photographer—he knew just the man—to send pictures of his own estate to them in Cathcart. That would be helpful.

The landscape he envisioned would cease being something they wanted. He was an exceptionally good salesman. A pool surrounded by ancient statues would become something they owned but did not yet possess.

He would assist them. He would facilitate. He would find someone to oversee the job—someone good.

This would have a cost, of course. But these things do.

And he would show them the quarries from which the marble would come. Indeed he would—so he said to the Bartons. He guided them back to the table, now set with cakes and ices and a sweet wine to accompany their dessert.

"I wonder if you might join me tomorrow in a walk to the quarries," he said. He was not entirely certain whether Grace would be pleased or distressed by his apparent disregard for her handicap. He suspected the former. "We shall go in the morning if you can."

Grace and Argue looked at one another, trying to gauge their responses to the second unexpected invitation of the day.

"I like to make the climb from time to time," Morrow continued. "It does my soul good. The mountains are a rare combination of delights. And the walk is always much more pleasant with company."

He glanced at the sky. "The weather looks promising. I'm sure you'd find it an excursion of interest."

"Oh, Argue," Grace said, "it would be such an adventure."

*Part Three*

# THE CLAW CHISEL

*Bernini treated marble with such tenderness it would appear to be wax or even the flesh itself.*

—Abbé François Raguenet, 1700

CATHCART, ONTARIO. APRIL 2010.

I hope that Herkimer, Mulberry, Cannon, and Flatt have demonstrated to your satisfaction their dependability. Although this is not something I can be absolutely certain about, of course. Under the circumstances. It is April 2010. But things will change. I am here, writing this letter by an old pool, in the bright spring sunshine, confident of little else.

But Herkimer's has always been reliably unsurprising in my experience. They represented my adoptive parents—executing the straightforward details of Winifred Hughson's will in 1976, and then the conveyance to me of the Hillside Avenue property and the bulk of my father's estate following his death fourteen years later. Herkimer's—as once they were known by anybody who was anybody in town—used to be the firm of choice for established Cathcart families. The families Archie Hughson referred to as "the fine olds." Anglicans, in other words.

Archie and Winifred attended Montrose United Church. Archie had been brought up in a more austere tradition, but his shift from Presbyterian to United was inspired not by doctrine but by the proximity of Montrose United Church to their Hillside Avenue home. "Same tub," Archie summarized. "Slightly warmer water."

He was a schoolteacher. He saw this as an honourable calling—one that combined the greatest possible responsibility with the lowest imaginable salary, as befitted the spare and earnest Sundays of his childhood.

But then he wrote a geography textbook. He had no literary aspirations and no hope for commercial success. He wrote *Our World* only because the dreary textbook from which he was obliged to teach was so terrible.

*Studies in Geography* had been first published in the late 1920s. Archie ignored it as much as the curriculum would allow. It reduced the world to chapters that opened with small, blurry, black and white photo illustrations of "A busy street in Rome," or "Natives harvest cane in Africa," and ended them with questions of memorization for a test. Annual rainfall was a favourite subject. But the textbook's departmentally approved dullness was not its worst sin, in Archie's view. "Nothing in it is connected to anything else," he complained to Winifred. "Which is rather a problem. Since everything in geography is."

Archie was a popular teacher. There was an eagerness to him that he could never suppress—a sincerity that conveyed to his students that when he stepped into a classroom he was there not because there were curriculum requirements to get through, or a term to complete, or departmental exams to prepare for, or because it was his job. He was there—opening his worn leather briefcase at his desk; handing back carefully marked essays—because he had something very interesting to tell them.

Archie read avidly about the places he would never see, and he encouraged his students to put the Cathcart Public Library to good use. But he also encouraged them to learn about the world by paying attention to what actually was around them. He could teach something about the Amazon by taking his students to look at the marshlands on the outskirts of Cathcart in the spring. He could teach something about mountain ranges in Europe by guiding his students along the limestone trails behind his home in Cathcart. He hoped that what could be immediately observed would arouse curiosity about what could not. A melting bank of snow was a retreating glacier. A puddle beside the playground was a prehistoric sea. A widening crack in the sidewalk at the Girl's Entrance was the drift of continents. There was never a reason not to learn.

Archibald Hughson was famous—famous, that is, in Cathcart—for his kindly nature, his tough marking, his bow ties, and his geography hikes. But it was a legendary final exam on which his reputation most firmly rested.

It only happened the once. It was not an examination that could be repeated. But for years—indeed, for every year until Archie Hughson's retirement—the exam's impact was undiminished. Any student preparing for a geography final with Mr. Hughson did so with the knowledge that he was capable of asking anything.

On that memorable June day, his students—filing anxiously into his classroom, their heads brimming with the memorized names of rivers and precipitation rates and potash production tables—were confronted not with a page of printed questions on each desk but with two objects displayed on a small, white metal table at the front of the class: a rough chunk of limestone and a miniature marble replica of Michelangelo's *David.* On the blackboard, written in an unusually large and solidly chalked script, were three double-underlined words: "Compare and Contrast."

"I want them to think," he had told his wife the day the idea had come to him. "I don't want them to regurgitate."

*Our World* was the product of the same pedagogic instinct. It took Archie three successive summer holidays to write it. The new geography textbook was an entirely unanticipated success.

This made him an unusual client of one of Cathcart's most highly regarded law firms. Archie had never expected to have money. Herkimer's was favoured by the Cathcart families who had every expectation they always would.

I can remember the high ceilings of the old downtown offices of Herkimer's. They were soon to be torn down when

I sat there with Archie a week after Winifred's death. The wood-panelled rooms were on the top floor—the sixth—of a building with a marble foyer, polished hardwood corridors, brass mail chutes, and even then, elevator operators who wore white gloves.

I am not exactly ancient. But I learned from a young reporter at *The Chronicle* with whom I once made the mistake of having a coffee that the gradual disappearance of the old Cathcart has been followed by the much faster disappearance of the knowledge that there ever was one. The young reporter graduated in history, he told me. Perhaps so. But his degree had not given him much grasp on the recent past.

For some reason I was telling him about the pedestal drinking fountains in Cathcart. The fountains were on downtown corners, usually where maple or elm trees provided dappled shade to the thirsty passersby. The sidewalks in Cathcart were wide in those days.

These fountains ran continuously, and the central bud of water tasted exquisitely cold in the pure clear light of those stainless basins. "Really?" my reporter friend said. "And was it safe to drink?"

As far as he was concerned, the old incline up the bluffs of Hillside—its overgrown stone foundations still visible among the trees—might as well have been built by Ozymandias. My early memories of Cathcart—of the tawny sidewalks, of the awnings of china shops and dressmakers, of colonnaded movie-theatre lobbies, and of cool marble washrooms under a civic meridian of tended flower beds and Victorian fountains—were as exotic to him as Babylon. I enjoyed my conversation with the young reporter less, the more I reminisced. By the end of it, I felt a lot more antique than when I'd started out.

There is only one transformation that can compare to

the physical when it comes to growing older. And that is the change that occurs when you go from thinking that nothing disappears to realizing that everything does. There are now discount stores and Money Marts on the main downtown streets. Submarine sandwiches and pizza slices are available.

The Cathcart my parents knew has mostly vanished. And it won't be long before the last of those who remember it are gone too. That's how things get lost. And that, I suppose, is why, before I pause here for some lunch and probably a short nap, I'm asking you—my daughter, my only child—to undertake the occasional remembrance of something you never knew.

It would not be accurate to say that I fell in love with your mother the first time I met her. What would be accurate is: the first time I met your mother I knew that I was going to fall in love with her were I to meet her once, maybe two times, more. In a small town like Pietrabella, meeting Anna again—on the street, in the Café David, at the market—was inevitable. So that much was settled the first time I met her. The only question was how long this would take and whether Anna would ever find out.

She animated what might have been ordinary features—her narrow face, her long nose, her wary, brown eyes—with an energy that had every appearance of great beauty. Her hair so perfectly matched her personality it was usually the first thing that came to mind when anyone thought of her. It was comparable, so I once said, in its wild, abundant splendour to the cascading folds of the cloak in Bernini's *Santa Teresa and the Angel.* I am embarrassed to say those were my exact words.

Sculpture was one of the subjects Anna had decided to teach me about that summer. Her love of stone seemed bound up in everything. There were dinners when we talked about nothing else. I'd always had respect for art—a middle-class attitude that Anna felt could do with some heightening. She took me on day trips to Florence, and the first thing we always did when we got off the train—before we went to the Accademia, or the Uffizi, or the Bargello—was to go to a grove of trees in the Boboli Gardens and smoke a spliff.

Once, we went to Rome. Anna gave me her paperback copy of the treatise on Bernini by Rudolf Wittkower to read on the train. It was held together by an elastic band more than by its crumbling binding. It was underlined so much, there was little text that wasn't.

As was the case in the other subjects of her curriculum that summer, I was an eager student. And I was eager to show off what I'd learned. But when I brought up the subject of Saint Teresa I was crushed to discover I wasn't the first to comment on the baroque associations—high baroque, actually—of Anna in bed.

Pietrabella was a town full of sculptors, and Anna had made morning coffee in her cluttered kitchen for many of them. It's a place where a name such as Bernini—like Michelangelo, like Brancusi, like Canova, like Moore—is almost a household word. Everybody knows *Santa Teresa and the Angel.* So it's not all that surprising that more than a few of her lovers would have made the same association I did. In Pietrabella, it wasn't exactly obscure.

Bernini was drawn to these ecstatic, transformative split seconds. And as great a sculptor as he was, it was this dramatic compulsion that makes him less great than Michelangelo. This, at least, was Anna's opinion on the matter.

Bernini's mastery of the point, the punch, the claw chisel, the rasp, and the trimming hammer was unequalled. Few objects are less stone-like than Santa Teresa's cloak. And few heads of hair were more like a luxurious disarray of heavy silk than Anna's.

Bernini was incapable of creating anything as gracelessly unfeminine as some of Michelangelo's worst female figures. But he lacked something that was in every piece of stone Michelangelo touched.

"He is terrible, as you can see, and one cannot deal with him," said Pope Julius II of Michelangelo, and it is this quality of the *terribilità*—more so than the century that divided the two great artists—that distinguishes the furious preoccupations of Michelangelo from Bernini's smooth genius. It was as if Michelangelo conceived of figures that, no matter the niche or plinth they were to inhabit, would exist most importantly in the infinite space of the viewer's imagination. Bernini, on the other hand, placed his figures in elaborately contrived settings—dramatically coordinating sculpture and architecture. He dictated the viewer's perspective and experimented with the theatricality of concealed, directed light. He was a showman. Not only did Bernini go for a story, he usually went for a story's most spectacular moment.

By Bernini's time, the marble of the Apuan mountains was the material of choice for sculptors (and, more importantly, for the patrons of sculptors) in Holland, Spain, England, Italy, and France. By geological happenstance, it was a material that held within its composition the strength required to support the most delicate carving. Bernini was a virtuoso of marble. *Santa Teresa and the Angel* was carved in Carrara stone.

The recumbent figure is about to be pierced by the arrow of the Holy Spirit wielded by the angel above her. Her eyes seem to have just closed.

The piece is often referred to as *The Ecstasy of Saint*

*Teresa*—a title that Anna preferred. "That is what it is," she said. She peered at me closely as we stood together in Rome, in the grey light of the Cornaro Chapel. She wanted to be sure I understood. She suspected I didn't. The innocence of a Cathcart upbringing was a source of endless fascination to Anna. "It's the statue of orgasm," she felt obliged to make clear, as if explaining something to a particularly slow student. And because I have no photograph of Anna, it's a black and white illustration on a page that had separated from the crumbling binding of her Wittkower that I keep pinned above my desk down at the house: *"St Teresa and the Angel, 1646–52. Cornaro Chapel, Santa Maria della Vittoria, Rome. Bernini."*

In May 1968 I arrived at Richard Christian and Elena Conti's apartment on Via Maddalena in Pietrabella after three miserable days of hitchhiking from Paris. My last, and the only lucky, ride, a skinny Dutch sculptor, picked me up outside of Genoa. He was smoking Marlboros—non-stop, judging from the ashtray. And he had been listening to Ramblin' Jack Elliott and Jerry Jeff Walker all the way from Holland, judging by his lack of interest in playing any other tapes for the rest of the trip.

He was going to Pietrabella. He was going to be there for the next six months. Maybe longer. He'd been there before. He had a studio.

Not only that, he knew the address scrawled on the piece of paper that Richard had given to me in the Louvre. He was happy to drive me right there.

With a crank of handbreak his Deux Chevaux stopped on the steep road in front of the garden wall of number 19.

The steps cut between the terraced vines to the big, old home. The front buzzer clicked on the timed lights in the interior stairwell. The white marble hallway didn't echo very much. But somehow it gave the gleaming, cold impression that it could—quite a lot—given half a chance.

Elena stood beside Richard at the open door of their apartment. She was looking at me and my backpack with suspicion. I could hear voices and the clattering of cutlery behind her.

"Well, well," Richard said. "Will you look at this. It's my dying captive."

There were many such dinners in that apartment during the time I spent in Pietrabella. As a result, I am not certain if I am remembering my first or an accumulation of similar evenings. There must have been a few of the young Italian artisans there—Giuliana, for one, who worked in one of the town's studios, and who had a smile so broad and white it was as if it had been made that way by the marble dust of her work. As well, there would have been some foreign sculptors. Perhaps Luc, tall and gaunt, with dark frizzy hair, who made long, polished totems of marble that he sold through a gallery in Zurich. There were two Swedish sculptors who were often at Richard and Elena's: they worked together on commissions for California wineries and developers in Florida, they lived together in the same mountain house with their girlfriends and jointly tended children, they wore the same denim overalls, and, on occasion, they dropped acid together. They were trying to raise the money to carve a memorial to the workers of the region who had died in accidents in the quarries. Their idea—born of Michelangelo's unfulfilled plan for a mountainside colossus—was a sixty-foot-high figure of a quarry worker, carved directly into one of the flanks of Monte Altissimo. It was the kind of thing you came up with on LSD.

And, of course, there was your mother.

---

Elena and Richard were probably roasting chicken and vegetables that night. They often did. I was ushered in. I was introduced to their guests. Your mother was intrigued, so she later admitted, when Richard repeated what I had hastily explained at the apartment door. His version was shorter but more colourful than mine. He told his friends I was someone he'd met at the Louvre who was now on the lam from the French police.

I put my knapsack in the spare room as instructed.

When I returned to the kitchen, Elena turned and laughed—I'm not sure at what. It was not a particularly significant moment. She was quite small—small, that is, for someone whose quick laughter always became the centre of any room she was in. She was wearing bright colours. She had a wide, expressive smile. "Eyes like pools," Richard once said. "Deep brown pools of mischief."

Elena turning and laughing, at that counter, in that kitchen, is a memory I've always kept. Because I was lonely, I suppose. And because she was kind. There was no part of her laughter, and no part of the way her open face addressed everyone in the room that excluded me.

Elena turned and laughed, and then she asked if I would go outside and get more rosemary for the chicken. It felt like I'd been welcomed in some special way. It wasn't something you'd ask a stranger to do.

At the back of the house there was a slope of vegetables and herbs. It rose in carefully tended terraces from a low stone border to the old town wall. I leaned forward and ruffled through the plants. I felt as if I were hunting through files.

When people talk about their travels, they seldom mention the air. They mention sights, and sounds, and events, and the people they encounter. But they seldom mention the air—or if they do, they mention a partial aspect of it, perhaps its warmth, perhaps its salty briskness. They seldom make reference to its overall feeling: the combination of humidity, elevation, and temperature that makes everything so different in a different place.

I'd never felt air like the evening I met your mother. The sky was mauve and the temperature was so fresh it felt to me as if gravity did not have its customary hold on things.

I could find no rosemary.

The kitchen opened from the central hallway of the second floor. There was jazz on the record player. The air was full with tobacco and hash, heated oil and garlic turning gold in a frying pan.

My empty-handed return was not noticed quickly. Those were dinner parties at which everyone held forth on everything: on Coltrane and Brancusi, Django Reinhardt and Henry Moore, Kerouac and Donatello. The few supper gatherings that the Hughsons hosted in Cathcart were staid, formal, sober affairs. I think that first dinner on Via Maddalena was the first time I understood that talking and laughing and joking and telling stories were what dinner parties are for.

Richard particularly loved talking about music and sculpture, and it was not always clear which was which when he did. He was like Anna that way: not all that big on distinctions. He was not always easy to follow, but there was something about his Texan accent that made him sound sensible—sensible, that is, for an artist, sensible for someone who refused to take any money from his wealthy parents, sensible for someone who could go all the way to Paris to see a single piece of sculpture.

Richard always had about him the wild contradictions of exile. He had fallen in love with Italy as completely as he had fallen in love with Elena—and he lived with a kind of glee, as if this addition to his life was entirely miraculous. But he was dodging a war with a sense of outrage and of justice that seemed, somehow, very American in its confidence. And sometimes late at night, usually when he was drunk, he suffered the sadness of those who adopt a country. Sometimes his bushy eyebrows drooped as if to hide his shining eyes. Sometimes his drawl halted as if he were not sure he could control his voice.

Elena and Richard's kitchen had tall windows and a small stove. There was a terra-cotta pot on a gas ring. There was an oven. There was a cutting board on the kitchen table. There was a salad underway. There was a jug of oil. A chunk of hard cheese. A grater. There were open bottles of wine.

The room seemed old-fashioned even then, with its basic appliances, its high taps, and its small, deep sink. The little table—around which a surprising number of people could be seated for a dinner—had a grey marble top. The windowsills were also stone.

No rosemary? Elena smiled patiently at my stupidity. Everyone laughed. But it was Anna who got up. She was wearing an untucked man's white shirt, rolled khaki slacks, and sockless old sneakers.

She led me out of the apartment, through the high double doors at the end of the marble-floored hallway.

Anna stood at the back of Via Maddalena 19. She pointed. There was a rosemary bush there. It was the size of a large boulder.

"You are not so bright," she said. "For a desperado."

I told Anna what I thought rosemary looked like.

"*Spreegs*?" she asked. "What are *spreegs*?"

---

Now, here I am. All these years later. Back up at the pool. I am following young Robert Mulberry's instructions.

Here I am, cursed by the fury of your mother to still be in the land where rosemary can come in sprigs and spaghetti in cans. And rightly so. I was a coward. Most people are. Here I am, still in Cathcart.

I have a clipboard and some paper. With any luck this chaise—which must be as old as the pool—won't collapse for a few more days. I am drinking Prosecco and grapefruit juice. For old time's sake.

I have now almost concluded what business I need to conclude with young master Mulberry—which, at three hundred dollars per hour, is just as well. And I have now finalized my plans for my visit with you at the end of this month.

You'll note that I say "visit." The sale of the Cathcart property does not mean that I plan to stay in Italy any longer than a visiting relative should. Which is not long—in my opinion.

Not that I am opposed to the idea of staying longer. Staying longer is one of the possibilities that comes from having no place, and no job, and no family to return to. It's one of the things that can sometimes happen to travellers. It's always possible that I'll encounter someone who will change everything.

The weather is warm in Cathcart this April—the result, no doubt, of catastrophic global changes in the climate, but for my isolated purposes, a happy coincidence. The fine balance between the warm sun and a wind that has just passed over the last snow in the Hillside woods reminds me of Pietrabella. There is the same lightness of air that I felt when your mother showed me the rosemary on my first night in Italy.

Your mother used to maintain that she had seen me falling

in love on the evening I arrived in Pietrabella—but not with her brown eyes, and her rumpled white shirt, and her wild hair. She said she could see me falling in love with the air.

"That was the beginning for you," she said. "That was where your changes started. You felt everything first. The details came later."

"You are the details?"

"Love is the details."

"I think you're getting a little carried away."

"Your big problem," she replied, "is you don't get carried away enough."

That was true—although much less true by the end of August than in May. Your mother was very good at getting us carried away.

Our presence in Rome could not have been unknown to the other guests of the poorly soundproofed *pensione* we had chosen near the Campo de' Fiori. We didn't make it to the breakfast room in the morning. And when, that afternoon, we stood together in the Cornaro Chapel, it occurred to me that the tragedy of art appreciation was that it could not always be taught by Anna on the afternoon after a morning of making love.

"Imagine her body," she said to me. Her husky whisper made it clear there was very little innocence in the instruction. We'd been staring at Bernini's *Santa Teresa* for almost ten minutes without speaking. "Can you picture her body under all that luscious garment?"

Anna looked directly at me at that moment. Her eyes are exceptionally beautiful. Then she returned to Saint Teresa.

"Do you see? Bernini catches her when she is just starting. You do not know this feeling. So let me tell you. Don't bother trying. You cannot imagine how delicious this feeling is."

She kissed me quickly, as if in commiseration for this unfairness.

"Bernini catches her when her climax is just starting. To rise. She is just starting to lift herself to meet the angel's arrow." Anna swept her hair away from her eyes. "Everything about her is saying the same thing. Do you see?"

Anna's hand moved through the air as if caressing the form she was describing.

"Even the folds of her cloak are like waves of . . ."

Anna's head was cocked slightly to her left side. T-shirt. Red bandana. White coveralls. Old tennis shoes. No socks. Her hair was in its usual disarray. There she was, *Anna: Cornaro Chapel, Santa Maria della Vittoria, Rome.* Her English sometimes deserted her.

"Pleasure?" I suggested.

"Exactly," she answered. "Waves of pleasure. Coming right from the centre of the stone."

I've always felt lucky to be able to remember something like that . . .

# CHAPTER SEVENTEEN

THE GOATHERD CAME RUNNING to the village on feet like little hoofs. It was August 1944. The men had gone away.

*O partigiano portami via / O bella ciao, bella ciao, bella ciao ciao ciao!*

The goatherd moved uncertainly. His legs were bad. He moved with stiff, awkward difficulty. He looked much older than thirty-three.

When he was small, Italo Cavatore watched his older brother Lino play in the square of the little hillside town. Lino was cunning in his feints and in the unpredictable dance of his slight body as he ran. But even though the two brothers were entirely dissimilar in movement, they bore a resemblance to each other that went beyond their lean faces. It was as if a pathology cast specifically over Italo's stringy legs and curled-in feet had been visited more generally and less severely on his older brother. Lino was one of those taut, wiry boys in whose sharp features can be seen exactly what age will do. He had never looked youthful, exactly. But he was very quick.

Italo liked to imagine that he was the one who was racing and leaping with the other children. Dusk fell and the blackbirds circled and the old bells from the villages across the valleys rang flat. And he ran and he ran in the daydream he liked to have.

He smelled the capers on the stone of the old wall that he leaned against. His legs were splayed and his feet tucked under his pale thighs, and when dinner was ready their mother called the two boys.

*Lino. Italo.*

Sometimes he still thought he heard his mother's voice. *Leeeeno. Eeeeetalo.*

When he was minding his goats when it was dry, the wind had a long, familiar sound. When he sat still, he could hear it. And in the sound of the dry summer heat he could hear: *Lino. Italo.*

He had dreams of visiting his brother one day. Lino lived in a house with electric lights, and hot water pouring from silver taps, and carpet on every floor.

Lino had been away for thirteen years. A long time. A long time for their mother not to see one of her sons. Lino had sent money to their mother every month until the war.

Italo felt special to have such a brother. The olive trees and the mountain crags and the birds and the butterflies and the little wasps treated him with respect when he hobbled along the goat trails with his herd. "That's Lino Cavatore's brother," he liked to think they were saying when they saw him sitting motionless on a hillside in the shade of an old tree.

Lino Cavatore brought young men out from the hillside villages to work for him as apprentices. "I was given a chance," Lino explained, "and now I can make the same offer."

But the war had interrupted. The war was interrupting everything.

Italo kept careful track of his herd, but not by turning his head to watch them. He didn't move a muscle. He listened to the shifting proximity of their tinkling bells. Butterflies landed on him.

He had dreams of girls. They were like clouds.

He was sitting in the shade on the hillside trail that day. His eyes were closed. His dreams were drifting around him. That was when he heard the noises: far below.

Ears like hawks' eyes, people said of Italo.

He knew at once. He could hear danger coming up the trail.

So he ran. He ran as quickly as he could. He made his stiff, clumsy way under the grey wall of Castello and the stone foundations of the church.

He hurried up through the olive grove. He climbed the dusty path. He came up through a hedge of bramble and into the cobbled street.

The goatherd was running on his strange-looking hoof-like feet. They had no feeling.

"They have no feeling," he always said. When he laughed, his face wrinkled with his years in the wind and the sun. And when, as the children always did, they asked Italo if this could really be true, he amazed them. He took off a worn old boot. He pulled down his darned sock. He sat. He lit a match. He held it there. Their eyes went wide.

And now he was running on feet that had no feeling. He was running as best he could. And he was pounding on the heavy wooden doors and he was shouting.

He had heard a commotion of motors from the valley. Tires on gravel. The opening of truck-backs. The clanking of straps and boots and cartridges.

Italo was hurrying through the narrow streets. *Tedeschi.* He was shouting in his strained voice as he went from door to door. Germans.

Soon the word outpaced him. Soon his warning was racing ahead of him in the village of Castello, leaping nimbly from house to house.

# CHAPTER EIGHTEEN

No one is ever sure where Pietrabella is. This is the professional challenge Clara and I confront at the Agency of Regional Tourism every day. This was something my father and I had in common. Nobody knew where he was from either. Nobody had heard of Cathcart.

He'd been found there in 1948. He was in a cardboard box by an antique-looking pool. The box was beside a marble statue.

The fountain's grouping included two other nudes. They were smaller, less precise in their carving, and, by a trick of perspective, apparently in the distance of the tableau. They were approaching the pool behind the larger central figure with their urns on their shoulders. There were a dozen other stone figures—some more weather-worn—around the grounds. But it was the partly naked water-bearers that prompted the joke Michael Barton made when he first proposed that Archie Hughson buy his swimming pool.

MICHAEL INHERITED BARTON HOUSE and the extensive grounds when his father, Argue Barton, collapsed on the sidewalk outside the offices of the Cathcart *Chronicle* on August 15, 1945. The Barton papers were among the few in the world that didn't lead that day with Japan's surrender.

The pool had been so rarely visited by Michael Barton and his young, generally pregnant, English bride, that the Hughsons came to think of it in the years after the war as a kind of forgotten conservation area at the end of their own garden—a blank plot of snow in winter and an empty space of crickets and heat-buzzers in summer. In the spring of '46 the pool's never-very-efficient filter system broke down entirely. Frogs became part of the soundscape.

It was the first of several lots of the Barton property to go. But the truth was, Michael had never cared for the grounds. His mother had died when he was eight, and this was a well of sadness so deep and unexpressed he never spent a day without peering down into it. When, three months after her death, the tomb his father had commissioned was finished, Michael had been terrified by it. It was white and cold and not like his mother at all.

His father's need to sustain his wife's memory—honoured in her mausoleum, honoured in the gardens and pool, honoured in the establishment of the Grace P. Barton Memorial Travel Bursary—always reminded Michael of the honoured gloom in which he had grown up.

He'd had the pool area surveyed. He'd gone to Herkimer's and had it divided from the estate. But before it was officially put up for sale, Michael telephoned Mr. Hughson.

Michael was no longer wealthy. But the habit of appearing so never left him. His voice had the jovial ring of condescension used, almost always, by the well-to-do in conversation with their former teachers.

"Mr. Hughson, sir. I have a business proposition I'd like to make," he said. "Neighbour to neighbour."

Archie walked around the block to the front door of Barton House. They spoke for a while there, and then made their way down the paths past terraced flower beds and rock garden to the pool. It was while they slowly strolled around it that Michael Barton made the joke that Archie would, for some reason, always remember.

Michael Barton said he feared that townhouses might go in. The land could even accommodate a small three- or four-storey apartment building. The zoning regulations were alarmingly flexible. He did not want the Hughsons to be disadvantaged by his decision to sell a portion of land for which he had little use.

The long summer evenings that the Hughsons spent in their garden were not pleasures they were willing to sacrifice to what *The Chronicle* referred to—a little giddily, Archie Hughson thought—as the "Cathcart economic miracle." Cathcart was a long way from becoming anything like a major metropolis, but it prospered in the postwar years. It wasn't far from the American border. That didn't hurt.

Energy and enterprise were in the air, and one didn't want to get in the way of such robust civic ambition. But the Hughsons were thankful to have a retreat from the exhaust and billboards of this progress, and their retreat was their secluded back garden. Their quince tree and blackcurrant bushes produced the fruit for their excellent jam. The Hughsons worked together boiling and canning. Their carefully labelled Mason jars were much sought after at Montrose United's annual bazaar. They made excellent hostess gifts.

Their rose bushes bloomed profusely and the pink flowers were often the centrepiece to their simple dinners. At dusk especially, their garden often seemed as quiet as a country glen. Often, on warm summer evenings, they ate cherries in the garden swing while Mr. Hughson read aloud to his wife from one of the red-bound volumes of the set of Charles Dickens they kept, along with a few Royal Doulton figurines, on the shelves of their living room.

Hillside Avenue marks the point at which the lower, older town and its newer, upper tracts are interrupted by woods and rock ledges too steep to develop. The Hughsons were grateful for this rough geography. When it became too dark for Mr. Hughson to continue his reading, they often sat together in silence. The deep volume of trees rose up beyond the old pool at the end of their garden.

But the world was changing quickly. This was clear to Mr. Hughson. Were he not to buy the property from Michael Barton, someone else would—and that would not have been at all satisfactory.

"Can we afford it?" Mrs. Hughson asked when her husband relayed to her the startling proposal Michael had made. Her face was open and alert.

"We can't expect the royalties to last forever," her husband replied, "but at the moment the purchase is possible. I could take a small loan, I suppose, but I don't think it will be necessary." This was a rare departure from the fiscal certainty by which they liked to conduct their lives. It was a risk that, under the circumstances, they wondered if they might do well to take. They'd always admired the property. It had never occurred to them that someday they would own it.

There was nothing about the pool that admitted to imitation—the statues were worn with an age that seemed well beyond anything to do with Cathcart. The stone bathing pavilion at the deep end, the cracked tiled perimeter of the water, the thick marble flagstones outlined with thyme, the still, green reflection of the surrounding trees—everything about the pool was entirely convincing. It was as if a grotto had been transported from a Tuscan villa, complete with its moss-covered, ivy-shouldered proof of age. It was a secret place that backed onto the Hughsons' ordinary bridal wreath, and everyday wisteria, and their staked, practical rows of *tamatas*.

This was a pool that looked nothing like swimming pools in North America would soon come to look. This was no turquoise rectangle around which people sunbathed and drank soda pop and listened to transistor radios. This was from a much older world.

My father was never sure if the central stone figure—the one gently pouring her jug into the pool—was intended to be Mary Magdalene about to wash Christ's feet, or Rebecca providing water to the strangers sent by Abraham, or just an unnamed woman at an unnamed well.

These details are all answers to questions I put to my father. His letters tended to be answers to my questions. And when they weren't, they were usually reports of his day-to-day activity in Cathcart. "I'm just in from watering the garden" was more his letter-writing style. "The mosaic tile at the edge of the pool is chipping badly." Only his last letter—the one he didn't expect to be read for years—told stories I would not have known to ask him about. More usually he began his letters by telling me he was too tired to write much of a letter. The weather was a popular subject. "I can't remember a colder February." This was the written equivalent of the small talk that drove my mother crazy.

"NICE JUGS," Michael Barton said to Archibald Hughson, gesturing toward the fountain.

There was a moment of silence in which Michael waited for Archie to respond. It passed awkwardly. Michael was so accustomed to being amusing that his voice sounded unresolved when it was not followed by, at the very least, a chuckle. But Archie didn't chuckle. He didn't do anything. He was waiting on the marble flagstones of the old swimming pool, politely puzzled, for Michael to continue.

Michael cleared his throat—a nervously jovial habit. Recently this harrumph had been turning into a prolonged, two-pack-a-day rumble. The hack was, at first, a bit of a joke. Like his famous hangovers, it emphasized his reputation for partying. He'd always been too young and too good-looking to have a smoker's cough. But that was a while ago. Things were not quite so amusing anymore. His eyes were tired.

It might seem a strange thing to say, but he was someone who had been very good at having summer holidays. He excelled at them, and as he grew older he made the mistake of thinking that he could turn his skill for docks and boats and girlfriends to commerce. But he wasn't a businessman. His commercial objectives, like his skills of serious communication, were rarely directed with any single-mindedness.

But Archie Hughson was good at deciphering things. He was a teacher. He was accustomed to finding good answers, like good students, deep in the midst of distracting detail. And the first cogent point he retrieved from Michael's confusing explanation was this: the pool lot had been legally severed from the grounds of the Barton estate. The second concerned some unpleasant possibilities: townhouses, or garages, or even a small apartment building.

"You follow?" Michael asked. He spoke as if it were Archie's hearing, and not Michael's explanation, that might give rise to misunderstanding.

"Oh, yes," Archie replied. "I do. Perfectly well, thank you. And I am quite interested in what you seem to be saying."

When, a few days later, Archie informed Michael Barton of his and his wife's decision to purchase the pool, Michael marked the occasion by presenting Archie with a miniature replica of Michelangelo's *David.* It was a souvenir of his parents' trip to Italy, the summer before he was born.

ARCHIE HUGHSON'S STATUS in the community was largely based on his occupation, on his old-fashioned manners, and on the calm dignity he brought to his duties as an elder at Montrose United Church every Sunday. He was a beloved figure—a public persona that in no way differed from the more private view of him held by his adopted son or his wife. He was a shy man. He had a kind and quiet heart.

He met Winifred when he was at the Cathcart Teachers' College. She really was five-foot-two with eyes of blue. On their first date he took her to the beach. They parked their bicycles under a willow tree, beyond the purple-shadowed spans of the high-level bridge. It was only a short walk to the lakeshore. Just past the railroad tracks, with the water gleaming through the dune grass like the Côte d'Azur, he took Winifred's hand to help her over the deep, hot sand. And, as he was always proud to say, "I never let go."

But the respect he enjoyed in Cathcart had also to do with the fact that he was "quite well-off." The description seemed never to vary in Cathcart conversations.

Entirely to Archie's surprise, *Our World* sold many, many copies. It was first published in 1946. And for close to twenty-five years, it was widely distributed and frequently reprinted. Its unexpected success only made Archie wealthy by a schoolteacher's standards, which wasn't saying much, but that was a perfectly adequate windfall for the Hughsons. Anything more would have been unsettling.

It was the absence of financial anxiety more than the possibilities money presented to them that made the Hughsons thankful for their good fortune. Being "quite well-off" was not a condition with much applicability to their lack of consumption. But it had its advantages. For one thing, Mrs. Hughson devoted herself as a volunteer at the Cathcart General Hospital—an activity that neither she nor her husband considered less than a serious and demanding occupation because it earned her no income.

Their needs were modest: they ate simply, travelled rarely, attended church regularly. They kept an unassuming, comfortable home. The Hughsons were in their mid-forties when they found Oliver—not at all old, of course, but old for a childless couple to adopt a baby.

CONTRARY TO THE ADVICE of almost everyone—and no one had been more outspoken on the matter than his own father—Michael Barton had turned his back on the family's newspapers, took the money he had inherited on his twenty-first birthday, and, before the war was even over, started his own business. He wanted to oversee an enterprise that more suited his own sense of who he was. This motivation was not (as his father had argued, to no effect) much of a basis for profit.

The greyness of newspapers was not in dispute. The business of running them was not a colourful occupation. This, Argue Barton admitted. But in a town the size and modesty of Cathcart, newspapers were a much more reliable commodity than speedboats. On this Argue Barton insisted, uselessly, to his only child.

There were losses in the start-up of Barton Marine. And there were more losses in the quarters and year-ends that followed. It wasn't that the product wasn't good. On the contrary, the long-prowed, beautifully varnished runabouts were well made and well designed. They were soon in great demand. But Michael's financing was not structured to accommodate the expanded production necessary to keep up with success. This was the first in a series of stumbles.

The direction in which things were heading soon became apparent. But they headed that way for a long time without much resolution—long enough for friends to learn to decline Michael's invitations to unnecessarily long lunches at the Cathcart Club. His cheery confidence that he would find investors among old school pals, among regimental buddies, among business associates of his father turned slowly, over many Scotches and water, into the disappointment he became. He drank more heavily. He fought more frequently with his wife. He woke in the middle of every night for a cigarette. But for years Michael was able to prolong his company's decline and his own downward spiral by unloading parcels of the Cathcart property.

Even so, for years Michael remained convinced that his father had been wrong. The war was long over, but he still believed the country to be full of men with no better way to celebrate their good luck at being alive than by laughing in the spray of a speeding Barton Runabout—one hand on the steering wheel, the other around the girl in the bathing suit at his side.

Archie Hughson bought the pool in late 1947. This transaction was one of the early signs of the protracted disaster of what was always referred to in Cathcart as the period of Michael Barton's "financial difficulties." It lasted more than a decade. And it ended badly.

Michael shot himself in Toronto in early November 1958.

The hotel was just across from the bus terminal. The ticket stub from Cathcart was found in his pocket. He had nothing else with him—if, that is, you don't count his clothes, his wallet, an open package of Silk Cuts, a Zippo, a half-empty bottle of Cutty Sark, and a Luger.

# CHAPTER NINETEEN

"How very beautiful!" Grace Barton exclaimed.

"Yes," said Julian Morrow. "But I've learned that it is not called beauty by those for whom it is the everyday. It is who they are. Not what they see."

And Morrow was right. The inhabitants of the hillside and mountain villages didn't think of what surrounded them as beauty. What they recognized was more a pride in their cobbled streets. And in their pale walls. And in the dark escarpments of evening across the valley. It was something they didn't articulate but that they would miss terribly were they ever obliged to leave it behind. As many were. It wasn't beauty—not to them. It was more the sadness that would someday attend its loss.

It was a clear summer day. They had been climbing all morning—Morrow, along with his guests, Grace and Argue Barton. They had lunched at Morrow's villa the day before.

As they walked, Morrow kept a sharp eye for the wild herbs growing amid the rubble that fell away from the road.

He stopped, snapped open a jackknife, and cut the oregano he had spotted. The air expanded with scent. He pulled some cord from another pocket, tied the little bunch deftly, and dropped it in his pocket for his cook. He liked to bring her these little gifts.

They continued the climb.

He had been forced to change his plans. There had been an accident the day before in the quarry to which he usually took guests. These events were upsetting. He was not accustomed to marble's sudden mishap. He doubted he ever would be.

But the quarry to which he was guiding Grace and Argue Barton was just as spectacular. Perhaps even more so. It was, however, a more difficult climb.

Eventually they reached the floor of a working quarry that they would have to cross. They would pick up the trail at the other end of the smooth, rink-like surface. He explained that their climb would follow the steep incline of an old *lizza*—the wooden slide on which blocks of marble had once been lowered.

Because the narrow road opened so abruptly to the wide, flat plain of the quarry floor, because the sun was now higher, and because the smooth, grey-veined white stone reflected the brightness of the cloudless day so strongly, Julian Morrow, accompanied by his friends, moved sharply from shadow to light. It was like stepping from the woods onto the wide, open expanse of a glacier.

The day changed with this transition. Even the sound of their footsteps changed immediately—from the crunch and slide of gravel to the padding of soles across cool stone.

The surrounding peaks, the green hills, the roads that twisted below for miles, the haystack of Corsica on the blue horizon—the clarity of these distances kept the scale of the quarry from becoming frightening. Or so it seemed to Grace, who was in the habit of assessing landscapes with a painter's eye. But the smoothness of the floor, the sharp right angles of the walls, and the levels of marble that had been worked by the quarrymen made Grace feel suddenly very small.

She laughed. "We are church mice crossing the cathedral steps."

Two tightly drawn lines of cutting cables were strung overhead, across the sky. They continued up, out of sight, beyond the lip of the marble above, and they disappeared below, down the slope of the mountain.

"Will the marble ever run out?" Grace asked their host. She was walking beside him with a determined energy.

Morrow smiled. "Like your buffalo?"

"Yes," she said, "I suppose. Like my buffalo."

Morrow was not a small man. He grunted as he hoisted himself over a shelf of stone.

"Someday the sun will die. Someday time will end. I don't think we need worry ourselves about marble running out. Do you?"

"I suppose not," she said.

"At least, not on a day as lovely as this."

The narrow, steep path of the old *lizzatura* was the most difficult section of the climb. The slope seemed unreasonably severe and steep. Argue Barton's new walking boots were not as comfortable as he had hoped, and he stopped several times to adjust their laces. But eventually the three hikers found their pace. They established the steady rhythm of their climb.

The only sounds were their shoes on the loose marble pebbles, the squawk of circling swallows, and the rattle of some abandoned metal siding in the wind.

Occasionally, Grace would stop. She would lean back, eyes closed to the sun, and let the mountain breezes wash over her.

It was noon by the time they reached the upper quarry. By then, it felt as if their sweat was sparking against the mountain air.

"How are you?" Morrow asked her. He was worried about her leg.

"Ecstatic," she replied.

# CHAPTER TWENTY

BEFORE YOU READ what I have written about my twenty-year-old father, I should tell you about the god. It was an idea that my mother came up with. This was in the summer of 1968. This was about the same time she was coming up with me.

She stole the idea from Constantin Brancusi—one of her favourite sculptors. Carve like a god, Brancusi said—something my mother took very much to heart.

This particular god isn't much of a god, though. He's not exactly all-powerful. He's only ancient in the sense that he isn't Christian—an important qualification for my mother. He's pagan, or sort of pagan, or at least he's a god more interested in wine and food and beauty and falling in love than in being the fount of goodness from whom all blessings flow.

He's omniscient because he's a god. But he's lazy. This means he is observant but not likely to engage in the complications of doing anything about what he sees. His great advantage (so my mother decided in the process of inventing him) is that he is not encumbered with the plodding order of time and space in which mortals are customarily confined.

She thought the god was an idea that might prove useful to my father. Because he was, in her view, a bit of an idiot.

My mother believes that the universe is ordered—just not in an order apparent to most mortals. She thinks that any attempt to proclaim a more sequential alignment of past, present, and future is propaganda for the forces of the unimaginative that are, unfortunately, in charge of most things. Most especially, the news.

She was afraid that Oliver was not sufficiently aware of this. Not only might his misguided sense of duty return him to North America, much worse: he was in danger of becoming a journalist.

To understand fully my mother's disdain for the media, you'd have to know how implicated she believes it to be in the general decline of civilization. The short answer—not that she ever has one—is very. And there was no representation of journalism she disliked more than the assured, orderly voice that seemed so often to deliver it.

She thought this was a dangerous distortion of reality, a confidence that belied what she believes is the one essential fact of existence: that we don't, as she always put it, know what the fuck is going on. The measured, certain tone of a weather report could infuriate her.

She thought the two things my father most needed to do were: learn more Italian and be less reasonable. They seemed to go hand in hand. She decided that were he to take on the more attractive qualities of a reasonably fluent, slightly drunken pagan demigod, that would be a good thing—and at the farmhouse, that morning, she told him so.

This was an appropriate setting for such an announcement—as my father pointed out to me in one of his letters. Although he did not want me to imagine that his reasons were authoritative. His sense of the region's history came almost entirely from what my mother told him—a collection of local stories she'd picked up over the years, some true, some probably not.

She knew very little of her own history—very little, that is, beyond the story of the Castello massacre. Its prominence seemed to obscure everything else about her background. This, she resented.

In 1944, before their retreat became complete, the Germans had pushed back not many kilometres to the north of Pisa. But this reversal was not what the Germans imagined it to be. The temporary collapse drew the German forces back south into a deep and what would prove to be a disastrous salient.

But when the German armoured corps retook Pietrabella they did not imagine their triumph would be so brief. They returned with the authority of occupiers. And when they found the bodies of five of their soldiers, all of whom, it seemed, had been burnt alive, there would be no escaping their retribution. The bodies were on the Aurelia, not far from the cemetery, just beyond a small bridge on the outskirts of Pietrabella.

There must have been a vehicle. But the steel, even the shards of tire, had already been scavenged by the locals. The bodies had been left unburied.

It was my mother who told my father how the Germans took their revenge. They staged their assault on Castello from the site of what was once a sacred spring. It was said that in pagan times, women from the region who were slow to conceive came at dawn of the summer solstice to bathe in the pool in the hillside grove of trees. Mothers of infirm children brought their babies. My mother—generously disposed to any spirituality so long as it had nothing to do with priests or nuns—thought the place had great powers.

And it was at that same spot—temple gone, convent gone, villa gone—that my father stepped from the kitchen door of a modest rented farmhouse out into the sunshine late in the summer of 1968. He had by then received a letter from Archie telling him of Winifred Hughson's illness—a tumour discovered in a routine checkup. But Oliver never mentioned this to Anna. He was aware that he would be using it as an excuse.

The news from Cathcart didn't make Oliver decide what to do. It made him realize he already had.

He was going to go down to Pietrabella later that morning to buy a railway ticket—an intention he had not mentioned to my mother.

MY MOTHER TAKES PRIDE in the fact that she has never—"Not once," she always makes a point of saying—paid for a piece of stone. Any countertop or cutting board she has ever had is a castoff from one of the marble yards in Pietrabella. All the pieces of sculpture she has carved have been made from fragments of local Statuario or Bianco P or Bardiglio or Arabescato.

She knows all the marble workers in town. And they all know her. Everyone knows my mother.

For her table she acquired a bevelled panel of Ordinario—the grey, workaday marble that is used in train stations, washrooms, and undistinguished office lobbies. The slab was about the size of a door. It had been discarded because, after it had been cut and polished, a corner had somehow been cracked off. My mother set it up outside the farmhouse on two carpenter trestles.

A remnant of the old villa's terraced garden is there—a grassy plateau about the size of a generously proportioned dining room.

And it was there, that summer, that my mother and father often had their breakfast. This is how I picture it.

Anna turned to smile at his sleepiness that morning. "How is Mr. Up-Early-to-Write?"

The day was already hot and she had been sitting at their outdoor table with her coffee and her first smoke of the day—both of which were finished by the time my father appeared.

She was wearing the man's white T-shirt in which she always slept. Her brown hair was in its customary morning disarray. Oliver wore a towel around his waist.

She said, "I've been thinking about what you were saying last night. Do you remember what you were saying last night?"

He closed his eyes and lowered his face for a moment into her hair, as if doing so would allow him to fall for a few seconds back into sleep.

"You were saying it isn't paragraphs that worry you . . ."

His voice was still thick. "It's the spaces between them."

"Ah, you do remember," she said, rolling her shoulder and head into his kiss. "So I have been thinking."

"Have you indeed?"

"And I've decided that you must be more like Brancusi. You must be more like a god. As Brancusi carves stone. This is how you must write."

"I see," he said.

His writing was not what they were really talking about—my father knew that. What they were talking about were his obligations as a recipient of the Grace P. Barton Memorial Travel Bursary.

The reason I know the official title is not that my father ever used its full length. It's because once my mother decided to talk to me about my father, she used nothing but. She only ever used the award's full, formal name—as if anything shorter would have contained insufficient syllables for her sarcasm.

The Grace P. Barton Memorial Travel Bursary was an endowment established by Cathcart's one newspaper, *The Chronicle.* It was irregularly presented to the winner of an essay-writing contest open to university students. The trust awarded $1800 for "a summer in Europe to broaden the recipient's cultural horizons," and "part-time employment throughout his or her completion of an undergraduate degree." It was understood that the bursary would lead almost certainly to a job at *The Chronicle.*

And so this was what my mother was thinking about when she came up with the idea of the lazy, ancient god. My father could return to Cathcart—as the Hughsons and the trustees of the Grace P. Barton Memorial Travel Bursary expected. That would be sensible. That would be within an established order. That would be reasonable. Or he could, as my mother believed, do something unreasonably and unpredictably godlike. He could do something really unexpected. He could stay with her.

"You must not give this up." This is what my mother said the first time my father read to her a passage from his journal. Her voice was surprisingly stern. And although he peered closely at her eyes, he couldn't tell whether she was joking. Nor was it clear whether "this" referred to the words he had written or to what they were describing: the dusty olive groves; the sweet, curling smoke of a farmer's brush fire in the still, blue air; the flat, thin bell of the church in the hillside village above.

He treated this idea of my mother's—the notion that he would not be a visitor to Italy but a resident—as the wildest fantasy at first. Although one way of describing his summer would be to say that each day of it inclined him more to the idea's possibility. By the time he had to make a decision, the options were almost in equal balance. This was a shift in which my mother played no small part.

To begin with, she taught him to cook—lessons that started with her standing at the marble cutting board in the farmhouse kitchen. She turned slowly around to him with a bud of garlic in one hand and a paring knife in the other. Her eyes were wide in disbelief.

And there were other lessons. On late weekend mornings they sat in the sun at the outdoor table smoking spliffs and drinking Prosecco. They passed the time with the stories they invented. But usually, when the day got hot and drowsy, they ended up going back to bed.

My mother has always insisted on being frank with me about sex. It is one of her personal measures for countering the strictures of the bourgeoisie. I was never comfortable with this. But my comfort wasn't the issue. This was a struggle my mother expected to take generations. She felt she had an example to set.

My mother wasn't an exhibitionist. That would be an exaggeration. Let's just say, she was never quiet—a recurrence of moans and sighs and shrieks that, as a child, I took to be something like thunderstorms, only more frequent. At a very young age, I knew what a lover was because I met so many of them at our breakfast table.

Once the subject of the young Oliver Hughson was out in the open, my mother saw no reason to be discreet just because he was my father. "At first, he knew as much about lovemaking as he did about cooking," she told me. There was a pause. "I had to tell him what garlic is."

On the occasions (usually late at night, usually after lots of wine) when my mother persisted in arguing against my father's conviction that he should be reasonable—when, no matter how light her tone, she made it clear that she wasn't joking about how important it was that he stay—he avoided confronting her directly. His claim that he didn't know enough about the region's history, or about marble, or about the history of sculpture to write the kind of book she had envisioned for him at least shifted the discussion away from immigration. Concern about talent was a safer subject for him to raise than his doubt about commitment—certainly it was less likely to infuriate my mother.

"It's connecting things that's the problem" was what he had said to her. He knew she was susceptible to exactly this kind of abstraction.

My mother's flaws have largely to do with her relationship with the future. Her retirement, for example, couldn't possibly be less real for her than it is. "I'm an artist," she says. "Not being an artist is not something I'm saving up for."

As my ever-practical husband tried to explain to her, this is not a responsible attitude. People get sick, Enrico said. People get old. But there is a saying in the mountain towns that goes: the pail of strength and the pail of weakness are drawn from the same well. That's my mother.

Her lack of regard for the future has always been maddening. But it finds alternative expression in how fully she occupies the present. I am familiar with the look: her eyes closed, her lips parted, her neck arched back slightly, as if she is pausing, instructing herself to drink in every sensation of being alive. She moves through the air with an open, attentive saunter.

Faith in the improvisational nature of the present is a kind of personal creed, one that is connected to her most important artistic pursuits. My mother believes that great sculptors—whether they be masters of the figure, such as Michelangelo and Bernini, or masters of more abstracted form, such as Brancusi—move from plane to plane without thinking about anything other than the instant of their carving. "They are like ancient gods, looking down on their world of marble," she once said. "They are in the piece. They are outside it. They are close. They are far away. It's a talent sculptors have."

She paused.

"It's why we are so bad at everything else."

ON THAT LATE AUGUST MORNING Anna smiled at how obviously Oliver Hughson's sleep still clung to him.

"But I think you are too sleepy to do magical things," she said. "So you will have to be a lazy, ancient god."

My mother's relationship to the past is more complicated than most people's. She inhabits it more wilfully than anyone I know. What she chooses not to think about, she puts away, as if in a locked drawer. She is very disciplined in this. As one good example, she was so angry with my father, she didn't think of him for forty years.

This doesn't mean that she was unable to remember him. It means that when she sensed his memory looming on her horizon, she turned away from it, the way someone with a stutter learns to avoid the approach of a troublesome consonant. In fact—as I eventually learned—she remembers quite a lot about the summer of 1968.

"Ask him if he remembers the lazy, ancient god," she instructed me. We were sitting at her outdoor table on a spring evening in 2009. I had just told her that I was going to go to Cathcart to meet my father.

She pulled on her hand-rolled cigarette, exhaled unhurriedly into the still evening. She considered the smoke carefully. I remember being surprised. This was the first indication that she might lift her embargo on his memory.

And so that's how I picture him: on a chaise, in the afternoon, looking up into the sky. But he could just as easily be looking down. Direction is immaterial when it comes to lazy, ancient gods. It's almost as irrelevant as chronology.

This is why my mother says she prefers Michelangelo's unfinished sculpture to the most polished of an artist even as great as Bernini. She doesn't love anything that insists on being observed from a single point of view—a staged theatricality on which Bernini usually insisted. She likes to move around objects. She says that's what space is for.

Even a lazy deity could probably locate the right Italian town through the parting clouds—but it's not easy. From way up, where the gods drift, there isn't much colour to be seen down below. Everything is a grey, hazy map—like a polished marble floor. The pigments and earth tones become clearer as he descends, but even that isn't much help. All the Tuscan towns look like the opening credits of movies. It's the light.

The lazy, ancient god looks down, past the bell towers and red-tiled roofs, on the right piazza. He's got the right time of the day, in the right year. It takes some doing.

It is late summer of 1968. At a table of the Café David, in the main square of a little town in the northwest corner of Tuscany, there is milk-foam on the rim of young Oliver's cappuccino. He is twenty years old.

His journal is open. The smoke of his cigarette is drifting from his table on the southern side of the central piazza of the old town of Pietrabella. He has a train ticket in his pocket.

# CHAPTER TWENTY-ONE

By the early afternoon the three hikers had reached a height in the mountains at which the sunlight felt coated with a thin veneer of cold. The upward climb had taken four hours. Grace Barton had refused to be slow.

About thirty metres below their destination, the path seemed to end. A steel-cable ladder was staked into the outside edge of a wall of stone. Morrow stood at the base.

"This is a little dangerous," he said to Grace.

She looked at him with alarm.

"But," he said with a reassuring smile, "rather fun."

She placed her foot on the first rung. He reached around to guide her.

She started up, not daring to look down. The ladder ended at a wide ledge high above the spot from which her anxious husband watched her climb. Julian Morrow waited for her to complete her ascent before he helped Argue Barton begin his.

Grace had been standing alone for several minutes, looking out to the red roofs of the distant towns and the flat blue of the sea, before her husband joined her. Morrow followed.

"*Ecco,*" he said. Morrow gestured, and when she turned, she was astonished that she had not seen what was behind her. It was a high cave, cut into the side of the mountain. It felt as if they were standing at the portal of a cathedral. "*Luci di marmo,*" Morrow said. "The light of marble. It's like this nowhere else on earth."

They would eat their lunch on the picnic rug he opened in front of the long-abandoned quarry. From there they could peer up into the cave. They could see the high ladders and scaffolding. There were rusted stakes driven into the walls of the high cut of rock—From what original vantage? she wondered. How did the cobwebs of wire get so far up there? It was impossible to imagine working there under the calmest of circumstances. "What would it be like, she asked, "to be climbing the scaffolding, traversing those catwalks in a driving winter wind?"

"Difficult," Morrow said. That was the only description. "Work in the quarries can be very . . . difficult."

The accident had occurred in another quarry the day before. Julian Morrow felt how truly cold and implacable these mountains could be, and the thought saddened him. As it always did. His manager would provide him with the details.

These scaffoldings and ropes and dangling ladders were climbed and crossed and clung to, Morrow explained. "The workers' job," he said, "was to cut away the loose stone high above the vast blocks that would be cut from the wall." Here and there, the sunlight caught an angle of broken white stone, sparking the crystalline glint sometimes called "tears of Christ."

Or, he pointed out, his guests could look in the other direction. They could look from a great height out toward the coastal towns. There, said Morrow, were the marble yards, the loading docks, the saws, the studios, and the offices where marble agents made the connections with buyers in London, in New York, in Paris. And there was the sea.

"My world," he said.

He was unpacking their lunch from his rucksack. The wine for their meal in the quarries had been wrapped in damp canvas by his cook to stay cool.

"Simple fare," Julian Morrow said. "But I hope to your liking."

# CHAPTER TWENTY-TWO

I DIDN'T KNOW who my father was until a year before his death. I was forty years old when I made the discovery. And the first thing I did when I learned Oliver Hughson's identity was figure out where he lived.

Getting any information from my mother on this particular subject was not easy.

At first she said, "He's gone." Her response to hearing a name she had not heard spoken for decades was calm but resolute. "Forever," she added, as if she were a judge recalling a sentence from a long-ago case.

"But he was important to you."

"Once."

"Would you ever see him again?"

"It would take a miracle."

She stared at me with her characteristically maddening combination of unreasonableness and concern. "Why do you want to get to know him? Now."

"Because he's my father."

"So?"

"I need to learn who I am."

"You don't need to," she replied. "You want to. There's a difference." And for a while we left it at that.

But when my mother eventually admitted to me that she could remember who my father was, she said she didn't really know where he was from. Not precisely. She never had.

"Somewhere near New York," she said. "Or Chicago. Or Hollywood, maybe."

This was not a help.

What little information had found its way to her did not add up to a country. She was relieved to learn that no baby seals had ever been clubbed in Cathcart. Once, as a child, she'd read a book by Grey Owl, but she couldn't remember anything about it. Sometimes, when she was crossing the smooth white surface of a quarry floor, she wondered what could be done with chisel blades that were built into skates. There was a Joni Mitchell song she liked about a frozen river. This was pretty much the sum total of her thoughts about Canada.

Anna thought the name of the town Oliver was from and the name of the province the town was in were a single word. When I mentioned this to my father on the evening of our first meeting in Cathcart, he smiled, a little sadly. "I haven't heard that for a very long time," he said.

Pietrabella is in Italy, but nobody knows where it is either, because it is not very distinguished and it is surrounded by places that are. It's a dusty, noisy town, and probably only my father, who had hardly visited anywhere else in the world in his life, could have found it as magical as he did. He told me that, on his first morning there, he pushed open the shutters of the spare room in Richard Christian and Elena Conti's apartment on Via

Maddalena—the same room, it so happens, in which I am writing now. He said he had never seen so beautiful a place.

This is not the common view. Pietrabella is not at all what people picture when they think of Tuscany—even when I instruct them to forget scenes from movies about people discovering picturesque properties requiring renovation and the intervention of handsome local tradesmen in the lives of lonely women. I tell them to think of the ordinary northwest corner of Tuscany on the ordinary flats between the Apuan mountains and the sea. Still, I am often surprised by the blank stares I receive, even from Italians. So then I say, "Not far from Carrara," and usually people know where I mean. At least approximately. Although I have noticed that North Americans sometimes remain confused. As they often do.

Carrara is one of those names that Americans think they know. It sounds familiar, but they aren't quite sure why. Sometimes they think it is a make of downhill skis. Or a kind of sports car. Or a line of fancy kitchen appliances or a condominium complex. "The marble quarries," I then say. Which still doesn't necessarily help.

My father was carried by two paramedics from his seat on the Alitalia flight from Toronto to Milan on the morning of April 23, 2010. He was carried because the wheels of the ambulance gurney would not pass down the plane's narrow aisle. There were too many seats for that.

As we went through the papers he had with him in the airport, it became apparent that he had sold his house in Cathcart shortly before his departure for Italy. This was unsettling—partly because he had said nothing to me of this decision, and partly because the officials with whom I had to deal began referring to him as someone "of no fixed address."

"He is not a nomad," I told the immigration officer. "Obviously."

Actually, it wasn't that obvious. If my father had an address, we couldn't find it.

"But where does he live?" the immigration officer asked. There was an edge of frustration in his voice, a bureaucratic reaction to an unsettling absence of necessary information. Apparently, the processing of my father could not continue—not satisfactorily—if it appeared that the body came from nowhere.

Nobody knew what to do. And there I stood, in the harsh, modern light of the airport, surrounded by a semicircle of police, immigration officials, airline representatives, and the two bewildered baggage handlers with a wooden crate the size and shape of a casket on the dolly between them. One of the airline employees—a woman—thought I had not heard the question. And after a few moments of silence, she repeated it more gently.

"Do you know his place of residence?" she asked.

A few more seconds of my silence passed. A delay in a flight to Nairobi was being announced.

"Cathcartario," I answered—as much to myself as to anyone. And this, finally, was when I began to cry.

# CHAPTER TWENTY-THREE

THE YOUNG OLIVER HUGHSON was not athletic in his build. His arms were a little slender; his chest was a little caved. It was late in the summer of 1968, at a table of the Café David, in the main square of a little town in the northwest corner of Tuscany.

Pietrabella isn't very far from the marble quarries of Carrara. It's a town that sculptors have known for centuries. But it's a place that Michelangelo didn't care for very much, if you want to know the truth. It was an irony not lost on my boss, Pier-Giorgio, that a place that has always been so noisily, dustily, and charmlessly devoted to the industry of stone, seemed only to get in the way of Michelangelo's chief obsession.

Michelangelo was one of those geniuses who seemed to have the history of art coursing through him—not because history interested him particularly but because both inspiration and instruction were to be found there. Anna used to say that the past wasn't something Michelangelo studied. It was part of who he was.

It was in 1506, on the Esquiline Hill in Rome, that a man came across what he thought at first was a buried grey rock. It appeared as if it had been worn into furrows by the passage of time. He was digging in a vineyard. And as he continued to dig, he was surprised by the size of what he was discovering. And then he began to see that it was not a rock at all.

A bearded male nude and two smaller, younger figures emerged. They were pulled from the mud and the pebbles and the shards of terra-cotta that had surrounded them for centuries. It took the farmer a good hour of digging before he could see that the three figures were of a single piece. They were struggling with two large serpents.

The discovery was sensational. Possibly, it was the Greek original. Possibly, a later Roman copy. Crowds gathered. Artists travelled great distances to study the marble statue.

The ferocious dignity of Laocoon's struggle and the violent torque of the central figure fascinated Michelangelo. So did the serpents—sent by the gods to kill a father and his two sons. But Michelangelo was as interested in the practical function of the coiling snakes as much as anything. He admired the ingenuity. The serpents upheld the weight of Laocoon's extended and otherwise insupportable arms.

By the time Michelangelo was in the Carrara area looking for the stone for the pope's tomb, his first *Pietà* and the *David* were both behind him. He was no longer a young man, but he still had a young man's passion for stone. He didn't much like the place where, at the pope's orders, he had ended up. He was impatient and restless and irritable.

There are more beautiful towns. It is the tragedy of Pier-Giorgio that he kissed only enough asses to be appointed executive director of the tourist agency here, and not in Lucca or Florence—municipalities better suited to his goatee and his Milanese suits. Here, things aren't so grand.

Most of the artists who work in Pietrabella are unknown foreigners. Most of them are young. And most of them are destined eventually to see for themselves, if they are not told by others, that they are not going to be great sculptors. In most cases they are not going to be sculptors at all. But there is a time of life when this doesn't matter very much. There is a time of life that is, for some, the most beautiful of all. It can be a few days. It can be a year, sometimes two. It usually happens away—somewhere we can be who we want to be, instead of who we are.

For aspiring sculptors—their heads spinning with Brancusi and Moore, Bernini and Michelangelo—Pietrabella was that somewhere. It may be a centre of the marble industry in the Carrara area—the bustling headquarters of bathroom tiles, condominium lobbies, and kitchen backsplashes—but it is also a capital of artistic aspiration.

There are established artists who live in the area. And there are others who visit regularly, coming to choose stone, or to work, or to oversee the transposition of a small clay or plaster model into a piece of marble big enough to command a public square in Berlin or the entrance to a cluster of corporate towers in Shanghai. It is the local artisans, almost more than the stone itself, that make the place famous.

Henry Moore used to visit Pietrabella often. On occasion my mother was hired by one of the marble workshops to act as a guide for his excursions to the quarries. She remembered that his nose was very red. Botero lives not far away. Giovanni Belli's photographs include portraits of Jacques Lipchitz and Jean Arp sitting in the Café David after their day's work. But for the most part, Pietrabella is populated by freight handlers, diamond-saw operators, lorry drivers, marble workers, and commercial stone carvers. This is not, as Pier-Giorgio makes clear, very glamorous.

Above the Café David in the main square there is a plaque marking the gloomy upstairs room where Michelangelo signed a contract for the stone he needed for one of the many projects that he never completed. But the bidets for the sultan of Brunei also came from the workshops of Pietrabella. Crucifixes and *Pietà*s, telephones and sinks, cupids and communion chalices are churned out morning and afternoon by the artisans of Pietrabella, men dressed in blue dust coats and folded newspaper hats who could carve the curls of Christ's beard or the folds of Mary's gown in their sleep. These traditions, passed from generation to generation, are ancient. But they are not, as Pier-Giorgio frequently points out, very sexy.

Our office hears regular complaints from hotel guests who imagined their holiday as picturesque tranquility but who are awakened at eight in the morning by the whir of dozens of pneumatic chisels and the beeping of front-end loaders from the town's marble workshops. The tourists who sit on the terraces of our cafés object to the noise and the fumes of passing lorries and stone-laden flatbeds. As a result, Pier-Giorgio rejects any marketing initiatives that emphasize the region's industry. He takes particular pleasure in reminding us that our most important visiting artist did nothing but complain about what a shithole he found himself in.

The combination of Michelangelo's displeasure at being here and his disinclination to leave much evidence that he ever was, do not make him a very obvious marketing tool for regional tourism. He presents challenges, I admit. But Pier-Giorgio's attitude, when I am foolish enough to bring the subject up in her presence, drives my mother crazy. "Greatness is greatness," she says. "And morons are morons."

In order to get the full impact of Anna Di Castello's aesthetic theories you'd have to sit at her outdoor dining table with her as she talks—at some length—about art. This is what my father did on the last, long evening he spent with her. He was going to buy his train ticket the next morning. He was going to sit for the last time at a table at the Café David and write in his journal the next day. And then he was going to come back to the farmhouse from Pietrabella to tell Anna that he was leaving her. But the night before all this would happen, she had talked about art until the light had fallen.

My mother believes that art is a spirit, not a museum of objects, and that the work of the truly great—of whom there are very few—becomes part of what mankind is, not what it observes when it takes the time to visit an art gallery. Of course this spirit is visible in institutions such as the Accademia and the Louvre, but it is also apparent in the everyday. In fact, it is especially apparent in the everyday because the reason great art is great art—at least according to my mother—is that it is the everyday. The patterns of beauty that are apparent in a cobbled street, a mountain stream, or in the arch of boughs over the curve of a hillside path, are the same patterns found in the curves and planes, the light and shadow, of *David,* or *Santa Teresa,* or *The Kiss.* My mother conceives of art as being an ongoing song, to which centuries of voices contribute. And a few of the voices—Michelangelo is always the example she uses—are so great, they become the melody with which others harmonize.

On that last evening, when she sat at her uncleared outdoor table, drinking wine and talking happily with my father, she insisted that the song was audible for anyone who cared to listen. She crumbled her hash, rolled her tobacco, set the spliff in the corner of her mouth, scratched a match on the rough underside of the marble slab—all without ceasing to speak. And her descriptions to him of the music she heard were various. It was energy. It was a magnetic field. It was a global grid of mystical points, responsible for outbursts of genius such as Charles Dickens, Dizzy Gillespie, and Leonard Cohen among others. She believed the stir Michelangelo created in the universe when he carved stone was something that could be felt still. She blew out the match with the exhaled smoke of her only pause.

I'm not sure who would be more horrified by this—my mother or Pier-Giorgio—but I do sometimes think that even the most harried and exhausted tourist is still hoping for something magical to happen on a trip to Italy. Even the one whose feet are hurting the most, whose back is the most sore, and who is most bored by what a museum guide is saying must want to feel the ruffled air of the ghosts my mother feels all the time. It isn't the fact that Michelangelo was once in the vicinity of her farmhouse that excites her. She thinks he still is.

In the 1920s and 1930s, Giovanni Belli spent a good deal of time looking for evidence of work undertaken by Michelangelo during what was, apparently, his unhappy time in the Carrara and Pietrabella area. When my father wondered how it was that Michelangelo could have been so grumpy about a place that seemed—at least to a visitor from a small, unremarkable place in North America—so very beautiful, my mother said that Michelangelo's moodiness was not caused by where he found himself so much as by what he found himself doing. Which was not carving marble.

IN 1968, AS HE SAT ON THE TERRACE of the Café David, Oliver had something. And what he had was being twenty. He thought it was his being in Italy. He wasn't the first to confuse the two.

Oliver had come to Pietrabella with no intention of staying for more than a few days. This was how long he had expected it would take for the Société Générale in Paris to transfer his funds to a bank in Pietrabella. Once that was sorted out, he'd recommence his travels. This proved to be an unrealistically optimistic view of the efficiency of European financial transactions in the late 1960s.

Being an artist's model was a job that he had never previously imagined for himself, nor one that he would ever feel capable of undertaking again. But during his four months in Italy—his four months with Anna Di Castello, his only four months anywhere that wasn't Cathcart, half of which were spent waiting for the Société Générale to release the funds of the Grace P. Barton Memorial Travel Bursary—he was perfectly poised between his youth and his adulthood. This was a moment of grace he was able to put to some advantage. He needed to make some money and so he worked for Richard Christian: standing, sitting, squatting, twisting, and, for one of the figures in *The Pope's Tomb*, simulating as best he could, without actually strangling, being hung naked in Richard's studio. For Richard's idea was that his captives, the figures that would populate the pedestals and niches of his tomb, would be the grotesqueries of the modern age: the murdered, the tortured, the starving, the war-torn. But this wasn't going to be easy—certainly not for his model. "This figure," Richard explained as he demonstrated the cowering crouch he wanted for one of his captives, "has just been sprayed with napalm. I want to feel his skin bubbling." They were, as Richard put it, "killer poses."

But Oliver was up for it. It was work. It was enough money to get by. He had arrived in a town of sculptors at the one instant in his life when artist's model was an occupational possibility.

SEATED AT A TABLE AT THE CAFÉ DAVID on his last day there—with the milk-foam on the rim of his cappuccino, with the smoke of his cigarette drifting across the piazza, with a train ticket in his pocket—Oliver Hughson was copying a verse of poetry in his rounded cursive into his journal. He liked the quotations in his journal to be neat. He wrote carefully:

*And you wait, you wait for the one thing*
*that will infinitely increase your life;*
*the mighty, the tremendous thing,*
*the awakening of stones,*
*depths turned to face you.*

It was a verse from "Memory," and it wasn't likely that Oliver was the only young person who, at that moment, was sitting down in an outdoor café to copy Rilke carefully into a journal. It was late in the summer of 1968. The youth hostels and train stations and art galleries of Europe were full of Olivers.

At a café in the main square of Pietrabella, Oliver took a last inauthentic pull on his cigarette. He was not really a smoker. He just liked the way he looked with a cigarette. He finished his coffee. He put his cap on his pen. He tucked his journal and his Rilke into his rucksack. He stood to go.

It was a slow time of morning, the midpoint between the early caffè *corretto* of the artisans on their way to their workbenches and the later cappuccinos of the lost-looking tourists who found their way, usually by accident, to Pietrabella.

Oliver left a tip, more generous than usual. He'd be back someday, he was sure. Perhaps next summer. Or the summer after that. He had not quite thought things through.

He looked around, taking in the red geraniums on the old brick balustrade, the tobacco shop, the cinema, the fountain, the wide, vacant steps of the cathedral. He looked to the east, up beyond the town wall to the hills. He could see the steep grey bluff that marked the western ridge of the Apuan mountains. He wished now that he had been more rigorous with his journal entries during the past four months. He wondered how vividly he'd remember the evenings when Anna sat at her marble table and taught him about the figures of beauty that so commanded her imagination. "Form," she said. "Michelangelo was great because he understood that form is all we have. Here. Now." Oliver wondered how clearly he'd remember the details of Anna's face, her voice, her instruction.

On one of his journeys along the region's hillside trails, Michelangelo conceived of the idea of carving a giant into a craggy face of bald stone. This had great appeal to him. It would be enormous, for one thing. For another, carving directly into the bluff meant there would be no wagon contractor, no barge captain, and no rogue of a stone agent involved.

Michelangelo's letters to Rome hardly stopped. "I think I have been gulled," he wrote in April 1518. "And it's the same with everything. I curse a thousand times the day and the hour I left Carrara!"

Michelangelo oversaw every aspect of quarrying, from choosing the face to be cut, to supervising the cutting itself, the sledding of the blocks down the mountainside, and the loading onto ox-drawn carts. He hired barges. He accompanied the blocks to the coast—an arduous and dangerous journey.

In Pietrabella's main square, Oliver stepped away from his table and gave a brief, ordinary wave to Claudio Morello, the café owner. Claudio was banging away, as usual, at the espresso machine.

Anna liked the Café David. She was a fixture there. Claudio enjoyed her. Their political differences could not have been more extreme. Given her history, it was hard to imagine that a friendship between them could be possible. But it was. Their disagreements were swept away by their major point of agreement. They were both impatient with any artist who did not insist on comparison with the greatest. It was Claudio Morello, bar owner and fascist, who most outspokenly shared Anna's belief in the uncompromising importance of beauty.

At the Café David, Anna tended to become the centre of the tables full of foreign sculptors. Her English, her knowledge of all things local, and her looks meant that she never sat at a table by herself for very long.

So Claudio tended to undercharge her. The *stranieri* wanted to drink grappa with her. And talk about Brancusi with her. And ask her where to buy the best olive oil, the best pancetta, the best claw chisels and fine rasps. And late at night, not long before Claudio presented them with the sobering reality of their bar bill, they wanted Anna to sing "Bella Ciao." It was a song of the partisans, from the war.

Oliver liked to go into town with Anna in the evenings. They got dressed up, a little. Which is to say, Anna got out of her cut-off jeans and construction boots, her T-shirt and bandana. She showered, or sometimes, when it was very hot, washed herself with the cold water from the old hand pump at the end of the garden.

Oliver never knew anyone who looked better in a man's white shirt and a pair of blue jeans. In the Café David, he sat back, slightly removed from the centre of the pulled-together tables. The wine and the grappa were ordered and reordered. He watched Anna. She was at the centre of everything. And when she was laughing and clapping her hands it was the rhythm of Anna's muscular arms and shoulders and the movement of her shining hair that became the beat of everyone's singing.

*O partigiano portami via / O bella ciao, bella ciao . . .* It was the song of a partisan fighter leaving his beloved. It was the song of all young men off to war.

*Bella ciao ciao ciao!*

Anna enjoyed these gatherings. But Oliver liked their departures from the bar best. Then the cool nights tumbled down to the square from the mountains. The air smelled of damp stone as they started their way up from Via Maddalena to the olive groves, to the hillside path that led to Anna's farmhouse. There were fireflies once they got beyond the town wall. "We are walking through what Michelangelo would have known," Oliver said. "It's like we go back in time."

Michelangelo walked the mountains, surveyed the quarries, tested small pieces, searched for breaks, studied veins. He listened to the stone, rapping it with a hammer to hear either the clank of imperfection or the clarity of a faultless ring. Marble can hide surprises—accessory minerals, or faults, or pockets that are not visible. And as Michelangelo studied the stone, he studied the quarry workers. His gaze returned to them again and again.

They lifted, they pulled, they heaved, they strained. He watched their taut muscles and their tanned skin and the way the sweat ran down the crevasses of their necks. He watched their twisting, turning, bending bodies accommodate themselves to the demands of their work. They were usually young. But they had about them something even more irresistible than their youth: they had the camaraderie of young men joining together closely in dangerous work. They were soldiers of sorts.

Nobody did male figures like he did. Vasari says that at the Santa Maria Novella job-site in Florence, the young Michelangelo "started to draw the scaffolding and trestles and various implements and materials, as well as some of the young men who were busy there."

From the café Oliver crossed the square and disappeared under the rooks' nests in the portal of the town's old wall. He'd always liked the walk from Pietrabella.

He passed the train station where, earlier, he had bought his ticket for Paris. He passed a restaurant where he liked the bean soup. He passed a little hardware store where he bought some string once. He passed the doorways of a few vegetable stores he had come to know. He passed a good place to buy wine and olive oil that Anna had showed him. He crossed an intersection on the Aurelia. He took all this in. He was aware that these places were now no longer where he was. They were what he was leaving.

It was never an argument. It was never even much of a discussion. It was more like a running joke that Anna had with him, one that took the place of argument or discussion. But the subject never changed. "You are being pointed in a whole new direction," Anna said one afternoon in their bedroom. "By fate. By destiny." She always closed the shutters on the daytime heat. They could hear the landlord's tractor in a distant patch of sun. Drying hay was on what breeze there was. "You are being shown your true path." She tried, without success, not to laugh at herself. "Why can't you see that, you *stupido*?"

He continued south on the shoulder of the road, protected by the plane trees from the traffic: cars and scooters and rumbling lorries. He walked beside a pale wall that, twenty-three years after the war, still bore pockmarks of the Allied advance and the German retreat from the Gothic Line. "It was at this unhappy site," a plaque explained (and that Oliver's bad Italian could just work out), "that five German soldiers were ambushed, resulting in the terrible retribution by Nazi forces and the tragic events of Castello on August 12, 1944."

Beyond the cemetery, Oliver was in the countryside.

Oliver had no point of comparison, really. He was not greatly experienced in love. Which is to say, until he met Anna, he was not experienced at all.

He once said to Anna that the smell of her hair was what he imagined a forest would be like if he woke in its shadows after a midsummer nap.

She laughed and said, "You're crazy."

And he kissed the back of her neck and said, "Oh, you've got that right."

So it wasn't that Oliver didn't know he was in love. What he didn't know (but what any lazy, ancient god could have told him) was that he would never be so happy and so in love again.

The light was a combination of haze and precision. The cut-out hills. The veins of smoke from the little fires at the edge of olive groves.

Michelangelo once came to the region to sign a contract for marble, and he must have walked along the same road. More or less. And if he didn't, Anna and Oliver had decided that they could say he did. Who was to say otherwise?

"He was on his way back to the convent where he's staying," Anna had decided. "There is a fountain where the old abbess always sits. It needs his attention."

# CHAPTER TWENTY-FOUR

MICHELANGELO WAS WEARING BOOTS of cordwain over his stockings. He had a task to perform. It was a favour for an old holy woman of great wisdom. A correction to a piece of marble statuary—little more than smoothing out a knot of stone where a piece had broken and been inexpertly rejoined.

The rejoining technique was something that he'd learned from old stone carvers as a boy—a very finely cut tongue and groove of stone, implemented in an elongated zigzag to maximize its strength. Sometimes there was a flaw in the stone that no one had guessed was there. And no worker wanted to abandon a piece when an arm, or a hand, or a curling beard that had been carefully worked over for hours and hours suddenly broke away.

Resin and marble dust were mixed to create an epoxy. Then the joint was carefully and finely polished. It was a useful trick, known to any experienced hand in a marble studio. It amused

Michelangelo that the repair—almost invisible—would resemble an *M*.

The flaw in the convent fountain may not have been a carver's mistake so much as an artist's rush to complete a job for an impatient patron. Michelangelo was familiar with the problem.

The tomb of Pope Julius II was to be a project of unsurpassed scope. Michelangelo's pupil Ascanio Condivi wrote that the "tomb was to have had four faces, two of eighteen *braccia,* that served for the flanks, and two of twelve for the heads, so that it was to be a square and a half in plan. All around about the outside were niches for statues, and between niche and niche, terminal figures; to these were bound other statues, like prisoners, upon certain square plinths, rising from the ground and projecting from the monument."

The reasons for Michelangelo's bad temper were obvious. His days were too full of contracts—contracts with quarry owners, contracts with transport drivers, contracts signed in airless second-floor rooms with obsequious marble merchants and greedy stone agents. It would be good for him to grip a chisel.

Michelangelo hurried over the millstream.

The task Michelangelo would perform at the convent wasn't much of a job, but it would be a welcome change. The duties he was called upon to perform for Julius—all preliminary to the carving he longed to do—were wearisome. "I have ordered many blocks of marble and handed out money here and there, and had the quarrying started in various places," he wrote in one of his letters to Rome. This was all necessary, but he did not enjoy becoming entangled in the business of marble. It gave him a headache. He wanted to get back to what he loved most. He wanted to get back to working stone. He always did.

During his time in the Carrara area, it was unlikely that Michelangelo left anything to chance—or at least not to the very good chance that somebody would be less a perfectionist than he was. He climbed and clambered and searched for exactly the right whiteness and sparkle of Statuario, exactly the right overcast Bardiglio, exactly the right creamy patterning of Arabescato.

Still, he made some mistakes. A marble quarry has its specialists. But not even the most experienced can know for certain what will be found when marble is cut away from a quarry face.

On one occasion, when a block was being hoisted to a wooden sled, it shattered, revealing a hollow at its core that none of the *minatori* had guessed was there. This was a constant and curious fact of a marble quarry: that a place that seemed to be so monumentally still could possess the potential for such sudden, crushing movement.

Uncharacteristically—for Michelangelo was furious at almost any setback in his schedule—he commented in a letter not on the delay but on the fact that everyone in the work crew, himself included, had escaped disaster only by chance.

# CHAPTER TWENTY-FIVE

THE FIRST PART OF THEIR WALK that morning had somehow not been pleasant—or at least not as pleasant as Grace Barton had imagined it would be when she and her husband accepted Julian Morrow's invitation. The first two miles, up the gravel switchback, were steep and difficult, especially for her. The gravel was thickly strewn.

The sun was not yet high enough to warm them. Occasionally, through the trees, they were able to glimpse the peak to which they were headed. It seemed to Grace to be very far away.

"Michelangelo's mountain," Morrow said. "The only place he got his stone in the region—or that, at least, is the popular myth." The Welshman shrugged amiably. "There are three or four other 'only places' in the next valley."

After a mile or so Grace wondered not so much whether she could make it but whether she really wanted to. She found herself thinking of what she might have done instead. She might have spent the day reading on the balcony of their hotel room in Carrara.

It was a gorge, more than a valley, through which they were climbing. The side of the road fell away steeply to their left, through a tangle of trees and goat paths and overgrown thickets of vine to a small river. They could hear the water, but the stream was too far below, too hidden in branch and shadow, for them to see.

They reached the end of the road and the entrance to the working quarry. They had to pass through it to get to the trail that would continue to the abandoned cliffs above.

As they crossed the quarry floor, they noticed a figure in the distance. Neither Grace nor Argue could identify what it was doing. Not until they were closer did they realize it was a man crouching over a tripod. He was in knickerbockers, hiking boots, a mountaineer's worsted jacket, and a silk scarf. He had an owlish, intelligent face.

Giovanni Belli travelled throughout the Carrara region on a motorcycle, his tripod and cameras loaded in his sidecar. He was friends with many of the famous artists who came to Carrara to work the stone. He played American music on his trumpet at their boisterous parties. His portraits of stone carvers at work in Carrara studios were much in demand.

But it is Belli's documentation of the quarries that is his most celebrated work: the Piranesi-like catwalks and high, angled ladders, the stone lunch-huts and the black thinness of cables strung like cracks in the air. He captured the rolled sleeves and cloth caps of the workers, and the unbuttoned vests, walrus moustaches, and battered Borsalinos of the *capi.* He took long aerial views of distant valleys. He recorded the smallness of the crouched, the straining, the bending men in comparison to the enormous, tilted vaults and cut-away faces of the grained white stone.

"*Ciao, Maestro,*" Julian Morrow called.

"*Ciao, Padrone,*" Belli answered. He looked up and nodded, politely enough. But Belli was not going to stop what he was doing. "The light . . ." he began to explain.

Morrow signalled his understanding with a genial flick of his hand. "Come by soon, my friend. For lunch. I have a project I'd like to discuss with you."

"With the greatest pleasure," the photographer replied.

They continued past him. Belli bent back over his camera.

When they had continued a short distance beyond, Morrow spoke to the Bartons in the low voice of shared confidence. "A brilliant photographer. And an interesting man. He is convinced that he will find evidence of Michelangelo's time here. In the area. Time spent, perhaps, on the very trail we follow now."

Grace was enchanted. The climb had become easier—or rather she had accommodated herself to its demands.

Morrow had an inquisitive nature—especially when it came to women. It was one of his great attractions. He had a love of women that he expressed with curiosity. He showered them with questions about where they had grown up, what their interests were, their politics, which artists they admired. He was indiscriminate in this enthusiasm. He asked about suffragettes. He asked about perfume. He asked about the books they were reading. He asked about their travels, and their education, and their beliefs. He asked about their childhood. He wanted to know everything about them. He couldn't help himself. It was the most effective form of seduction he knew.

He asked Grace about her work, and she told him about her painting. And then she told him about the work she did for the Barton papers.

"Ah," he said. "A journalist."

"An art critic" was her immediate correction.

He asked with the gentlest deference about her leg. He assumed it had been a condition of her birth. But on this he was also corrected. She told him of the art school in Cathcart where she had taught when she was just a teenager, and the loft where the art supplies were kept.

"The boys pulled the ladder away as a joke," she said. "They meant no harm."

It was just to show them. She had jumped, skirt billowing, auburn hair streaming, just to get the better of their grinning, upturned faces.

"It was a very foolish thing to do," she said. And for a while she was silent.

Eventually, he raised the subject of sculpture. Morrow always did.

"There is a village," he said, "called Pomezzano." He gestured to the hills to the south. "It is a place that specializes in making a carver's tools, each with a specific name—*gradino, subbia, dente di cane*—and each with a special purpose in the process of carving." The claws followed the points. The rasps followed the chisels. With marble, he told her, the bite depends less on the strength of a hammer blow than on the angle.

"Whom do you admire?" he asked.

The question puzzled her.

"What sculptor?"

She searched for a name that would not be too obvious. "Brancusi," she said.

"Ah. You are a modernist."

"No. Merely a lover of pure beauty. An admirer of direct carving. And you? Do you have a favourite?"

"Michelangelo," he answered without hesitation. "No one else comes close."

As they began to eat their lunch that day, Grace and Argue

both became aware of how keen their appetite had grown. Later, when they recalled their time in the mountains, they both admitted that they had to restrain themselves from wolfing down the food, from gulping down the wine. It was all so good. So very, very good: the soft give of the bread beneath its crust, the bite of the cheese, the salt of the olives, the smokiness of the crumbling meat.

The wine was young and crisp and surprisingly thirst-quenching. It wasn't quite effervescent, but it tasted somehow as if it were. Were she to choose one meal from her life as her favourite, it would be that lunch, there, at the mouth of that abandoned marble quarry.

She nestled against her husband's shoulder. They listened as their host talked. And talked. It was mesmerizing: his Welsh voice, the rich history, this astonishing place. "There," he said. "Out there, somewhere on that blue horizon is where Shelley drowned." He recited "Ozymandias" without mistake, and in the prolonged silence that followed their impressed applause, they all became aware that the food and the sun and their morning's climb had bestowed a drowsiness that was becoming irresistible. It was like a charm in a fairy tale. Morrow said, "There's a warm spot. Over there. Behind that rock. Out of the wind. You'll find the long grass quite soft when pressed down around you. I've napped there myself often. Why don't you rest for half an hour or so before we start back down. I have some exploration of the ledge below that I have been meaning to undertake. You need only call down when you are ready to deal with the ladder again. You are experts now. But I shall hold it steady for your descent."

She hesitated briefly. As did her husband. There was something about the idea that seemed bold somehow.

"Go," Morrow said. "I'll be on the level below. Meditating on vast and trunkless legs of stone. Contemplating what stretches far away."

He rose. He repacked the rucksack and whisked away the crumbs. He crossed toward the top of the ladder. He hoisted the pack over his shoulders. He turned. He gave a last little wave, signalling the couple toward the spot he'd suggested for their after-luncheon rest. Then, swivelling his weight over the lip of the stone, he started cautiously down.

The warm, sunny spot was softened by moss and the promised long grass. It was secluded. Even sound seemed muffled by the breezes that curled around the protecting rock. It was away from everything. It was a place in the blue sky that proved too delightful for them not to give in. How had it happened? She always wondered.

It was so unlike them. But the luncheon had been particularly delicious. And the air, of course, was clear and splendid. "A rare combination of delights," Argue said while they were straightening their clothes after. They'd laughed together at that. Argue's Welsh accent was surprisingly good.

Michael was born close to nine months later. She chose to believe that's where it happened.

It had been shocking behaviour—a thought that always made her smile. How could it have happened like that? Outside. Practically in public. And her only answers were: because the day was so clear; because the sun felt so good; because they had just fallen in love; because, perhaps, the wine had gone to their heads.

# CHAPTER TWENTY-SIX

Oliver stopped on the footbridge. It was the last point on the walk at which he could change his mind.

He wasn't certain. Looking up at the terraces of olive trees and the distant grey walls of the hillside town above, he wasn't sure at all about his decision. A little ridiculously, and with a deep, hollow sadness that he was only just beginning to get to know, he was thinking: Anna has the most beautiful back.

Oliver continued across the footbridge. He was aware that he could be making a mistake. But he was not bold enough to share Anna's belief in the unforgivable. He was naive enough to think that there were mistakes it was sometimes necessary to make.

He headed up the road, beneath an empty sky.

He crossed between the windbreak of bramble and through the buckled, wire gate toward the little farmhouse at the top of the narrow valley.

A country road, little more than two ruts made by the landlord's tractor and hay truck, cut across the bottom of the garden of the little house. There was a red blur of poppies in the hedgerow.

The farmer's rabbit pen was between the fields. It was built of wood and screening where once there had been a swimming pool. The villa had been destroyed in the war.

Tanned and slender and naked from the waist up, Anna was at the hand pump at the property's edge. The well there is deep. However hot the day, the water is always cold. She filled a jug. She was rinsing a rosemary infusion from her hair.

Something was different about her that day. A lazy, ancient god could see that, even if she couldn't. Yet.

She mistook her flush for the late-morning sun. She thought her shivers were caused by the cold water on her back and shoulders. She thought her drowsiness was only the remains of a long sleep.

Oliver did not call out. He did not wave. He decided that there was no way to soften this. He walked directly to her.

They stood together, face to face. He spoke.

And that was when she shouted. That was when she reached back as if swinging something.

Anna shouted *you fucking coward* and swung hard and hit Oliver's smooth unfinished face.

*Part Four*

# THE RASPS

*No block of marble but it does not hide*
*the concept living in the artist's mind*
—Michelangelo Buonarroti

Cathcart, Ontario. April 2010.

Eventually, I gave up expecting any kind of correspondence with Anna. She never replied to the letters I sent after I returned to Cathcart. But I can't decide whether the fact, as you report, that she kept all twenty-three of them means that she held me in higher regard than I'd hoped. Or whether, because they were all stored at the bottom of a cardboard box crammed with equally unopened bills and tax notifications, her opinion of me was lower than I'd feared. In either case, there was never any encouragement to write.

So far as I can bring to mind—up by the pool on this very bright, almost brittle April afternoon—the only people who have ever asked me to write letters are you (my newly found daughter), Robert Mulberry (my extremely well-dressed lawyer), and Christopher Barton (for a time, my closest friend).

The Barton property was adjacent to the Hughsons'—separated by the pool fence and, on the Bartons' side, by a barrier of the lilac and forsythia and wild grape that nobody ever looked after. But Christopher and I might as well have passed our earliest years ten blocks apart. From his pre-kindergarten days, he attended Charlton House—a local private school. The Hughsons, naturally, were great believers in public education.

But even without its high chain fence of rampant morning-glory, even without its wall of untended bramble, the Barton grounds seemed distant and impenetrable to its more modest, more ordinary, more contemporary neighbours. This had as much to do with the stories that enshrouded the grounds as with any physical distinction. The place was famous—famous, at least, in Cathcart—as the wild flower beds, the overgrown statues, and the untended terraces of grief.

---

At Argue Barton's instruction, Grace's crypt was inspired in its formal, austere design by a tomb his wife had admired in Paris. It was in a chilly grey church they had visited the day before their departure for Italy on their honeymoon in the summer of 1922. Grace had always been a great one for museums and old cathedrals. Things of that sort.

The choice of Carrara stone for her tomb—supplied to Lino Cavatore with all possible haste by the Morrow quarry—was a more appropriate decision than Argue Barton fully appreciated. It was the kind of thing his wife would have explained to him. His interest in art, although entirely authentic, had only ever really been his interest in being in love with Grace. The finer points of cultural history usually passed him by.

Argue Barton noticed, in the many letters of condolence he received after Grace's death, a slight disinclination to acknowledge the tragedy he knew it to be. This general sentiment was probably not conscious and, in any event, only hinted at. It was apparent more in what was not said than in what was. His well-meaning friends and colleagues had certainly been surprised by the wedding almost a decade earlier. Now they conveyed, in their black-trimmed notes, that they expected him, with God's help, to weather this storm.

There was nothing mean-spirited in this, he realized. There was nothing heartless in their assumption that he would recover. He wasn't a youth after all. He had just turned fifty-five when Grace died. She was not yet thirty.

But the truth was: in the slowed pace of the way, for the rest of his life, he walked to and from his office at *The Chronicle*; in the unwavering seriousness he dedicated to the business of running Barton newspapers; in the way he stood in his frozen garden on the coldest winter nights. He felt that his heart could have been no more shattered had he been as green as Romeo. It would have been easier had people assumed that he would hurl himself, wailing, on her stone crypt. He had to be privately inconsolable—a condition he disguised as the stern, humourless demeanour that his employees and his neighbours and his son came to know.

Because, like that, she was gone—a finality that the arithmetic of his age made more cruel, not less.

Her grave wasn't anything they had ever talked about. Nothing was ever further from his mind during his time with her. And anyway, even if it had been something they had discussed, he was certain he'd get it wrong. He'd always got his gifts to Grace wrong—the jewellery he later realized she would never have chosen herself, the peignoir she pretended so kindly to like. But what else could he do? Someone had to make a decision.

Something more Italianate might have been appropriate, but marble tombs did not come to mind when he thought of their time in Italy. The only occasion on which he could remember Grace saying anything about her taste in memorials had been not in Italy but in France.

They had walked beside a lake in a Paris park on the morning before their departure for Carrara. They had to hurry to an odd, deserted café for their luncheon when it began to rain. Her fine hair was up. The hem of her skirt had come partly undone. "My goodness," she said when she noticed it, but somehow the ballooning silk struck her as very funny. "Perhaps I shall establish a new style." She said the Café de la Paix would soon be full of society beauties trailing the lining of their skirts.

This was something he would miss. This was something he would miss terribly: the way she could make him laugh. She could even make him laugh at his own not-laughing. He could hear her voice clearly sometimes. "Oh, Argue," she would say, "don't be such a stodge." And then, embarrassed by how long it had taken him, he laughed too.

Sometimes he could feel the tilting rhythm of the way she used to walk beside him. He could remember her arm on his later that afternoon in that chilly grey church in Paris. She was an indefatigable tour guide. They were making their way through the crypt of Saint-Denis.

Isabella of Aragon, the first queen of Philip III of France, died in 1271. Italian marble was used for effigy in France before it was used for that purpose in Italy. The elegant, modest depth of the recumbent figure has led art historians to conclude that it was carved from a Roman column, probably quarried in Luni, near Carrara.

"Oh my," Grace said to her husband. "Imagine being remembered by something as exquisite as that."

Grace glanced around quickly, to make sure no attendant would witness what she was about to do. She reached a gloved hand to the stone figure and once, unhurriedly, stroked the straight, carved folds of the stone bodice.

"I can't resist," she said to Argue.

She let her hand drop and, for a long and silent pause, just looked. Her husband stood slightly behind her left shoulder, and during the same pause he wondered whether there were many men who had ever had such a view.

She was never severe in the way she put up her hair. There was always some of it unfurling at the back of her neck. Before meeting Grace, Argue had not realized how pretty the back of a neck could be. He admired the cut of her coat and the elegant swoop of her hat. When he wasn't looking at Grace or her hat or her collar, he was looking at the tomb she was so obviously admiring.

"I suppose," said Grace, "that even if death is cold, it is still somehow beautiful."

"I suppose," he replied. "In the grand scheme of things."

She rested her arm once more in his. They moved on.

And that was all he had to go on. That was all he could think of when he spoke to Lino Cavatore, the young artisan Julian Morrow had appointed to oversee the design and installation of the Barton House gardens. Cavatore's English was rudimentary, but Argue managed to make himself understood.

Argue Barton found someone at the paper to do the necessary research. He provided Lino with reference photographs.

Lino began in stone by roughing out the block with square hammer, point chisel, and punch. Then his strokes, made with his flat and his claw and his tooth chisel, became steadily more oblique and, very gradually, more and more refined. The figure that emerged under the applications of his rasps looked more like suspended liquid than stone. He finished with the increasingly fine abrasives of sand and emery. The tomb took almost three months. It was widely admired.

I remember when you asked me to write. I'm sure you do too. It's not, I suppose, an unusual request for a daughter to make of a father. But in our case, it seemed momentous.

Your request came when you returned to me through the crowd at Security at the Toronto airport. You were on your way back to Italy after your surprise arrival in Cathcart last summer. Surprise being—as I'm sure you intended—an understatement.

I'm sure you are very good at your work. You have a talent that must be very useful in an office. You are quite skilled at not making it obvious that you are asking as many questions as you are. I'm sure I would have asked much more about the Agency of Regional Tourism and about your husband's teaching position at his community college and about your sons. But I spent most of our time answering your questions about me.

Still, I managed to get a few queries in. I was curious, naturally, about the child, the teenager, and the young adult I'd missed when you were growing up. But it was not until the last night that we were together that I finally asked the question that I'm sure you'd been worrying I was going to ask. It's one I'd often wondered about over the years, but until the day you came striding up through the garden it didn't have much connection with reality.

What if? Who doesn't have their share of paths they didn't take? I'd always thought this pointless conjecture. But your arrival changed that.

Do you remember? We were sitting in the dark, in the bathing pavilion, by the pool.

"Do you think your mother would ever see me were I to come and visit you?"

You surprised me with your answer. "I asked her that before I left."

"And?"

"Do you really want to know?"

"Of course I want to know."

"She said it would take a miracle."

This did not sound encouraging.

Still, not hopeless. The more I thought about it the more I found myself wondering if there might be some ambiguity in the reply. There often was with Anna.

You said nothing more about your mother that night, although we stayed up for quite a while as I recall.

The wooded slope rose up beyond the hedgerows at the deep end of the pool, like a bank of dark clouds. Against them, framed by the shadows of the trees that surround it, was the turreted outline of what I still call Barton House. You asked me about it that evening. But it wasn't for sentimental reasons that the view led me to the past. On warm summer nights, up by the pool, I honestly don't know what else is there.

Christopher Barton rarely joined me and the other neighbourhood boys on warm, sunny Saturday mornings. Christopher kept to himself. He almost never played baseball.

He was tall for his age and, as a result, a little awkward. But we never thought of his lack of athleticism as the reason he stayed away from the vacant lot where we had tramped down something that looked almost like a baseball diamond. We had the sense that Christopher had better, more important things to do.

He knew how to countersink. He knew the difference between a crosscut and a ripsaw. He had a workbench. He was comfortable and careful with power tools.

He couldn't catch a ball to save his life—a fact that I never thought of as significant. It was simply an aspect of Christopher's character—no more meaningful than my own inability to hammer a nail straight. I never gave his rare, hopeless swings at sucker balls any thought at all.

Pickup baseball took place on Saturdays. But my time with Christopher always had to do with the second half of my childhood weekends. Christopher and I often spent our Sundays together on the Hillside trails. But unlike many childhood memories, this one ended abruptly.

It was a rainy evening in early November of 1958. I'd had my dinner early. I'd be leaving for Montrose United in a few minutes. It was the first of Miriam Goldblum's rehearsals for the annual Christmas pageant, *The Wayward Lamb.*

Archie Hughson shook out his umbrella at the front door and then leaned it, only partially folded, against the round, dark-stained table in the vestibule for it to dry. He took off his raincoat, and after clearing a space in the front closet so that its dampness would have no contact with Winifred's lambswool, he hung it up.

Then he turned toward the living room, where I had the comics of the Cathcart *Chronicle* open on the carpet. Winifred Hughson, weightless as a bird on the green chesterfield, waiting for Archie's return before she ate, was reading the front section.

Archie said, "I'm afraid I have some very sad news."

Barton House seemed to turn in on itself in that bleak autumn. The curtains were drawn for a long time. And then, suddenly it seemed, the house was empty. Soon after Michael Barton's suicide, his widow and their children moved away.

A month or so later I received a postcard from Christopher. It was from Bristol. They'd returned to his mother's family in England. It said: "Dear General Eisenhower; Please write. Ready, aye, ready. Yours, Monty."

But I didn't. Eventually, I lost the return address, but that wasn't the real reason I never answered. I didn't know what to say.

I hadn't spoken to anyone about Christopher for a long time until that night when we stayed up in the bathing pavilion talking. I remember that occasion very fondly. It was the same evening that you gave me your text for "Michelangelo's Mountains" to read. And it was the next day that I drove you—very nervously, as you noted—to Toronto to catch your flight.

"I have never seen that before," you said at one point on

the busy highway. You turned in the passenger seat to get a better look.

"You've never seen what?" My eyes did not shift for an instant from the bumper in front of me.

"Your knuckles. They actually are white."

I have never taken much pleasure in driving. And the more crowded and fast the highways, the less comfortable I feel. I suppose this must seem to you a sign of my age, but I see it differently. It's a sign of the age in which we live. But somehow we arrived safely at the airport. Somehow we parked.

You got your boarding pass. You checked your luggage. I had no idea how to say goodbye to a grown daughter I had only met three days before. But our farewell—our first one, anyway—was oddly unemotional. We had a quick, awkward hug. I waved you off at the security gate as calmly as if you were a visiting journalist returning home after an assignment.

Your re-emergence was the surprise.

At that particular moment I happened to be thinking it would be nice to meet my grandchildren someday. I was also worrying that I never would. I can't help these anxieties. They occur whenever I have to remember what parking level my car is on.

I have a fear of being trapped forever in a complicated, multi-tiered parking garage. I worry that the machine won't accept my credit card at the exit or that I'll cause some paralysis of the entire system by ending up stuck going the wrong way on the ramps. I don't picture objects in three dimensions very easily—especially when they are filled with floor upon floor of similar-looking automobiles. I've had difficulty finding my own more than a few times. Hospital and airport parking lots are the worst.

I looked up from the ticket that would not, I was sure, guide me very easily back to the right floor, and right colour code, and right parking spot. And there you were: pushing back through the oncoming throng of your fellow travellers as if you were digging your way out of what had almost buried you.

Robert Mulberry's request for a letter was much less dramatic. He suggested calmly, from the enormous black leather chair behind his desk, that I write the letter I am writing now. The miniature marble replica of Michelangelo's *David* that I had just given to him stood amid the files of our recent transaction.

Herkimer's law firm is now situated on the eleventh floor of an office tower out near the highway, and not in the wood-panelled downtown offices that I remember visiting with my stepfather at the time of Winifred Hughson's death in 1976. The demolition of the old offices was a shame—but hardly a surprising one. Things change.

By the time my adoptive mother passed away, central Cathcart was deep into the throes of its urban renewal. A misnomer if ever there was one. During Winifred's protracted illness, the trees that lined the elegant little park between Cathcart's two main streets were cut down: because they were grand and mature, and because their grand, mature boughs obstructed the views of the rushing motorists on Cathcart's newly established system of one-way streets.

Once the trees were gone, it didn't take long for the benches and fountains to go too. Who wants to sit in a park with no trees? Surrounded by traffic? Apparently, these were not the kind of questions that arose at city council. One wonders, looking at the ravaged remains of downtown Cathcart now, what kind of questions did.

Soon after the trees and the benches and the fountains were removed, the public washrooms were closed and the cool, damp stone stairs bulldozed. The facilities of the newly completed downtown shopping mall had made the underground washrooms redundant.

The marble floors and walls and counters are sealed like a pharaoh's tomb now, along with the empty sherry bottles of the last regular users. Across the busy street, a bingo hall and some cheque-cashing outfit occupy the ground floor of an address that was once the front door of the Victorian building in which Herkimer's had its brass and mahogany downtown offices.

Robert Mulberry was well paid for his work, of course. Lawyers generally are. Even so, he devoted himself, clause by clause, to the protection of the interests that now are yours in a way that seemed beyond professional obligation. That's why I brought him the souvenir replica of the *David.* I wanted him to have a memento of the transaction through which he had proven to be so dedicated and skilful a guide. I knew he would be pleased with the gift. He was aware of the statue's provenance.

Julian Morrow had sent it, with his business card, to Argue Barton, who had left it among his belongings for his son to wonder what to do with. And then Michael Barton, marking the sale of the swimming pool, had given it to Archie Hughson. Thus had it come to me.

Robert Mulberry was touched by my gesture. It's the little things that stick with people.

I know that the pool will be filled in by NewCorp. It's land they want, not an old, mosaic-edged rectangle of green water. There was no way around that. Sad as it is for me to imagine that this gently splashing grotto will soon not exist, preserving it was not an outcome I was going to be able to achieve. That was obvious from the start. It was a necessary surrender.

But that was my only accommodation to the developers. Once the pool was conceded, my bargaining position was strong. I was able to press the purchaser a little more aggressively than most sellers can.

I wanted a very good price for the property—well above market value, frankly. And I wanted to save the swimming pool statuary and some hint of the original terraced gardens of the pool and the old grounds of Barton House. These were conditions of sale on which I could insist.

I wanted all the statues to be incorporated into the landscaping of the new condominiums—all the statues that is, except one. The three-quarter life-size partial nude in white Carrara marble, the central figure of the fountain, is excluded from the chattel of sale. That one piece—a female, leaning forward, pouring water from her jug—will remain in my possession. It's the gift that I will bring to your mother.

Robert admitted that my conditions were unusual, but he was not in the least deterred.

He knew that the land I owned was central to NewCorp's development plans. The swimming pool property happens to be a lot that would connect an interior laneway in the block. Construction would be difficult without this access. Parking for townhouse and condominium residents would be awkward were I to cling to ownership. It was not a piece of land on which NewCorp actually intended to put a building, which may have been why its importance to the development was not given the careful pre-consideration that it deserved. But their package of neighbourhood properties was much less commercially viable if the pool were not part of their acquisitions. Without it, the cavity at the centre of their holdings threatened everything.

NewCorp's initial response to my demands was outrage, naturally. But Robert's politely but firmly stated rejections of their first three offers eventually resulted in a price generous enough for us to entertain. "A good starting point," Robert informed his counterparts in negotiation.

This was not what NewCorp expected to hear, but a starting point was what their fourth offer proved to be. We had even more unreasonable demands to make.

Robert Mulberry was adept at appealing to those commercial interests that could most easily be disguised as philanthropy. He pointed out to NewCorp that history is a great thing. They weren't so sure. But then Robert went on to say that local history is something new homeowners like to buy into. People like to think they are purchasing a past when they are buying a home.

"My client isn't causing you a problem," Robert said with great forbearance. "He's giving you a branding tool."

It was Robert's idea to frame my demand as an effort to make an important gift of public art. And once the Cathcart city hall and *The Chronicle* got involved, NewCorp began to see that our position was not without merit. There had been some pushback from concerned local residents about the development, and Robert pointed out that a few statues would go a long way to demonstrating good corporate citizenship and concern for community—whether or not NewCorp possessed either. The sidewalks, the lobby entrance, and the underground parking garage of what will now be known as "The Carrara Estates by NewCorp" will be decorated with the statues that Lino Cavatore installed along the pathways and by the pool of Grace and Argue Barton's landscaped grounds so long ago. There were even tax benefits.

To be perfectly accurate, the estate is Archibald Hughson's. The earnings from his geography textbook, and the stock portfolio he established once he had some money to invest have always remained its core. My income from my work has not greatly added to it, I'm afraid. My salary as an arts reporter for *The Chronicle* and as the host of a cable-television program, along with my going rate as a luncheon speaker and occasional lecturer are rarely more than honoraria—a level of remuneration, typical of the cultural sector, that pretty much requires either an indifference to poverty or an inheritance.

Archie's financial success has allowed me to live comfortably in my adoptive parents' Cathcart home. My lifestyle has been far from extravagant. I almost never travelled, for one thing—a curious fact that makes me think that your mother really did place a curse of eternal provincialism on me in her fury. But this strange inertia was something I managed to keep quite successfully to myself. For some reason, people I saw in the fall whom I'd last seen in the spring assumed I'd been away—somewhere in Europe seemed to be what they imagined. So I let them. But the truth is: I hardly went anywhere.

I lived beyond what would normally be the means of a freelance culture critic in a small town not exactly obsessed with culture. Let's put it this way: I was the only columnist at the Cathcart *Chronicle* who spent his summers sitting beside his swimming pool.

Of course, living at Hillside Avenue on the trust fund Archie established for me was not what I had ever planned to do. I came very close to having another life entirely—the life that would have included you. But that's not what happened.

What happened was I left your mother. And what happened was time passed.

Time passed in a sequence of little things that I was not observant enough to see as a sequence. And as it did, something else happened: I became the oddest thing.

The blue jeans gradually disappeared. The conversations

with neighbours about what I was going to do and where I was going to go gradually stopped. I slowly became the no-longer-young man, in pressed slacks, open-necked oxford cloth shirt, and loafers, who, for reasons people always wondered about, never moved away from the house in which I had grown up.

I liked my work at *The Chronicle.* I found something satisfying in meeting deadlines, having beginnings and endings, working within the limitations of the quotidian. Such work is not inglorious—much as your mother thinks otherwise. Writing my column at *The Chronicle,* lecturing the bored camera operator at the Cable 93 studio about Impressionism and Renaissance sculpture, giving the occasional luncheon speech to Rotary, and teaching an adult education course on art appreciation at the local community college kept me busy. Occasionally, I wrote program notes for an art gallery or a local theatre company.

I settled into the idea of never moving away from the Hillside Avenue house a good decade after I had settled into the fact. I helped Archie during Winifred's long decline. Then I stayed put, helping Archie look after the house and the pool. I filled the niche of Cathcart's roving freelance cultural expert—a niche that was extremely small but, probably for that reason, entirely empty.

Archie came to rely on me. First, for company after his wife died, then for getting the groceries and returning his library books. I took over the driving when the policeman who was very kind about a red light suggested that might be a good idea. I got used to helping Archie in and out of the bath. I became the cook. I looked after the bills. I dusted the Royal Doulton figurines on the mantelpiece. I got up to turn over the Reader's Digest symphonic classics when, on winter nights, we sat in the living room listening to the hi-fi.

The pool was always Archie's job. When he was frail and shaky and old, he sat on a white patio chair while he worked. Cleaning it was his job, and so long as the pool was open—so long as the old filter was humming in its shed and the water was not yet covered for the winter—the job never ended. He poled hand over hand, drawing the head of the vacuum slowly across the bottom. He had mastered this task long ago.

But I shovelled the walk, raked the leaves, and took out the garbage on Sunday nights. And I was the one who, at Archie's suggestion, went down from the pool to the kitchen to get crackers and lemonade when visitors came to call in the summertime.

The time it took me to make my way through the garden, put the crackers on a tray and fill the plastic tumblers with lemonade was about the amount of time it took for Archie to manoeuvre the conversation to the point at which someone asked him something about his late wife. Winifred Hughson was Archie Hughson's favourite topic.

"She was no bigger than a minute, you know" was what I heard Archie say. I was often coming up the steps of the pool gate and across the flagstones to the bathing pavilion with the tray when I heard his introduction. This was always how he began.

Like most stories, it had departed from certain facts and had taken on certain embellishments over time. Not that I doubted the story's essential truth. It was just that when I listened to Archie Hughson telling it to his poolside visitors as he raised a trembling iced lemonade to his lips, I could always picture the ghost of Mrs. Hughson leaning forward on the brown and yellow and green plastic weave of her patio chair. I could picture her bright eyes, and her girlish posture, and her cropped bowl of white hair. I could see her smiling at her husband with more pleasure than embarrassment. She was saying, not so much to Archie as to the friends who had come to call, "Well, dear, no, that's not quite how it happened."

The success of Archie Hughson's geography textbook had allowed Mrs. Hughson to devote herself entirely to her volunteer work. She took this seriously. She sat on hospital committees, chaired the ladies' auxiliary, oversaw the candystripers, organized bake sales to raise money to refurnish waiting rooms and replace the drafty windows of the Victorian brick hulk of the Cathcart General. She was devoted to her work. But it was the Second World War that gave her a calling.

"You see," Archie would say, "when she became president of the women's auxiliary, she asked for a tour of the whole hospital. She'd been working there for some years by then. But she did not know all the wings. There were floors she hadn't been on. And it was while she was being shown around that she noticed a door that said No Admittance.

"Oh, Archie. It said no such thing. It was just a door."

"And there they were," Archie would continue. "A dozen or so of them. In this dark, airless room. In those old, straight-backed wicker wheelchairs . . ."

"Honestly, Archie . . ."

"Sitting there. Just sitting there."

She called them her boys. They were the soldiers, airmen, and sailors in the burn ward that had been established in a wing of the Cathcart General: young men whose war stories ended with being trapped by mined tanks, caught by plane wrecks, captured by explosion, encircled by flaming fuel.

She went back to visit them a few days later. Then she went back again. Soon it was part of what she did, every day. "Oh, I just try to cheer them up" was her description of a task that was often impossible.

She helped them write letters to their families. She brought them treats of butter tarts and sodas. She read them stories. She comforted them when, as they sometimes did, they cried.

And then she invited them to her house on Hillside Avenue. For a luncheon.

The guests had all been instructed on what to expect. There were always a few young women there from the Cathcart Teachers' College because Mrs. Hughson thought that pretty girls were probably what the boys worried about most.

The girls had been told not to stare.

They passed sandwiches. They chatted. And they laughed with young men who had probably thought they'd never laugh with pretty girls again. Someone played the piano. And they sang the songs that everybody knew in those days.

It was after two or three such luncheons that Mrs. Hughson had what she called their graduation. One by one, she took the young men out to a restaurant.

"Out into public, you see," Mr. Hughson would explain to his poolside visitors. "The one thing that they didn't think they could do. Out to the tea room of the Royal Cathcart Hotel."

The staff knew her, and the waitresses were kind. But always there was someone—a girl at a nearby table, a new busboy, a child out for a treat with a grandmother—who would point. Or laugh.

At a bulging eye. At a smooth flank of skin where half a face should have been. At a twisted reconstruction of jaw and nose. At a lipless mouth. At a wispy island of hair.

And when a little girl gasped, or a child pointed, or a busboy tried to hide a snicker, the young man who had already been so brave—brave enough to have gone to war when he was scarcely older than a boy—would feel something on his knee. It was a firm, small hand, under the tablecloth.

"Be brave," Winifred Hughson would say. "Be brave, and you'll be just fine."

Her decline was long and slow and awful. She was in and out of the hospital more than a dozen times. It was the better part of a decade before she finally died.

I remember the green glow of the nursing station, the untouched dinner trays, the faint, persistent smell of urine. Archie and I took turns reading Dickens to her. And it was there, in that hospital room, that I found myself reading about what I had left behind eight years before. I was reading to pale, exhausted Winifred Hughson about the greenest of green hills, the bluest of blue skies. She hardly moved. She wore woollen socks on her icy, grey feet.

"That's where you were," she said weakly. "In Italy. That summer you went away."

"Nearby," I said.

" 'The quarries . . .' Dickens wrote, 'are so many openings, high up in the hills, on either side of these passes, where they blast and excavate for marble: which may turn out good or bad: may make a man's fortune very quickly, or ruin him by the great expense of working what is worth nothing. Some of these caves were opened by the ancient Romans, and remain as they left them to this hour.' "

"Carrara," she said with a bit of a smile—by way of showing me that she was still on the ball.

"Yes," I said, "that's right. Not far from Carrara." And I continued reading.

---

Your mother thought that objects—actual physical objects—were one of the few things we have that eternity doesn't. As she often pointed out, light is useless without them. Her appreciation of objects in space—whether of a tree, or a body, or a piece of stone—was how she said she knew she was alive.

It was one of the lessons she felt was necessary to teach. She found me shockingly unadventurous. "Do you know," she asked me once, "that making love comes in three dimensions?"

And that's why I don't like forgetting objects. Even losing a car for a while in a parking lot upsets me unreasonably. Forgetting about things, so Anna used to say, is what happens when we die.

When I was starting out at *The Chronicle*, curricula vitae were not examined with quite the rigour that I'm sure they are today. Somehow, the vague notion that I was someone who had spent a lot of time in one place in Italy became the generally held belief that I had spent years travelling in Europe. People just imagined that I was an art historian, or a culture critic, or an expert on Renaissance sculpture by training. Somehow that became my reputation.

I've read a lot, of course. Over the years. I've always had a weakness for expensive art books. But more than self-education, I credit my brief time in Italy for any ability I have to discern what beauty is—and not only because of the great works of art I saw on day trips to Florence and on my one visit with Anna to Rome. Just as importantly, Anna showed me the staggering beauty of an old wall; a stone lintel; terra-cotta pots on deep sills; a lion's head fountain, green with age, in the stone wall at the end of an ordinary, narrow, laundry-hung street.

These were everyday things in Pietrabella—just as the dusty red-maples that surround the pool are everyday things in Cathcart. These were the icons of Anna's religion. They were how she worshipped. And as I've grown older, I've learned to pay great attention to things.

That's the beauty that I'll miss—the limestone bluffs of Hillside; the sun and shadow on the fountain at the deep end of an old swimming pool; a neighbour's roof, straight and grey as a fact in the rain. It's form that I'll be sorry to leave behind. More sorry than I'll be about leaving a lot of the people I know, to be honest.

When it is my turn to say goodbye to a too-brightly-lit hospital room, I will mourn the loss of the most ordinary piece of rock—something rough and heavy that could be picked up from a creek bed and held and looked at, its weight cradled, its dull facets turned against the sky as if it were a jewel. Something everyday. Something that catches the light. The beauty of shape is what the dead lose: hedges and maple trees, lawn chairs and pool vacuums, and the green crossbar of an old garden swing where the Hughsons used to read Dickens to one another until the evening grew too dark.

It will be nice to meet my grandchildren. This sounds a little restrained, I know—the kind of muted emotional understatement that drove your mother crazy. But the fact is, I do think it would be nice to meet my grandchildren. I hope it might be more than nice. I worry that it might be less—through no fault of your two handsome young sons, of course.

That was what I was thinking as I stood outside the security gate at the Toronto airport, trying to make some sense of the numbers on the parking ticket I held in my hand.

And that was when your figure re-emerged. That was when you were suddenly turning back.

I could see the torque of your compact size, the artful

disarray of your orange hair, the drape of a shawl around your shoulders, the folds of your ankle boots. You had a leather travel bag over your right shoulder.

To be honest: I find seeing people off at an airport an awkward ritual. It has the irresolution of scenes in hospital rooms where goodbyes are said to those for whom goodbyes are already beside the point. Except for the occasional sheepish wave, the travellers don't look back very much at the people who are wishing them bon voyage. Their attention is elsewhere: lineups, laptops, change in pockets.

I was more dressed up than anyone else outside the security area. Which isn't saying much. I'd felt the occasion demanded some formality. I was a father seeing off his daughter. Mine was the only tie in sight. I was surrounded by track suits and nylon basketball shorts.

The guard who had checked your passport and boarding pass was wearing heavy, black-framed sunglasses. This gave the impression that your papers had been scrutinized by a military junta—a form of dictatorship that your mother had probably warned you to expect in the most remote corners of the North American continent.

In fact, the guard did move toward stopping you from stepping back out of Security. But even with his heavy sunglasses, even with epaulettes on his short-sleeved blue shirt, he was not much of a dictator. There was something in the set of your expression that made him realize you were not going to be interrupted.

You were moving as quickly as you could. You were pulling the floral silk shawl over your shoulder. Your face was round, but its broad simplicity was balanced with the fine lines of your features. Your expression was very precise: it was, in the cast of its determination, the face of a woman who does not like to ask for anything but is about to ask for something now.

You were bumping through hand luggage and slipping between parting shoulders. "*Permesso,*" you were saying. "*Mi scusi.*"

The light was so sharp and modern it seemed white.

You looked up, directly into my face. "Write me," you said. "Please. You owe me that. You never told me any stories."

People moved around us while we clung to one another much longer than either of us expected. I was thankful for the handkerchief I'd tucked, as a jaunty accessory, in the breast pocket of my blazer.

The guard let you sidle your way back through Security. You gave a last little wave. Then your figure disappeared . . .

# CHAPTER TWENTY-SEVEN

THE *APOLLO BELVEDERE* WAS CARVED, probably from Carrara stone, about a century after the birth of Christ. It had been lost for many hundreds of years when it was rediscovered during an excavation in Rome in the late fifteenth century.

Its heroic spirit was admired, as was the grace of the left-turning head and the exquisite beauty of the form. The young man's left heel is raised as he steps forward, and because marble is so dense and so heavy, the technical challenge of stabilizing such massive weight had to be overcome with a stone carver's structural standby. A tree trunk supports the figure's right leg. The *Apollo Belvedere* was the most celebrated piece of carving in the western world. It's probably fair to say that it remained so until 1504.

That was the year Michelangelo climbed down for the last time from the rough wooden planks he'd had built around a block of marble in a courtyard in Florence. He was covered in white dust.

*David* was carved from an eighteen-foot-high block of Carrara stone that had already been started by a sculptor named Simone da Fiesole. It was felt by many Florentine artists—and, presumably, by Simone himself, who had abandoned his faltering beginning—that the roughing-out had been badly botched and the block left unworkable. It sat untouched for years.

But Michelangelo saw a figure in the stone that nobody else had imagined. What he had in mind would fit—just. There was almost nothing in the dimensions of the block to spare. There was no room for a mistake.

He measured. He drew. He made a wax model. He built scaffolding around the stone. And then, in the courtyard of the Office of Works of Santa Maria del Fiore, in Florence, he set to work.

Leonardo da Vinci was making fun of Michelangelo when he compared the sedate approach of a painter to the sweaty exertions of a sculptor. Leonardo and Michelangelo didn't like one another very much. But Leonardo's description is as good a way as any of picturing Michelangelo in the courtyard of Santa Maria del Fiore.

"The sculptor in creating his work does so by the strength of his arm by which he consumes the marble, or other obdurate material in which his subject is enclosed: and this is done by most mechanical exercise, often accompanied by great sweat which mixes with the marble dust and forms a kind of mud daubed all over his face."

Michelangelo's work in the courtyard went on. And on. It seemed sometimes as if it would never end. But finally it was done.

He made his way slowly down the ladder. The scaffolding would be gone the following day. Then people would see.

But Michelangelo did not possess an optimistic nature. It

was his view that there were not many artists to whom optimism very naturally accrued. If his experience was anything to go by.

Five years earlier, he had finished the first of his great *Pietàs*. It had taken longer than he thought it would. Everything did.

It is carved from Carrara marble in a strong, triangular form, and its base is established by the highly polished folds of the mother's garments. The sumptuously draped skirt is unrealistically full, but it is the apparent age of Mary that has been the subject of the most literal criticism. Michelangelo's Mary appears far too young to be the mother of the dead Christ.

This physical improbability has been traditionally explained by the notion that it is Mary's virginity that has preserved her so miraculously. Needless to say, this was not a theory to which my mother subscribed.

She thought that Michelangelo was creating the way a god creates. She thought Michelangelo was ignoring the irritating constraints of time. She thought he had carved two ideas at once. My mother insisted that the young Mary is looking down at what is both unseen and seen. Invisible to us, her baby is asleep in her lap. Visible, her grown son is sprawled in her arms. "That's how time works," my mother said.

As she pointed out, it was an idea familiar to Michelangelo. The sculptor who captured the sensual splendour of youth more completely than any other—and never more exquisitely than in his *David*—once wrote: "my passion only knows how to carve death: this is my skill's poor force."

Anna liked to picture Michelangelo coming down the ladder from the rough wooden scaffolding in the courtyard of Santa Maria del Fiore that evening. Nobody would have been around. The light would have been failing. He was hungry. Probably, he was wondering how long it would take before some idiot complained about the size of the hands.

# CHAPTER TWENTY-EIGHT

THE GOATHERD CAME RUNNING on feet like little hoofs.

In one of the houses in the narrow cobbled street, a baby was sick with colic.

Italo Cavatore was stumbling in his awkward haste. As he ran, he swerved abruptly left, abruptly right, as if in pursuit of his lost balance.

The young mother could not stop her daughter's crying.

Italo's warning was already ahead of him, racing through the street. It sped across the laundry lines. It jumped from window to window in the little hillside town of Castello. It was as if the word he was shouting over and over had become a swarm of fears. They flew over the wide stone sills and through the dark interiors of the rough, unadorned houses.

He pounded on the doors with the flat of his hands. "*Tedeschi,*" he called out in his strained, shrill voice. "*Tedeschi.*" And then he ran, as best he could, to the next house. And the next.

The day had been strange, its stillness interrupted by sudden eddies of wind. The artillery had seemed far-off and to the north, but then closer, to the east and the south. And then quiet.

The young mother heard the goatherd getting closer. She was in her kitchen, trying to soothe her daughter.

Except for the goatherd and a few old grandfathers, the men of the village were gone. They knew every trail in the mountains and hills. "*Bella ciao*" the partisans sang. "*Bella ciao, ciao, ciao.*" She thought her young husband very handsome.

Now the dust could be seen from the town wall. It drifted below, through the olive groves. It was a cloud, raised by tires and treads and boots coming up the switchback.

The goatherd was running as fast as he could. But he was clumsy and stiff on his little feet. When he was young the other children made fun of him by walking on their heels to imitate his awkward, poorly balanced gait.

And now he could not begin to keep up with the fear. He could not. He could not.

And the fear that was racing ahead of him, that was rushing in useless circles through the little square, that was spinning down the cobbled street, was this: there was nowhere to hide in such a little, walled-in place.

Forgive me, the young mother was saying to her baby. Over and over. The baby was sprawled, her fat arms and legs batting the air. But the mother couldn't think what else to do. She held the baby firmly in her lap. Otherwise, she could not be hushed.

Now the goatherd was pounding on her door. He was shouting. Now he was gone to the next house. And the next.

The baby was sick with the colic. She would not stop crying. And the young mother cradled her in her arms and poured grappa into her mouth, and the baby sputtered and choked. The mother soothed the baby and poured the grappa into her mouth, and the baby sputtered and choked, and the mother soothed her and poured the grappa into her mouth. Then, finally, the mother kissed her, and breathed in the smell of her daughter's dark hair.

She pulled the wooden slats across the lid of a marble vat. It was one of the small tubs in which she mixed the pork fat that her husband took with his bread to the quarry. Now it was empty. There had been no work for months. There was never enough food.

She folded a cloth over the wooden top. She placed a brown ironstone bowl there. And the baby was still, and the house was quiet.

It was all she could think of. Perhaps when the men returned—the next day, the day after that—they would hear a baby crying.

She wanted to get as far from the kitchen as she could before the Germans came. She wanted to get as far from the house. She ran. She ran from the doorway into the street and that was when she heard the first spitting of the guns.

# CHAPTER TWENTY-NINE

MICHELANGELO IS THIRTY YEARS OLD when he makes his way to the Carrara mountains. His journeys take him to the isolated abbeys and the convents that shelter the pilgrims on their way to and from Rome, by a route known for millennia as the Via Francigena.

Michelangelo hears vespers as he walks. These steep roads are switchbacks through chestnut woods, across tumbling millstreams. A thrush, frightened by the crunch of his old cordwain boots on the pebbled road, flashes through the branches. The golden light won't last long now. He is approaching the convent.

The sisters will welcome him. They always do. He will be given the same simple room.

He is anxious about the courier from Florence with funds for the men in the quarries, with funds for the captain of the ox teams, with funds for the ships. Has there been any word? The sisters say there has not.

Everything is difficult.

He hasn't changed his dogskin buskins in weeks. In the evenings, he sits in the cloisters with the abbess. It's best to avoid mentioning the pope in his presence. Michelangelo isn't exactly easy company.

He is a restless soul. He grinds his jaw.

But her quietude soothes him. He finds her manner comforting. Her face is so smooth it could be wax. He imagines in her peaceful countenance a spiritual contentment rich indeed.

She is thinking: here I am. Then, about half an hour after that, she is thinking: there is no water coming from the fountain.

Because she speaks so little her voice is like the rustle of a dry leaf. He isn't sure he understands her question. But as she makes her noises, she points at the central figure in the trio of figures across and to his right.

His expert opinion is being solicited, he decides. This pleases him, of course. He's an artist.

He stands. He walks around the stone. He says, "It is fine. You see the hair, here. This shift of weight, there. Contrapposto. This leg. The skirt. This is good work."

She is thinking: water. She is thinking *splash splash splash*. But Michelangelo is concerned about other things.

"It came from a good workshop," he says. Local, he guesses. "Although here, perhaps, here, this could be better." He indicates the contours of the upper right arm and elbow. He could see the break clearly. The joint was unfinished.

"Sculptors," he confides to the abbess, "are always being rushed."

She seems untroubled by this information.

With his index finger he traces a line over the ball of the shoulder that aligns more appropriately with the forearm and elbow and with the weight of the water urn the figure is pouring.

He sees that some slight adjustment could be made to the folds of her skirt. The abbess follows his perusal of the statue with what he takes to be great interest.

And then, after a moment's consideration, Michelangelo proposes something remarkable.

She listens to his suggestion with equanimity.

He would have preferred the abbess to protest—just a little. It would have not gone unnoticed by him had she said something like, "You are too busy, surely. You are a great artist and cannot devote any time to an inconsequential convent such as ours." Something like that.

He's sensitive about things like this. Ingratitude always reminds him of the pope.

His time is valuable, God knows. That's what Michelangelo thinks. Even if nobody else ever seems to think so.

He looks intently at the abbess. This is a habit of his: staring at people. She seems to be untroubled by his gaze.

Then he understands. Then he realizes what he is encountering.

This is beatific calm, he says to himself. This is saintliness. The expression on the face of the abbess is the same endless gaze that he carved into his *Pietà* in Rome—the piece that some ignoramuses in St. Peter's said was the work of that tunnel-digger, Gobbo.

Gobbo! They said this aloud! In earshot of Michelangelo!

Fuck them, Michelangelo thought. The next day he carved his name across the banner on the Virgin's cloak. It is his only signed piece.

The expression of the abbess is serenity itself. This, surely, was the grace of God.

His tools are with him. They are wrapped in burlap. They were lugged by his servant through thickets of whores and thieves along the Aurelia from Pisa.

He insists. Not that he needed to, exactly. But he enjoys emphasizing the generosity of his offer. So he insists anyway. He insists that he will make the correction to the shoulder and the elbow the following day.

It is an acceptable intervention, since so many different hands worked on the piece in the first place. It was the work of a studio, not a single artist. And even if it were the work of a single artist, Michelangelo Buonarroti of Florence is not exactly modest about how his talent compares with the talent of others.

Even as a teenager he was not shy about his skills. Vasari tells us that he "went over the contours of one of the figures, and brought it to perfection; and it is marvelous to see the difference between the two styles and the superior skill and judgment of a young man so spirited and confident that he had the courage to correct what his teacher had done."

So he sets to work, the next day.

He re-addresses the joint. He constructs a small armature in the hollow he has made. He applies the epoxy his servant has prepared. The chiselling and cross-hatching only take him a few hours. The filing and the polishing, the same again.

He studies his work. The line of the arm is now graceful. No one who didn't know exactly where the zigzag was would ever see the *M.* He wasn't sure he saw it himself.

He notices a wedge of leaves and dead branches at the base of the fountain. He bends down and, with a few digs of his chisel into the wet cavity, clears them away. He hears water burble from a source that sounds very deep and far away. No water runs from the figure's jug, but the occasional rumble from the cistern makes him think that eventually it will.

He is satisfied. He has enjoyed the little job. He feels much better. Now he has to get to his room. He always sleeps well when he has been working.

The next morning Michelangelo departs—long before dawn,

long before the nuns awaken. The route up into the mountain quarries is long and arduous, and it is best to cover as much ground as possible before the day gets hot.

That morning, when the abbess takes her customary position in the cloisters and the first angled rays of the morning light touch the upper arm and elbow: an amazing thing! Water. From the fountain. There is nobody to hear her thin, little gasp of surprise.

# CHAPTER THIRTY

EVEN A MINOR GOD has capacities far beyond our limitations. Even if he's been drinking Prosecco and grapefruit juice since before noon.

"Work like a slave; command like a king; create like a god," proclaimed one of the greatest of modernist sculptors. My mother loved this quotation. Constantin Brancusi's work is famous for its curving horizons and smooth geometric planes. Several of his most celebrated pieces are in Statuario from Carrara.

"There are idiots who define my work as abstract," the handsome, grey-bearded Romanian once said. Brancusi spoke with characteristic disinterest in diplomacy. In pronouncement, as in sculpture, his imagination was free of any obligation to the unnecessary. This was a quality my mother adored.

By the 1920s, the creator of *Sleeping Muse, Bird in Space,* and *The Kiss* was associated with the new abstraction by art's general public. In other words, Brancusi thought that most of the people who had ever heard of him were idiots—a contention that his dark, fiercely intelligent stare defended without a great deal of trouble. "Yet what they call abstract is what is most realistic," he continued in a rumble of a voice that some women were reported to have said made them feel distinctly faint. "What is real," he pronounced, "is not the appearance, but the idea, the essence of things."

It's something that distinguishes most mortals from gods, and most mortals from artists as great as Michelangelo and Constantin Brancusi. We don't often get to the essence of things. This shortcoming is particularly apparent when the object in question is time. When it comes to that particular dimension, gods think of us as morons.

Fucking morons, clarifies my mother.

Most gods aren't so blunt, but none would disagree. Even a mid-level deity can observe a beautifully varnished speedboat in the summer of 1939 with the same casual glance by which he catches sight of a black-handled German service revolver on the bedside table of a cheap hotel room almost twenty years later. Gods are catholic in their attentions. They see different ideas at once. Past and future are all the same to them.

It was the blue, beautiful summer that would always be remembered by those who knew it as the summer before the war. Michael Barton was sixteen. His flapping white shirt is open to his smooth, slender chest, his right hand raised, his dark hair flattened by the wind. He is laughing through the spray of his own speed. The boat is a beauty. This is a snapshot from the annual regatta at the lake. There is a girl in a bathing suit at his side.

It's the way any old god experiences time: the splashes of a runabout slapping across a summer lake are, in fact, the fumes of a bus terminal coming through an opened window in a cheap hotel. The waved salute of a handsome boy is also the neck of a half-finished bottle of Cutty Sark by a bedside. The edges of the table are marked with the cigarette burns of prostitutes and travelling salesmen. The silver wake of a mahogany speedboat is the steel between a finally determined clench of teeth. The police responded to a desk clerk's frantic call.

That's the difference, between mortals and gods. And that, so my mother thinks, is why lesser gods will admit they sometimes envy the one thing that separates the best of us from the worst of them. They sometimes wish there were things they didn't know.

GODS LOOK DOWN, through grey veins of sky. They look down through branches. They see that regatta on that blue lake. No young man can guess what twenty years will bring, particularly when those twenty years will include a war. But gods can. They see that cheap hotel and that bottle of Cutty Sark. And they can see, not long before Michael Barton bought a one-way bus ticket from Cathcart to Toronto, what happened on the wooded hillside behind the Barton's house. They can see two boys hiding there. One is Michael Barton's son. The other is Christopher Barton's best friend. It was Indian summer.

"No. Like this," Christopher whispered. He was lying beside Oliver Hughson, both of them on their stomachs. They were deep in the rank old smell of October bridal wreath. The cliff fell away steeply below.

They were both ten. With his right arm, Christopher reached around Oliver's shoulder.

This was 1958. That year all the boys were wearing sweat-shirts with the sleeves cut off. Christopher's breath was toasty with their smoking.

"With your whole finger," he said. His right hand covered Oliver's. "Not just the end."

"Okay."

"That's it." He was so close Oliver could feel the feather of his whispering on his ear. They had to be quiet.

The Luger had a well-tooled action. The magazine had chambers for eight rounds and slotted firmly into place in the handle. The two rounded steel knobs behind the breech had to be pulled up and then back for charging.

The gun was heavy, almost two pounds. Oliver needed to use both hands to keep it steady.

The vertical iron sight circled the rocking couple below. The pink of the man was blatant between his unfurled pants and the tail of his dark shirt. Oliver squeezed the trigger. Even without ammunition, the spring of the firing pin had a solid, satisfying release.

That Sunday was a final burst of autumn warmth. And the weather made the trails of the hillside exceptionally beautiful to the few who had ventured along them so late in the season.

The boys had spotted the couple below the ledge that they had established as their observation point that afternoon. The fact that the two boys had a single German handgun was explained by the difficulties that had followed their escape. It was a little-known fact of the Second World War that General Eisenhower and Field Marshal Montgomery had broken out of a POW camp together.

The steep wood of Hillside had once been the lip of a vast, ancient sea. It had been formed into a bluff as the softer layers of sandstone and shale eroded beneath the more durable layers of limestone. The grey ramparts on which the boys played looked upside down—more narrow in their bases than on their upper, bush-crested ledges. There were places where it looked like the roots of big old trees were all that held the bluffs from collapsing. The paths—through hart's tongue, lady's slipper, trillium, and wall rue—turned here and there, around large, fallen shards of stone. The terrain was uncertain. The brown slope was scattered with fragments of grey. The tumbled creek beds appeared as a torrent of stone even when their streams were dry. The woods always looked like the rock slide had just stopped.

The man on top and the woman underneath him were in a grove just off one of the trails. They had spread out their blanket quickly among alder and chokeberry. Her long, thin hands were digging for the bones in his back.

"Will wonders never cease," said Christopher. The accent he used made him sound like Alfred Hitchcock.

"Will you look at that," Oliver replied, hoping for the flat rumble of the Midwest and of Lucky Strikes in his voice.

Stumbling across Adolf Hitler and Eva Braun screwing in the bushes was quite a break for the Allies. The gyrating bum made the perfect target.

"Hold it still. But don't hold your breath," Christopher said. "Take it slow and easy."

"Like them?"

The barrel went all over the place. Oliver lowered the gun.

Their laughter was louder than they thought.

Now the dark-haired man was kneeling. Now the woman was sitting, yanking down her top with one hand while hoisting her panties with the other. Now the man's head was swivelling and he was looking up. His face was red. Now he was shouting.

But by then the two boys were gone—along the ledge and down an angled path that cut through the woods to the main trail.

The boys' homes were under the wooded slope of what in Cathcart was always called the Hillside. Oliver could see Christopher's house from his bedroom window. It was usually at night that he looked at it. The ugly brown turrets of Barton House were the last shapes of anything before blackness.

Sometimes Oliver sat on the side of his bed and pressed his head against the cool, metallic smell of the screen. Sometimes late-night laughter, sometimes singing, sometimes loud voices came over the gardens. Once, a tuba. For a time, the Bartons had parties. These were always referred to by the Hughsons as "a little wild." More recently, there were fights: a woman's voice, a man's.

On the Sundays that followed a late Saturday-night party, Barton House was dark, and hushed. The quarter-filled highball glasses and full ashtrays were still on the side tables and windowsills. Christopher knew by the thick, still air that his parents would not come downstairs until much later.

Christopher lifted the Rothmans from his mother's purse. As usual. And then the boys went down to the basement to get the gun. It was a souvenir of Mr. Barton's from the war.

The stale space of gloom that opened off the bottom of the stairs had all the contemporary fixtures of a rec room—the muted plaids, the casually low-slung furniture, the dartboard, the television, the shelf full of regatta trophies, the bar. But there was something about the basement's heavy drapery and unmoving air that never felt like fun to Oliver.

"That's strange," Christopher said. Normally, the gun was kept locked in the bottom drawer of a liquor cabinet. "The Luger's not here."

Oliver was the one who spied the angled black handle. He was looking right at it on the bar for some seconds before he realized what it was. It was unfamiliar because it was so out of place. It was beside a glass of brown liquid with a cigarette butt floating in it. Christopher slipped the pistol into his backpack.

They could never find any ammunition—and not for lack of trying. But the gun still had a heft and an action that made the daring escapes of General Eisenhower and Field Marshal

Montgomery throughout the occupied European countryside feel the way they imagined the game of battle to be. The gun added immeasurably to the veracity of their Sundays: like the time they were running down the path, after Adolf Hitler and Eva Braun had started yelling at them.

"You goddamn kids. If I ever catch sight . . ."

Christopher and Oliver were leaping from root to rock, their shoes skittering, their legs like flywheels. They'd begun with their feet sliding sideways, like skiers traversing a nasty-looking drop, but that hadn't worked for long. Now they were racing as if trying to catch up to their own weight. Oliver hid the gun by holding it by the barrel, its handle tucked against the inside of his forearm.

HILLSIDE ISN'T A HILL AT ALL. It's a ridge of sedimentary rock, a muscle of limestone underneath the soft floor of woods. It rises steeply, here and there, in grey, horizontal lines so clearly defined and stacked in such apparent regimen, it appears as if the fissures and planes have been carved into the face of stone. Archie Hughson was particularly knowledgeable about the process of formation. He led his classes on geography hikes along the same trail down which the two boys were racing.

Archie Hughson spoke plainly. It was a dialect, now almost lost, that blended a modest, rural tradition of language with the respect for Shakespeare and Milton and Dickens and Tennyson with which his generation had been brought up. Those students who did well on his famous final exam did so because they could remember that voice. They always would.

They would remember Mr. Hughson standing in a creek bed in the Hillside woods, his sample bag over his shoulder, the waxed paper of an egg-salad sandwich protruding from the right-hand double pocket of his tweed jacket. They would remember him bending down with surprising agility and picking up a rough grey chunk of stone. They could remember him holding it up, turning it slowly before them as if it were an enormous jewel to be admired. And they would remember his flat, unadorned accent: "Let us imagine that a rock with much the same origins as this was under an ocean. Indeed, let us imagine that this rock was created under an ocean."

THE ROOTS OF THE BIGGEST TREES held the same horizontal as the ramparts of the rock face. The boys used them like secret stairways for speedy escapes. They took pride in knowing the details of the terrain.

Oliver was the better runner of the two, which wasn't, actually, saying very much. He wasn't the fastest boy on earth, but he had a quickness that often seemed—particularly in contrast to Christopher's thudding strides—comic in its agility. He was a bit of a ham. And it was when they were on that path that day, racing down from the ledge after greatly diminishing the Führer's quality of life, that Oliver gave into the temptation to let the pistol's serious weight slip so that its handle was in his palm. The two friends were laughing, hidden from pursuing storm troopers by the hedge of long grass. Oliver was running through the woods with a gun in his hand like a Hollywood movie star.

Suddenly, Oliver braked, his sneakers skidding. Christopher stopped behind him, arms whirling back as if encountering a sheer precipice at his toes.

Oliver crouched. He spun.

"Sniper," he whispered to his friend. "Eleven o'clock."

Oliver took fast, deadly aim at the German hiding behind the tree trunk on the cliff above them.

The recoil jumped like an electric shock in Oliver's hand. The sharp, precise crack of the pistol scared them both to death.

They both stared, not believing their eyes, at the burst of grey dust, suspended in sunlight, drifting over the stone above them.

# CHAPTER THIRTY-ONE

One Sunday morning in the spring of 1968, about ten days after his arrival in Pietrabella, Oliver Hughson was taken by Anna Di Castello on a climb up into the Apuan mountains of the Carrara region of southwest Liguria and northwest Tuscany—what Boccaccio and Dante knew as the Lunae Montes, the "mountains of the moon."

Charles Dickens passed through the Carrara area in 1846. He wrote a memoir of his journey through Italy. He called his journal *Pictures from Italy.* It is included in volume XVIII of the red, cloth-bound complete works that was left to Oliver—along with a house, a swimming pool, several Royal Doulton figurines, some gloomy furniture, a miniature replica of Michelangelo's *David,* and an investment portfolio comfortably adequate for a bachelor to live on.

Oliver had no pictures of his time in Italy. His camera—not very good anyway—had ended up in several pieces on the kitchen floor of the little farmhouse in the countryside that for a summer he had shared with Anna. On that occasion, Anna had stood over it, glowering, knife in hand, as if watching for any sign of remaining life. Had the camera attempted one last, dying click of its shutter, she'd have run the blade of her paring knife—and the chopped garlic that still clung to it—through its Instamatic heart. Or that, at any rate, was what her expression conveyed to astonished Oliver.

As a result, Oliver's souvenirs were idiosyncratic, to say the least. He had a copy of Rudolf Wittkower's Slade lectures on sculpture, its binding long gone. He had a black and white picture of Bernini's *Santa Teresa and the Angel* pinned above his desk in Cathcart. And he had the Dickens.

"They are four or five great glens . . ." Charles Dickens wrote. "The quarries, or 'caves,' as they call them there, are so many openings, high up in the hills, on either side of these passes, where they blast and excavate for marble . . ."

ANNA LOOKED AWFUL that Sunday morning. This was characteristic. Before she had her coffee, Anna looked like she'd bite your head off.

But her scowl wasn't threatening. It was merely cautionary: a warning to anyone in her vicinity to steer clear until her second cup had been sipped in silence and her puffed eyes had sorted themselves out. And it was usually at her outdoor table, in T-shirt and underwear, that she eased herself through her disgruntlement at no longer being asleep.

Anna's hair had the lustre of mahogany. So Oliver had by then decided—although he tried a dozen different descriptions of Anna's hair in his journal that summer. None of them were quite right. Oliver thought her eyes indescribable. Literally.

His notebook was filled with his self-rejected efforts: almond-shaped, jewel-like, deep. "Flashing" was crossed out heavily. These were approximations—and wrong, in some important way, for being so.

Anna's eyes were brown. That was about as close as Oliver ever got to finding a word that worked. They were the visual equivalent of the vowels that, no matter how he applied himself to his copy of *Italian for Beginners,* he was never able to master. They were eyes that were unafraid of demonstration—whatever mood Anna was in the mood to demonstrate.

Anna's resistance to etiquette was such that she withheld her smile until moments when she actually felt like smiling. As a result, it seemed not so much an expression as a change of weather—intensely gratifying to anyone who happened to be studying the sky at the moment the sun broke through.

But, if forced to name a favourite of Anna's physical characteristics, Oliver would probably have first chosen her hair. He often let it spread through the rise of his fingers just for the pleasure of watching it fall.

Anna's hair was at its best in the evenings when she sat at the centre of several tables full of singing, laughing *stranieri* at the Café David. It looked like it had been swept by her day—by the swings of her head when she was working, and by the breezes she'd ridden through on her rusty old bicycle—and not by a hairbrush at all.

It was at its worst when she just got out of bed. The storms that passed across her pillows in the night left a mess that would have included tangled power lines and unpassable roads had she been a landscape and not, as Oliver suggested to her one morning—from a safe distance—"a grumpy sleepyhead."

Oliver had no photograph of Anna because Anna would never let Oliver take one—a prohibition that he did not fully appreciate until the day he snapped a picture of her chopping garlic on the counter beside the kitchen window. His camera was hurled against the wall as a result. She had wrested it from him with surprising, unstoppable fury. "I'm not going to be a fucking souvenir," she shouted.

"Fucking" was a word Anna used a lot. It was the word "souvenir" that she spat so violently it sounded like profanity. Oliver had never before imagined that anger could achieve such sudden gale-force extremes. On the plus side: he had never guessed that lovemaking could be so ferocious.

Anna made a rosemary infusion that she used instead of commercial shampoo—simmering it on the stove for hours, before cooling it in her not entirely reliable kerosene refrigerator. The water pressure in the house was just as iffy, and Anna washed her hair on the hot days of that summer under the creaking hand pump at the bottom of the farmhouse garden. Oliver watched. He was always amazed that this scene—Anna turning, brown-skinned, wrapping a towel around her head, and smiling at him—was real. It seemed impossible. But then, all of Italy seemed impossible to Oliver.

He had arrived in Pietrabella, after his long, mostly tedious journey from Paris, in the evening. When he awoke in Richard Christian and Elena Conti's spare bedroom, it was late in the morning. He had slept soundly. But the room was still dark.

Richard had gone to his studio early. Elena had already caught a train to Rome, where she had a share in an apartment and where she worked as a freelance translator.

There were high, heavy wooden shutters on the window of the guest room.

Oliver opened them. He only wanted some light to unpack his knapsack. He had not anticipated quite so panoramic a view. He felt as if he were in a movie.

There were the terraced olive groves and grapevines. There were the footpaths that bordered the fields. There were the dusty switchback roads and red-tiled roofs.

The sounds were these: a commotion of roosters, the distant horn of a bus coming round a sharp turn in the hills, the whirring of the pneumatic chisels of men working stone.

There was white dust in the air. There was the smell of brush fires. There was the quiet, oddly distinct sound of cutlery being set for lunch in the house next door.

And above all this—either close or far away, he couldn't be sure—there were the foothills of the Apuans.

It felt like falling, almost like fainting. Dickens called it a "cheerful brightness."

When he opened those thick wooden shutters for the first time, the light of Tuscany staggered him.

Oliver lost his balance that morning. It was the first time he could remember it happening. He fell backward, his small, bare feet suddenly uncertain on the cool terra-cotta floor.

THE ROSEMARY INFUSION gave Anna's hair a distinct, woody scent—as exotic as the rosewood of jewellery boxes or the cedar lining of drawers filled with perfumed silk. Not that Oliver had any experience with either. And not that he'd had any experience with someone like Anna. Her difficulties with mornings often had to do with being up late in the Café David with a group of foreign sculptors.

Dusk settled over Pietrabella's central piazza. More wine was ordered. The surrounding hills darkened. The strings of lights on the square came on.

The stories began. And then the arguments. And then the singing. And then everyone decided to go to the little place on Via Piastrone that made such good grilled quail.

There was more wine. There were many courses. There was more singing. There was dancing.

These were the kind of nights that preceded the kind of mornings when Anna looked most awful. This was what Oliver discovered when he knocked at the door of her farmhouse. It was eight o'clock on a Sunday morning.

Anna's invitation to Oliver to go up into the quarries on Sunday morning had been typically unadorned with small talk. The offer was made at the Café David.

They'd met once before—at Richard and Elena's on Via Maddalena, on the evening Oliver had arrived in town.

At the Café David, Anna was sitting amid a group of sculptors. She'd caught Oliver looking at her a few times.

She had a directness to her that had as much to do with the absence of nuance in her English as with her temperament. She was ending a relationship with an American sculptor at the time. Anna did not end her relationships with great diplomacy. And it was in response to a remark from him that she got suddenly, if not steadily, to her feet.

She walked to the table where Oliver was sitting by himself. She did not bother with preamble. She spoke loudly enough for everyone to hear. "Come to my house tomorrow morning. Eight o'clock. We will go for a climb in the mountains."

When she turned, she almost knocked over the empty chair opposite Oliver. "I live in the hills," she said. "On the way to Castello."

Anna gave a final glare in the direction of the table at which she had been seated. "Everyone knows where."

It was an impressive exit—although not impressive enough for Anna to remember it. Oliver's arrival at the farmhouse at eight o'clock the next morning was not something she was expecting. Apparently.

She wasn't going to say a word before she had a cup of coffee.

Her hair, the dark circles under her almost-closed eyes, her long, rumpled T-shirt, her bare, flat-footed shuffle through her uncared-for kitchen made the point. They conveyed precisely the only reply that could, with Anna's customary honesty, be made to Oliver's polite, "How are you this morning?"

The cure for a hangover of this severity—so Anna told Oliver as she poured her second cup of thick, hot espresso—was the combination of coffee, a spliff, and the crisp, cool air of the Apuans. She then set out to prove this to be true.

An hour later, Oliver's newly heightened appreciation for the beauty of the Tuscan countryside overcame what concerns he had about Anna's driving. They made their incautious, bumpy way down from Anna's place, and through the mostly empty, Sunday-morning streets of Pietrabella. They started up toward the quarries.

Anna's Cinquecento was so badly rusted the passing road was visible through the floor. The car was filled by their two bodies, the knapsack Anna hastily packed for lunch, and the satchels, books, sculpting tools, empty wine bottles, and dirty laundry that were already occupying what little passenger space there was.

Anna had no money, of course. Oliver didn't either, he was embarrassed to admit. But Anna thought she had enough gas to get to the point on one of the high, switchback roads where, she had decided, their hike would begin. They'd worry about coming down when they came down. If the worse came to the worst, she said, they could coast.

This made perfect sense to Oliver. It was the first time in his life he'd smoked hash.

After they parked, Anna lit the bottom half of what they had smoked with their coffee. The car filled with smoke. It smelled like someone had set a pile of dung on fire. Oliver wasn't used to the black tobacco. He started coughing.

"Is this dangerous?" he spluttered.

"The hash?"

"No. The climb."

"Ha," said Anna. "It is very healthy, the climb."

"What are we climbing?"

"We are climbing to the mountains of the moon."

FOR MOST OF THE SECOND HOUR of their climb they were below what looked like the loop of a giant clothesline. It was a Belgian invention.

The cables didn't turn on Sundays. But on every other day—except, of course, for Christmas—the valleys hummed with the steady revolutions of lines of thickly braided steel. They were so long they looked as if they were stays holding the mountains in position. Ever since the end of the nineteenth century, they'd been the principal method of marble extraction.

As it turned on its enormous loop, the cutting wire was lowered slowly into the marble. A slurry of water, ground quartz, and sand was fed into the deepening slice. There were workers who were so skilled at this they could judge the cable's progress through the stone without ever looking at it. They made adjustments by sound alone.

The steady friction made the cutting line dangerously hot. For this reason, far below the quarries, usually below the staging areas where the workers first entered the gates and where the wagons were loaded, water troughs were constructed. The cables ran through the water to cool before returning to the white caverns above.

BY THE TIME they stopped for lunch, the cooling troughs, far below them, looked like miniatures of themselves.

Anna knew a spot. There was a stream.

The current widened, fed by a fall of water over a ledge of rock. She kicked off her old tennis shoes—footwear that Oliver thought alarmingly flimsy for so arduous a climb. But they didn't seem to be bothering Anna.

She stood, barefoot, in the shallows.

She showed Oliver the different varieties of stone that she had gathered in a single scoop of the creek bed. She had been right. Her recovery from the night before was now complete.

Anna held out the handful of smooth, wet pebbles. "Look," she said. "They're marble. But each is different. Look. Washed from quarries up in the mountains."

Cautiously, for the rocks underneath her feet were uncertain, she stepped closer to him. "The grey one is Ordinario," she said. "Mostly for building. It is everywhere. Window ledges. Stairs. Floors. The *pissoir* on the way to Via Maddalena . . ."

"How do you know that?" Oliver asked. He meant the question as a joke, although Anna took it seriously.

"I was a curious little girl."

"And the white?"

"Statuario," she said. "The first prize for sculptors. We all want this, like we want snow. Or angels' wings. Or stars. Because it is so pure for carving. It is such clean beauty. It was why Michelangelo came. And maybe he saw this very Statuario before it got knocked from his block."

"Do you think?"

"It is possible. It could take centuries for a piece to be tumbled and washed, getting smaller and smoother, down the stream from up in the mountains where he was working—all the way to us, here, now."

She pointed out others. Oliver watched and listened, enjoying the rolling, generous vowels as much as her eloquent eyes.

She held up a smooth oval. It was the size of a quail's egg, veined with grey. She said, "Bianca Oscura. From the quarry where we are going. After we eat." She looked at Oliver matter-of-factly. "And after we eat maybe we take a little rest if you want."

One by one, she let the stones drop back into the stream.

They ate on a warm ledge of rock beside the pool. Light slanted through the apse of chestnut trees. After their picnic, with her eyes on Oliver while she spoke, she rolled her head slowly from side to side. *Arabescato. Bardiglio. Breccia.* He was listening to a cascade of vowels. He was watching Anna shake out her hair.

# CHAPTER THIRTY-TWO

Julian Morrow's mind was impossible. Or that, at least, was what his quarry managers and his workshop supervisors professed it to be. It wasn't that Morrow didn't pay attention to what they told him. It was that he paid attention in his own unusual way.

He insisted on regular meetings, and he could be counted on to appear unexpectedly at a quarry or in a studio, usually with questions. Morrow had about him something of the amateur enthusiast—a curiosity about everything to do with marble that could be exhausting to anyone in his employ. It was how he had picked up his expertise so quickly. It was the same with his Italian. His acquired fluency inspired him to become more fluent still.

If anything, he paid too much attention to what his staff and his employees and his servants had to say. But his attention was always embroidered with thoughts that had no obvious association to what was being discussed. Not obvious, anyway, to his managers and supervisors.

The quarry boss was sitting in Morrow's villa that Monday morning. His leather-covered notebook was open on the lap of his heavy trousers. His boots were cleaned and shined because he cleaned them and shined them every Sunday night in preparation for the weekly meeting with the owner.

Morrow's soaring optimism was subject, at times, to plummets of sadness. These came upon him rarely. But they rocked him. This was one such occasion.

"The boy's father?" he asked.

"Yes," the manager replied.

"And two of his brothers?"

"Yes. There were a few others at the table too. Not related. Or, at least, not related very closely. The villages are small places."

"This is sad," Morrow said.

The manager said nothing. This was the way it was in the quarries. It was always sad.

IN HIS SPEECHES Morrow usually referred to his Tuscan villa as his "home away from home"—especially if his wife and mother-in-law were in the audience. They often were. And it amused him, privately, that they never guessed that the statement—always made with a courteous acknowledgment of their presence—was open to interpretation.

The villa had an interesting history—so he thought. So he explained to his attentive audiences. For centuries the structure had been a convent, made of stone, freezing in bleak winters, home to several dozen austerely hushed devotionals, a stop made by pilgrims and by other holy travellers. It was said that Michelangelo had stayed there. But the claim that Michelangelo had slept in rooms, or dined in homes, or signed contracts in the offices of marble agents and quarry owners in the area was not uncommon. The region specialized in such fables.

Like the diminishing echoes of their vespers, the nuns faded to a last rough coffin and a final plain white marble cross. The building fell into disrepair and was eventually purchased by Julian Morrow. He tore down its two wings, saving the statuary and the worn marble of the floors and the bevelled panelling of the veined, stone walls for his own use. He built a pool at the spot where the ground was always sodden anyway. After considerable renovation, Morrow made the remaining central structure his home. It was his favourite office.

THE QUARRY MANAGER had already gone over the first item on his agenda. He'd given his report to Morrow of the accident that had occurred two days before.

Morrow continued to stand, as he usually stood throughout their weekly meeting. His hands were clasped behind his back. He was turned away, looking from the window of his villa.

The manager was relieved that Morrow did not appear to spend any more time on the accident. There was nothing to be done anyway. There never was. There were other items on the agenda. The manager consulted his own childlike scrawl.

There was a new kind of saw to be considered.

There were some repairs that needed to be made to the *lizzatura.*

Morrow was thinking the Bartons' grounds would be a very fine commission—although he already knew from his conversations with Grace that developing the plans would not be a fast process. He could see that she had a good eye. He could also see that she had an eye for detail. And details were what took up time. And money. And more time. And more money.

It would not happen quickly. He reminded himself that the grounds for the recently completed Morris-Jones estate in Suffolk had been almost ten years in the planning. So he would not rush Grace Barton. Patience was key.

The timekeeper, Morrow's manager was saying to him, had requested that a small stove be installed in the quarry gatehouse as the winter months were very cold and the poor man suffered most terribly from hemorrhoids that were caused, he believed, by sitting on the cold stone bench from which he conducted his important duties.

This was not a matter, Morrow felt, that required his undivided attention.

He nodded vaguely at what his manager was saying. His thoughts on the Bartons had led him to thoughts of the luncheon speech he would be called upon to give in Swansea a few weeks hence. Some of the information he had provided to the Bartons might work in the talk. With some few small adjustments.

Abruptly, Morrow wheeled around from the window. A new thought had just occurred to him. His Italian was surprisingly convincing.

"Does the boy have talents?" he asked.

"The boy?" The quarry manager looked up from his notepad.

"The boy you spoke of. The water boy."

"Oh," the manager said. It had been almost fifteen minutes since he had reported to Julian Morrow the details of the quarry accident. The manager thought they were well into other matters. "Talents?"

"Yes. Talents."

Morrow had a reputation for asking things that were unexpected. But for once this was a question to which the manager happened to have an answer. He knew the family. He had relatives of his own in Castello.

"They say he has a knack for modelling clay."

"Does he?" said Morrow.

"Before he started in the quarries, he made some pennies doing little clay portraits for birthdays and confirmations."

"Did he indeed?"

Then Morrow seemed to slip for a few moments into one of his private avenues of thought.

"Make sure the widow is provided for," Morrow said. He looked at the manager, whom he knew and admired as a thrifty man. So he smiled when he said, "A little more generously than you might think appropriate."

The manager nodded and made a note of this.

"And have the boy sent to me. I don't like the idea of his going back to work in the quarries. It is too much to expect him to return."

The manager began to point out that accidents were facts of life in the quarries. But Morrow cut him off.

"We have no shortage of workers in the quarries. If anything, we have too many. If the boy is a smart lad, we can find him a good apprenticeship in one of our studios in town."

# CHAPTER THIRTY-THREE

WHEN I RETURNED TO ITALY from my few days in Cathcart in June 2009, I told my mother of the conversations I had had with my father. Anna rolled a cigarette and listened. We were sitting at her outdoor table. But when, finally, she decided to speak, she remained typically oblique. She said, "I remember he asked me once what it was that made Michelangelo so great. So I showed him. All summer, I showed him."

That was how she started talking about him. Her recollections came slowly at first. But eventually, I could hardly get her to stop.

For forty years she had never mentioned his name. She had never alluded to his existence in any way more specific than the frown and the shrug that had, all my life, been her response to my curiosity about my lineage. She had always been frank about the reason for this. She would purse her lips and shrug her shoulders. "My life was a little wild," she would say. "That's just the way it was in those days."

I'd discovered my father by accident. I was still smarting from Pier-Giorgio's rejection of "Michelangelo's Mountains." And in order to get my mind off Pier-Giorgio's smug face and on to something else, I embarked on one of my occasional and not ever effective campaigns to get my mother organized in some way for the poor accountant who suffered through her tax forms. It was during this futile exercise that I came across my father's letters at the bottom of a cardboard box on a shelf in my mother's bedroom. The letters were under a flap on the bottom of the box. I happened to notice a corner of blue airmail stationery.

By then, I'd pretty much given up. Or it may have been that my curiosity was satisfied sufficiently by the on-and-off presence of a man in my mother's life who acted a bit like a father to me when I was a girl. He might even have been my father—a possibility that my mother's casual approach to my interest in my own conception never quite confirmed and never quite denied.

In Pietrabella there were sculptors who appeared from Holland, from America, from Germany, from Britain, from Japan, and who stayed for a few weeks, or perhaps for a few months, and who never returned. Others became fixtures, either staying for good or returning regularly. Pietr Henk was such a fixture.

Once or twice a year, Pietr drove down from Holland. He had not become a sculptor by profession. Few of the *stranieri* did. But even after he began working at the commercial art firm outside of Rotterdam, he continued to carve stone as something more than a hobby and less than an occupation. He lived behind a high, thick hedge of rhododendron in an old, leafy suburb—a grassy, overgrown double-lot of peach and chestnut trees that was populated with his chickens, his rooster, and his marble sculpture. But he continued to drive to Italy a few times a year to select the stone he needed and to take a workbench for a few weeks in one of the marble workshops in the town.

His cars steadily improved over the years. But the Ramblin' Jack Elliott and the Jerry Jeff Walker he listened to en route never changed. Nor did he—not very much. He never ceased being kind and tall and blond. He never gained very much weight as he grew older. He never stopped smoking Marlboros. And even after he married, he continued to stay with Anna when he came for his visits. Whether his wife was aware of this, or suspected it, was not something anyone in Pietrabella knew for sure, despite many years of communal speculation on the subject.

He was not someone whose presence in Pietrabella vanished behind him when he left town. He'd been coming for years. His Italian was more than passable.

There were restaurants he favoured. There was a spot at the counter at the Café David where he always stood for his coffee early in the morning when he was on his way to work. He was always at the cinema on the square on Saturday nights for the usually old, usually American movies. He was often accompanied by Anna. They made a handsome couple.

Anna loved the way angled light caught things in black and white: a trench coat, a .38 on a kitchen table, Veronica Lake's hair. She thought this is what America looked like.

Pietr took me to the gelateria or to the beach from time to time when I was little. He sent me birthday cards.

His visits became less frequent as he got older. I hadn't seen him for several years when the news came that he was ill. And the news, from the beginning, was not hopeful. I wrote to him, in care of his office address. I asked if, please, he would put my mind to rest? Pietr agreed to the blood test.

My mother was right. She had been a little wild in her day.

"YOU WERE NEVER MENTIONED," I said to Oliver on my first day in Cathcart. "I asked a lot of people. I am quite a thorough researcher."

"I can see that you are."

"But your name never came up."

Immediately, I realized that this would have to be hurtful. "*Mi dispiace.*"

Oliver shrugged. The fountain splashed gently into the black, unlit water of the old pool.

"The invisible man."

"I would not have found you had I not found the letters."

Letters that were never answered, Oliver was quick to point out. Not one. He'd been given no hint about me. He wanted to make this clear.

It was not hurtful to him so much as strange that a time he remembered so vividly had disappeared so completely. His four months in Italy—four months he had visited and revisited all his life in his memory—had been forgotten by everyone with whom he'd shared them.

True, the limitations of his Italian meant that he had little more than nodding acquaintances with most people in Pietrabella. And the fact that he had spent a good deal of his time posing for Richard Christian in an otherwise unpopulated studio didn't allow for much socializing.

Richard's studio was a single room with a high ceiling and large, frosted glass windows with an eastern exposure. It had the soft greyness of natural light and the pleasing combination of clutter and emptiness that often characterizes places where artists work. It was furnished with tools, and reference books, and propane tanks, and rulers, and calipers, and drawing pads, and various works in progress, and armatures waiting to be used. There were dusty wooden tables and workbenches and a high, long shelf for his finished pieces. There was a large poster of Ingres's *La Grande Odalisque* on the wall.

There was great discomfort in modelling: the damp chill, the awkwardness of certain difficult poses, the slight headache of a long, hungry morning. As well, there were levels of irritation: itches that couldn't be scratched, lashes in eyes that couldn't be whisked away. But these are not the worst of it.

The real pain was stillness. It did not matter if a particular pose was hard or easy. The piece that Richard was working on when Oliver modelled for him required poses of considerable difficulty. Figures huddled. Figures writhing. One of the figures hung, as if from the struts of a bridge—an idea that Richard had latched on to shortly after Oliver had shown up on the doorstep of the apartment on Via Maddalena.

"I try to use what comes my way," Richard said.

But it was not the difficulty of the poses that was Oliver's biggest problem. It was simply not-moving that became intolerable. Sometimes he felt sick with it.

He found that the most casually bent knee, the most relaxed emphasis of weight on a hip, the lightest rest of an elbow on a ledge built steadily in intensity. They began as nothing worth thinking about and, after only five or ten minutes, became his sole preoccupation. He knew that this would eventually end—Richard would usually work about an hour before calling a break—but that didn't help somehow. In fact, it made things worse. Oliver found that when he couldn't move he was constantly in danger of being able to think about nothing else. His daydreams were of feasts of movement: he was running like a boy on a hillside path; he was walking through thick summer nights of olive groves and valleys; he was making love with Anna. But these were never dreams in which he could lose himself. They were longing. He'd never found the present so endless. There was no straightening, no idle step, no stretch that could relieve its oppression.

But even with these stretches of time the four months vanished. Even with poses that felt more like eras to Oliver than afternoons, his summer in Italy disappeared. I never heard his name spoken by the sculptors, artisans, workshop owners, bartenders, restaurant owners, and shopkeepers to whom I'd turned for clues. Oliver had dropped through Pietrabella's past without leaving a ripple. It was like he'd never been there.

MICHELANGELO WAS IN ROME, waiting for the marble he had quarried for the tomb to arrive from Carrara, when, in 1506, *Laocoon and His Sons* was discovered by a man working in a vineyard on the Esquiline Hill. The piece fascinated Michelangelo. It was an inspiration. From the ancients came the heroic form that he held as the greatest expression of beauty. But even more importantly, from the ancients came the philosophy that transformed the sweaty, dusty drudgery of mallet and *gradino* into a process almost divine. Michelangelo's gift for uncovering an object's beauty was how he believed he reached the purpose of his soul.

This quest was so central to Michelangelo's sense of himself that every delay in the marble shipments from Carrara felt to him like disaster. Every obstacle wasn't just an obstacle—it was an idea that, impeded, might become ordinary.

By the time Michelangelo was back in Rome, by the time he set out to see the statue of Laocoon that had been discovered in a local vineyard, he was feeling the slow, dull wound that artists almost always get to know. Those who esteemed him, those who honoured him, those who encouraged him, those who once boasted that they knew him seemed to be turning away. He was feeling the hollow, lonely sensation of attention going elsewhere.

Michelangelo had always been drawn to the beauty of the male body in exertion: straining, pulling, struggling. And Laocoon—the sad, unheeded character in the *Aeneid* who warns his fellow Trojans of the Greeks' intentions—is a figure of such writhing anguish that some have suggested that Michelangelo saw his own struggles in the Trojan's furious effort to free himself from the two snakes twisting around his extended arms and between his powerful legs. By then, struggle was something that Michelangelo understood well. Nothing was easy. Least easy of all: working for Julius II.

It wasn't an uncomplicated time to be pope—which was just as well, since Julius thrived on his capacity for complexity. He had the French to worry about, and the Spanish. The Florentines were always difficult, the Venetians worse, and he was intent on regaining control of the papal fiefs of Perugia and Bologna. Still, with enough on his military and political agenda to occupy fully the mind and the treasury of a more modest man of God, Julius chose this moment in history to establish a legacy far beyond a mere tomb.

Designs for the new St. Peter's occupied those of his attentions not already busy with diplomacy, politics, and war. The project for which he'd commissioned Michelangelo—the masterpiece that Michelangelo had imagined would be the crowning achievement of his youthful triumphs as a sculptor—wasn't cancelled exactly. It was just that Julius was busy now with other, bigger things.

Michelangelo must have seen the tribulation of being an artist in the torment of Laocoon's face. Even the greatest artist had to worry about money, about schedules, about impatient patrons, about dishonest quarry owners, about conniving agents, about wagons breaking down on mountain trails, about freighted barges on stormy seas. It was all impossible. No wonder he ground his teeth in his sleep. But there was an even bigger worry. Everything depended on how importantly his work was regarded by those who hired him. He needed their money, of course. But money was only the measurement of something more important: affirmation. To be ignored was a cruelty he found intolerable.

IMAGINE A GREEK CARVER of marble *kouroi* in 600 BC. This is something my mother used to tell me to do when she felt it necessary to teach me about the history of carving stone. She told me to picture an ancient Greek banging away on a block.

He is working at right angles to the unaccommodating surface. He is using a mallet on a bronze punch. This is because he's a century or so too early for iron tools that can carve marble obliquely. As a result of this professional bad luck, he is obliged to create his figure with small, repeated indentations in the stone instead of the longer furrows that will soon become the bread-and-butter strokes of stone masons and sculptors. And let's say that he grows tired of his arms feeling like battering rams. And let's say he gets a little bored with figures that, even when they are finished, look a lot like the block of marble from which they've come.

The *kouroi* are majestic, in their way. They have . . . *something*. That's what my mother said. *Something*. She could have said magic.

But she imagined that this particular Greek sculptor begins to think about the stone differently than any Greek sculptor had ever thought of it before. He wonders: What if it's just stone?

And so, one day, with his mallet raised, and his face smeared with marble dust, and the sun glinting on the soon-to-be-obsolete alloy of his bronze punch, and his hands going numb with his constant hammering against a material that seems not to want in the least to be hammered, the ancient Greek sculptor thinks: fuck it. He's going to ease off—just a bit. He's not going to bother putting absolutely all the strength, and all the grace, and all the skill, and all the inspiration, and all the apprehension of physical beauty that sits at the heart of a stone carver's soul into every single stroke of his mallet. He thinks nobody will notice anyway.

It's a moment with repercussions. My mother is of the opinion that it changed everything.

She said, "It doesn't take long for everything to stop working the way it worked before. Soon the magical springs are just places to get water. Soon there are no spirits in the woods. Swans are just swans. Midsummer spells become stories people make up. Everything is different. But nobody notices."

Nobody notices, that is, until an artist as great as Michelangelo comes along. Because it's not only that he is inspired by antiquity, it's that he remembers something the world keeps forgetting.

Were you to stand in the Italian Sculpture Gallery in the Louvre, as the young Oliver Hughson did in the spring of 1968, and were you to circle slowly, around and around, *The Dying Captive,* and conclude that, in all your life, you had never seen a form more charged with beauty, you might decide that Michelangelo's struggles were against forces far greater than practical difficulties. His real battle was with beauty itself. It was never easy to find. He had no choice but to put everything that sits at the heart of a stone carver's soul into every stroke of his mallet.

THE KIND OF TECHNICAL VIRTUOSITY THAT, by the nineteenth century, came to be embodied by an artist as efficient and as smoothly successful as the Venetian sculptor Antonio Canova, would probably have seemed little more than skilful cleverness to Michelangelo. Canova's pieces were created by the transposition of a small clay maquette to a larger block of stone by studio assistants and by the use of a pointing system—a multiplication of the key exterior points of the model to the larger scale of the stone. This was mechanics, my mother always said, not magic. Oliver was never sure how, but he somehow knew exactly what she meant.

Even as a young man, even as someone who knew almost nothing about sculpture, Oliver Hughson was puzzled by the people who gathered around Canova's *Psyche Revived by Cupid's Kiss* in the Italian Sculpture Gallery in the Louvre, and who then hurried past the unfinished Michelangelos. How was it possible for them to get things so wrong?

That's what my mother always wants to know. "Why can't people see what there is to see?" she asks. Often. Because when it comes to the ability to recognize the importance of great art, her opinion of most of mankind is this: they are barbarians. Specifically, so she likes to say, they are the barbarians who came south and stumbled on the village of Luni, an outpost of the Roman Empire—the empire they'd got it into their lice-ridden heads to conquer.

Luni was on the flats below what is now the region of Massa-Carrara. It was a dull, provincial place that did nothing but supply white stone for the empire's capital.

Over time, the steady buildup of silt at the mouth of the Magra River, running not far to the north of the present-day city of Carrara, would turn the port of Luni into unhealthy and unprofitable marshlands. But the barbarians stumbled onto Luni long before that. And they were dazzled by it.

Dazzled by its one temple. And its one aqueduct. And its one bath.

The barbarians threw all their bearded, furious numbers at the handful of startled soldiers and workers stationed there.

There was the usual mayhem. Then, when it was over and the carrion birds were circling, the barbarians headed back north. They were very pleased with their great triumph. But they were idiots, actually. They thought they'd just sacked Rome.

WHEN PIER-GIORGIO CALLED CLARA and me into his office for his decision, he came directly to the point.

"This won't do," he said.

The brochure was to have been distributed throughout the area, left at train stations and at the reception desks of inns and hotels and restaurants popular with foreigners.

He held the text of "Michelangelo's Mountains" at the edges of the pages, as if holding it more firmly would have demonstrated a commitment to its content that he was disinclined to make. "You seem to think our job is to send tourists to Rome," he said.

Clara began to splutter a response, but he cut her off.

"No," he said. "Rome does not need our assistance. We don't need to send our tourists to the Vatican. We want them to come—" his pause made it clear that he felt he was stating the painfully obvious "—here. We want them to spend their money—" a pause of similar irony, only longer "—here."

The tomb of Julius II, as Michelangelo envisioned it, was never completed. The blocks of Carrara stone that Michelangelo had quarried had come to Rome from Carrara by ship. Likely they'd been loaded somewhere in the vicinity of Forte dei Marmi and shipped to the Ripa Grande port on the Tiber, and then hauled by ox cart to Rome. But it was not long after they were amassed in the square of St. Peter's, not far from Michelangelo's modest rooms, that it became apparent that the attention of Pope Julius had shifted. Julius pretended that this was only a small matter—merely a redirection of funds.

The truth was this: Michelangelo was heartbroken. He had to give up ambitions that are the hardest to surrender. He was being forced to abandon the artist he thought he was becoming. And this, of course, proved to be impossible.

During his eight months in the quarries, Michelangelo had studied the workers' daily fight against gravity—for that is what their work amounted to. The conditions were harsh, the demands of quarry owners terrifying, the rewards to the workers paltry. All this he understood. It was like working for the pope.

Whether Julius came to believe that building his own lavish tomb was bound to be an ill omen or whether Michelangelo fell victim to the whisperings of his competitors isn't clear today. It probably wasn't clear then. Julius let it be known that the tomb would not proceed in the immediate future.

Michelangelo was furious. So furious, he let the pope know that he was furious—a dangerous impertinence that only an artist of the stature of Michelangelo could have dared. But Julius's monumental self-importance made him oblivious to any reasons for an artist's outrage, even when the artist happened to be one of the greatest in the world. Michelangelo was still just someone to be hired. Or not. When Julius changed his mind about his own tomb, he considered himself generous and thoughtful to be giving Michelangelo an alternative commission.

The new job wasn't one that pleased Michelangelo in the least. He "made every effort to get out of it," Condivi wrote. He thought of himself as a sculptor more than a painter. But even more importantly, it was impossible for him to abandon an idea that had been so consuming. He had the splendour of his design for the tomb in his imagination. It was hard to let such a vision go.

This was the point Clara and I made in the text for our brochure. We claimed Michelangelo never did abandon his vision, not entirely. He drew on his hopes for it. He drew on what he had lived and seen and what he dreamed of when, sore with the scratches of bramble of mountain paths and stiff with his long day's work, he lay down on the hard bed provided to him by the holy sisters in their bleak convent in the hills.

When he was in Rome, when he was addressing the pope's new commission, the quarries stayed inside him. The sawing. The hammering. The lifting. The hauling. Nothing was easy, not the quarrying of stone and not the creation of beauty. Always, what he thought would take weeks, took him months, took him years. It was all impossible.

There are still visitors to the Carrara region who struggle up paths, scale fallen screes, and edge across long-forgotten trails, searching for an *M* carved into an abandoned and overgrown rock face—as difficult as it is to imagine Michelangelo carving an initial into a rock to amuse either himself or posterity. There are people who hike the ridges that they think must have been Michelangelo's cobbled roads, and who climb to the dark, surprisingly small caverns that they think must have been his quarries. Everywhere, there are rooms where he was said to have signed contracts for stone. There are buildings where he was said to have slept.

But the richest souvenir of Michelangelo's eight months in the Carrara area may well have nothing to do with stone. This is what Clara and I proposed. It may be that tourists who want to know something of Michelangelo's mountains can find what they are looking for well to the south of Carrara. It may be that they have to go to Rome.

Resigned finally to his new commission, Michelangelo drew on his efforts in the mountains for inspiration: on the energies of his youth and on his memories of the quarry workers who had laboured beside him, on the gleam of their arms, on the breadth of their backs, on the fall of their thick hair on sunburned necks. He saw them working in the thin air and he saw them reclining on a ledge of rock eating bread and pork fat in the sunshine. He saw them turning away, arms stretched back into the tension of a rope. He saw them seated for their lunch, reaching out, a cup of wine in their broad hands. He saw them straining, pulling, reaching, pushing—resisting the unassailable force they confronted every day. These images seemed to tumble from him, these crouched and turning and twisted figures, these outreached hands, these roundly modelled, uplifted faces.

It took Michelangelo four years to complete the Sistine Chapel ceiling.

# CHAPTER THIRTY-FOUR

GRACE WAS A TEENAGER when she jumped from the storage loft of the Cathcart Art School. She was, even then, fierce in her defence of women's equality. "Did you know," she had written in a prize-winning essay for her third form social studies essay, "that the question of votes for women is one which is commanding the attention of the whole civilized world; that during 1911 the press of this country gave more space to woman's suffrage than to any other public question?" This, like her belief in art, was a passion that never left her.

Grace always remembered the afternoon when she first set eyes on the villa's grounds. She often described it to friends. She was walking with Julian Morrow. They were making their way at a leisurely pace toward the pool. That was where their luncheon would be served.

Grace was adept at gauging the physical difficulty of anything she was about to do without alerting anyone to her caution. She didn't like anyone to know, but she needed to rally herself for these exertions. She had been in conversation with Julian Morrow as they had approached the stone steps leading up through his gardens to his pool. He was explaining to her that it was the terraces of the marble quarries that had inspired him to conceive of levels of flower beds and rockery divided by a single, long, central stair. "The inclines are constructed for the downward conveyance of the marble blocks from the quarry walls," he said. "I've always greatly admired the look of them. They are called the *lizzatura,* and they are oddly beautiful in their dangerous steepness." The last two words of this explanation caused Grace to glance ahead.

Within the constraints her accident had imposed on her, Grace moved with open, unapologetic vigour. She had the freckled, attentive beauty of a very pretty boy, and her slender athleticism made her condition seem less a handicap than a physical idiosyncrasy. It wasn't a limp. It was just her energetic way of climbing the stone steps, between banks of rosemary and lavender.

That was when she first saw Julian Morrow's pool. Her husband was a few steps behind.

"Oh my," Grace said. She stopped at the gate and took in what was before her: the rectangle of green water, the stone figures, the tranquil cascade. One statue—a centrally positioned female nude—turned an urn of gently splashing water into the pool.

This was the bluest of blue skies, the greenest green of chestnut and cypress. There was thyme between the flagstones of the patio. The heat of the sun raised its fragrance. The long grasses buzzed. An afternoon bell, distant and tinny, sounded in the campanile of the walled town above them.

"Oh my."

It was a fond memory. So Argue Barton would always think.

He would always remember how radiant his wife had been on that holiday.

Argue had not been enthusiastic about the trip at first. He had wondered aloud whether he would have the time for a honeymoon—until, as he was speaking, he looked up from the papers on his desk and encountered Grace's level gaze. Of course there was going to be a honeymoon.

She had won him over. Oh, hadn't she just. The Bartons' tour had been a great success. And as a souvenir: something special, something grand, something as bold as the touch of his young bride in the dark bedrooms of European hotels.

Argue Barton commissioned an identical pool for their own residence in Cathcart. He couldn't imagine how such an extravagant idea had come to him. But it had—a bolt of sheer inspiration, he liked to think.

His grounds, like Julian Morrow's, were tucked in levels into the sheltered rise of a wooded hillside. The similarities of landscape, at least in summer, were striking. Cathcart's winters were another matter.

Grace Barton and Julian Morrow worked together on the plans. Drawings were sent, by post, back and forth between Canada and Italy. Morrow had anticipated that this process would take a long time. Grace, he knew, would enjoy it too much to rush. But it took even longer than he had imagined.

Grace was at first preoccupied with the birth of her only child. Michael was born in May 1923. It had not been easy. Grace did not recover quickly. Argue was of the view that his wife didn't completely recover, ever.

Julian Morrow had expected that the landscaping and the ornamental gardens of the Bartons' private residence might lead to a few other small commissions in Cathcart. He had an instinct for these things. But, for once, his expectations were too low. Long before work on the Bartons' gardens and pool had begun, Argue Barton was recommending Morrow International for various important public works. And in Cathcart, Argue Barton's recommendation went far. Morrow had underestimated the economic energy that would prevail in North America until almost the end of the decade.

The 1920s were boom years for institutional construction, and the marble industry had grown with the expansion of the world's economy, just as it shrivelled, during hostilities, with its constriction. Demand for both raw and finished marble had all but evaporated in the years of the Great War. But the market steadily improved after 1918, and by the latter half of the 1920s, marble production in Carrara had reached 340,000 tons a year. Three-quarters of this was exported.

In 1926 a central meridian was planned for Cathcart's downtown. It was not quite big enough to be called a park. It was, in fact, an accident—an unusually wide gap between the town's two main streets that existed only because Cathcart's first farmers' market had been established there. This common would be grand, even on Cathcart's small scale—an expression of respect for the public realm that, by the end of the century, would be entirely lost to private development. There would be large, shady trees. There would be planted flower beds. There would be park benches and pedestal drinking fountains. And beneath all this, under the paths over which Cathcart's citizens passed, there would be public washrooms. Morrow International was awarded the contract for the marble panelling.

As well, there was the construction of Montrose United Church in 1927–28, an undertaking to which Argue Barton was a generous benefactor.

Then there was October 1929.

But newspapers survived. Quite well, actually. It seemed that people were happy to pay to read about how bad things were.

Ten years after Grace and Argue Barton's trip to Italy, the landscaping of their private residence was underway. It was overseen by the Italian artisan Morrow recommended for the job.

"Lino Cavatore is young," Julian Morrow said in his letter of agreement to Argue Barton. But even as he wrote this sentence, sitting at his desk, looking from the window of his villa over his own gardens, and his pool, and the several empty pedestals that awaited the replacement of statuary—he realized the statement was not exactly true. Lino Cavatore had never been young. At least not in Morrow's experience.

When he first met the boy, he had been struck with his seriousness. But that was not so surprising. The boy's solemnity broke Morrow's heart, but he took it to be the natural response of a child to the loss of his father and brothers, and to his sudden ascension to the head of the family. Lino Cavatore had a brother with withered legs and deformed feet. Lino had a mother to look after as well.

Who wouldn't be serious about these new responsibilities? Who wouldn't be grave and attentive when ushered into the office of the wealthy quarry owner to be told that he would not be returning to his job in the quarries? Who wouldn't seem older than he was?

Morrow enjoyed being kindly. It was part of the pleasure he took in his own personality. And so, in a gentle voice, he said that he understood that the boy had talents that should be encouraged. The boy had looked stricken at this information, but Morrow told the boy not to worry. His mother would be looked after during the time Lino was in Carrara. Lino was going to be an apprentice in one of Morrow's marble studios.

For purposes of his billeting, and his moral and religious upbringing, he would live at the orphanage in Carrara, on Via

Sacristi, run by the priests. He would learn the trade of carving stone under the best of Morrow's artisans. This was how skills were passed down. It was a tradition, Morrow was always pleased to say, that reached back, from generation to generation, to the time of the great Michelangelo.

Lino Cavatore was small. But there was something in his face, something in his gait, something in the way he held himself against the world that was the posture and the attitude of an older, more hardened man.

"He is not yet twenty-two," Morrow wrote to Argue Barton. "But he has worked as an artisan in one of my Carrara workshops since he was twelve. Lino is reliable. He is a hard worker. But more importantly, he has an eye. This may strike you as the minimum of requisites for your job. But believe me, my friend, it is not—particularly when it comes to the collaboration of landscape and sculpture and architectural form. Lino knows what is beautiful and what is not. That, you may be surprised to learn, is a rare talent. You will be pleased with his work, I assure you."

Argue had expected that he would be.

He'd pictured himself strolling with his wife along the paths of stone figures. He'd imagined that they would sit on a stone bench in a shaft of sunshine in a grotto. He could see the pool. He could hear the gentle splashing of the fountain. He wanted a memento for Grace. He wanted something that would always remind them of how they were when they began their life together.

"Oh my," Grace had said when she stepped onto the marble flagstones that surrounded Julian Morrow's swimming pool.

Argue Barton wanted to give that happiness a physical form. But by the time Lino Cavatore's work was underway, a husband's gift to his wife had become something else entirely.

The peritonitis was the result of a ruptured appendix. An

operation would be risky. As such, it was a procedure that required her husband's permission. But Argue Barton was in Halifax on business. The efforts to reach him had not succeeded in time.

THE FOUNDATION OF GRACE'S youthful politics was her suspicion that women were, in many ways, superior to men. The world being what it was, this was a position she kept to herself. But it was an opinion held without arrogance. It was more like a kind of sadness in her own self-appraisal. As a teenager, she couldn't help but observe that she belonged to a gender that, to a considerable extent, was attracted to fools. It's not as if there was a shortage of evidence to support the view.

And they were fools. Worse, they were little fools. She wanted to best the boys who had pulled away the ladder from the art-supply loft of the Cathcart Art School. She was up there getting a new number-six sable brush. She would show them.

She moved from the supply cabinet at the back without hesitation. There was no slowing of her pace as she approached the edge. The foolish little boys must have seen her blue smock billow and her auburn hair stream behind when, with a confident smile, Grace stepped out into the air above their upturned faces.

# *Part Five*

# SAND

*Carving is an articulation of something that already exists in the block. The carved form should never, in any profound imaginative sense, be entirely freed from its matrix.*

—Adrian Stokes, *The Stones of Rimini*

Cathcart, Ontario. April 2010.

You are a daughter possessed of a thorough and inquisitive disposition. I knew this to be true by the time your visit last summer was over. Your questions were motivated by curiosity, not obligation. I could see that. And I can see that your writing has the same impulse. Beneath the well-organized information of your brochure was an idea that you raised quite irresistibly: What would it be like to go back in time? What would it be like to meet Michelangelo on one of the mountain paths he must have walked?

And so I'm guessing. But as an attentive reader of this letter, and as an asker of many excellent questions, you might be wondering how it was that Miriam Goldblum, daughter of Hannah and Haim, came to be the director of the Christmas pageant at Montrose United Church. It's the first question about the story that comes to mind these days. But I never wondered about it when I was ten years old and in love with her.

To me, Miriam's raven-haired involvement in our church's Advent season was natural—as natural, I suppose, as the readings from the Old Testament that prophesy the merry celebrations of the New. Still, I learned much later from Winifred and Archibald Hughson that Miriam was the subject of intense discussion within the church. She first expressed her desire to direct the Christmas pageant in the fall of 1947.

"But you're Jewish," said Norbert Owen, the church treasurer, who liked to think he spoke plainly.

"So what's this?" Miriam replied. "The Führerbunker?"

The gesture was worthy of Bernhardt. The sweep of arm took in the pale chintz sofa, the framed watercolours, and the wall sconces of the Elsie McClintock Christian Fellowship Room of Montrose United Church.

The discussions that addressed this issue in the autumn of 1947 were not always as broadly ecumenical as might have been hoped. Feelings ran high. There were moments of the one joint meeting of the church's management and youth activity committees that were downright unpleasant.

The debates wandered into what most participants considered were unnecessarily obscure theological realms—but then, unnecessarily obscure theological realms were a specialty of Reverend Arthur Gorwell, the minister of Montrose. He had delivered many a Michaelmas sermon on prophecy and revelation.

In the end, what was revealed to the Hughsons by the controversy was something nasty and stupid. Winifred and Archie suspected it lurked somewhere in the pews of a congregation of which they were faithful members.

It was the following June—the June, that is, that followed Miriam's directorial debut at Montrose United Church—that Archie, coming up to the pool for his morning swim, discovered a dripping, crudely executed swastika emblazoned on the side of the bathing pavilion.

He had his swim anyway, since it was a lowering, muggy morning, rain was imminent, and he could see no reason not to. As he passed back and forth over the patio furniture that had been dumped into the deep end, he contemplated the nature of evil and the grace of forgiveness. With ten lengths to go in his morning regimen, the heavens opened, but as he had heard no thunder, he continued his stately breaststroke.

It was Archie's custom to swim with his glasses on—he

enjoyed looking at the stone figures that surrounded the pool. He was particularly admiring of the three maidens at the corner of the deep end with their water urns. The central figure—the one actually pouring the trickling cascade into the pool—was convincingly ancient and very well done. His gaze seemed always to fall on her. There was some quality to her that separated her from the others. Nice jugs, he always thought.

His lenses were wet and streaked, but his vision was not so obscured by the heavy rain that he didn't witness a sign of a just universe. At each of his consistently unhurried turns at the deep end he looked back to the pavilion where the water-soluble red paint, clearly not intended for application to stone, was being washed down the wall. By his eighth length the marking was gone, leaving only a puddle of watery pink on the flagstones. By his tenth that was gone too, seeping into the cracks of earth and grass between the old, worn slabs of marble.

That same afternoon a teenage boy from the neighbourhood—pleased to be asked to undertake such a mission—arrived at the pool with his swim mask and flippers and snorkel to fasten the ropes by which Archie and Winifred would pull the furniture from the water.

It might have been a random act, perpetrated by idiots too stupid to ascertain who was, in fact, a member of the group they claimed to despise. Were this the case, the Hughsons resisted what comfort might have been found in mistaken identity. They couldn't see that hate was any less hateful because it missed its target.

The Hughsons suspected motives a little more specific, for it was generally thought that it was Mrs. Hughson's burst of impatience at the joint meeting of the church management and youth activity committees the previous November that had carried the day for Miriam Goldblum. Mrs. Hughson's opinion was influential because of her reputation as a dedicated churchgoer, a long-time member of the women's auxiliary, and a devoted volunteer. "Oh, for goodness' sake," she exclaimed when she decided she had heard quite enough. "If our Lord was Jewish, I don't see why the director of the Christmas pageant can't be."

At the heart of the matter was not the dialectic of Judaic and Christian narratives—contrary to the presentation Dr. Gorwell made during the meeting of the committees in the Elsie McClintock Christian Fellowship Room. It was young romance. Miriam had a beau before the war who had been a drama student. His family went to Montrose.

He wrote poetry—mostly about Miriam. She had jet-black hair and the palest skin, as dozens of his sonnets made clear. He'd won the poetry prize in his last year at high school.

He was on the swim team. He was president of the drama club. He'd directed *Charley's Aunt.* He'd played Romeo.

Miriam's mother and father said that was all very well. They were sure he had many fine qualities. But it was hard to imagine anyone less Jewish than Bryson Scott.

"Yes," Miriam admitted. She spoke with the exasperated defensiveness she always ended up using in fights with her parents. "He's active in his church."

"Active?" Haim Goldblum said. "In a church? I don't like the sound of that."

Miriam shared Bryson's enthusiasm for Chekhov and Ibsen. And she shared his calling. She was an actress. "Since before she was five," her mother said, rolling her eyes. "For her, the mumps was Garbo in *Camille.*"

Miriam helped Bryson with the Montrose pageant the Christmas before the war. She was listed in the program as assistant director—an acknowledgment that raised no eyebrows so far as anyone knew. She was Bryson Scott's girlfriend. That was all. He had been mounting the pageant for several years.

Bryson suffered no illusions about the amateur production standards under which he was obliged to labour. But he thought that he could bring some real theatricality to the annual tradition. True, his experiment one year with actual barnyard animals hadn't worked out so well. But otherwise it was generally agreed he did an excellent job. And anyway, nobody else wanted to do it.

One terrible aspect of the war—insignificant in comparison to many others but relevant to the story at hand—was the way it distorted things by freezing them in time, like a photograph of a handsome young flyer in fleece-lined boots and leather bomber jacket. Had the war not intervened, Bryson and Miriam might well have stayed together, weathering the complications of religion and family bravely, and finally bringing together the Montagues and the Capulets at their happy, non-denominational wedding ceremony. On the other hand—and probably the more likely possibility in the more ordinary, more peaceful run of things—they might have just broken up. Young sweethearts often do.

They might have wondered, for a while, if they were going to get back together, and then, as time passed, they might have grown accustomed to the realization that they would not. Other boyfriends, other girlfriends would come along.

Over the years the two of them might occasionally have thought of one another. There is a place of special affection for a first love, and they might well have resided there in one another's memories: a kiss on a grassy hill by a college walkway in the autumn sunshine, a trembling hand on the snug white angora sweater it was daring to touch.

But that's not what happened.

Bryson ended up at the bottom of the English Channel along with the rest of the crew of a Lancaster bomber returning from a U-boat raid in 1945. Miriam ended up alone.

She decided—unwisely but with the conviction of the young and broken-hearted—that she would never love anyone else again. The photograph of the handsome flyer in fleece-lined boots and bomber jacket who didn't know pickled herring from gefilte fish sat on her mantel for the rest of her life. And Miriam Goldblum, the daughter of Haim and Hannah, continued to oversee the annual production of Bryson Scott's *The Wayward Lamb: A Christmas Story* at Montrose United Church.

My earliest association with the waxy, ecclesiastic sensation of marble occurred in 1958, when I was chosen for the role of the shepherd boy in Miriam's pageant. By then, *The Wayward Lamb*'s association with Bryson Scott was growing more archival for everyone except Miriam. His name appeared in the program that was run off every year on the Gestetner machine in the church office. He was credited as playwright and originator. But there were fewer and fewer people in attendance every Christmas who were sure who he was. Over the years, the annual production settled unquestionably into Miriam's domain.

The historic details of her association with Montrose United faded until it was only dimly known to the younger members of the congregation that there was something about it that was sad—but no more sad than the word frequently used to describe her. At what today seems a very young age to be defined with such apparent finality, she became a spinster.

Bryson Scott had written *The Wayward Lamb* because, when he was first asked to take on the pageant, he was enough of an undergraduate drama major to know that there were serious challenges to staging a story in which nothing happens. "Chekhov notwithstanding," Bryson always added. More challenging still: a story everyone knows.

Bryson couldn't see that there was a lot of stagecraft to be employed in the business of abiding in the fields, however frost-covered he was able to make the choir stalls and pulpits in which the shepherds stood. There's not a lot of action when it comes to watching sheep. And so Bryson Scott invented the story of a little shepherd boy who, searching for a lost lamb, becomes lost himself on a cold December night. But not just any cold December night, needless to say. His father sets out to find him.

The text was performed each Christmas at Montrose as faithfully as if the story had originated with one of the apostles. But in 1958—partly because I was quite small—Miriam Goldblum contemplated a change to the traditional staging.

Miriam could see possibilities in me that she had not previously imagined in the role of shepherd boy. I happened to be as slight and pale as any Hollywood casting agent would like a lost child to be. It wouldn't hurt that most of the people in the congregation knew that I was adopted.

Preparations for the Christmas pageant always began in November. This extended Advent always ended with a post-performance buffet dinner at Miriam's parents' modern, single-storey home. The cast, the stage crew, their families, and anyone who had helped with the pageant in any way—a good third of the congregation, usually—were invited. Miriam served a feast: potato and onion knishes that were made with enough schmaltz to oil a tank; moist, tender brisket; smoked whitefish salad; and gefilte fish with red (it had to be red) horseradish.

Reverend Gorwell was particularly fond of the rugelach. "My," he said at one of the first of what became a popular annual tradition for Montrose parishioners, "yours is a rich culinary heritage."

"We do what we can," said Haim Goldblum.

The appearance every November of Miriam's silk scarves, red lips, and black hair at Montrose was a clear sign of the passing of fall to winter. The caretaker took her arrival as the signal that he should soon retrieve the Christmas candles and wreaths from the cupboard above the tea service in the pale-blue kitchen behind the Sunday school piano. The choir began practising "The Trumpet Shall Sound." The Women's Circle started their careful planning for the carol service and poinsettia deliveries and white-gift Sunday.

Miriam threw herself into the challenges that each new production presented, insisting on more rehearsals than anyone ever thought necessary but that always proved, somehow, to be barely enough. Partly because the choir robe acted as a convenient duster, but mostly because it gave her a swoop of drama and authority, Miriam's cashmere breasts and nylon stockings always preceded a black, billowing train as she worked through her blocking on the chancel steps. Rehearsals took place on Thursday evenings in the sanctuary.

Miriam liked everyone to go off-book as early in the process as possible—even if this meant her chief role for the first several rehearsals was prompting. "Frankincense," she would intone from the shadows of one of the rear pews when Melchior forgot his line. "I have travelled far, bearing Frankincense for the king foretold."

My costume was a bathrobe and a towel. Everyone's was. Miriam was a good sport, which, of course, made me love her all the more. She laughed along with everyone else when Melchior read his line in one rehearsal as: "I have travelled far, bearing toothpaste for the king foretold."

I remember feeling very grown-up to be included in the enjoyment everyone took in his joke. I felt I was part of a special team, one that met in the evenings in the spooky, darkened church. The grey marble floor felt cool and strange under my bare feet.

Miriam clapped her hands. "All right, all right. Thank you, Mr. Brown. Now, shall we pick it up at the second shepherd's 'I see by the richness of your garments . . . ' Mr. Hannaford, if you please . . ."

I was required to hide—a concealment of the lost shepherd boy that could work to much greater dramatic effect, so Miriam Goldblum hoped, than in any previous production of *The Wayward Lamb.* But in order for the trick to work, I had to take my place on the chancel steps before the congregation began settling into the pews for the service—a process of muttered good mornings, clearing throats, rustling church calendars, and organ prelude that might take as much as half an hour. I had to lie perfectly still on a marble step, concealed by a cardboard outcropping of biblical-looking rock. I was obliged to remain there, unmoving, until the moment when I heard my cue.

This wasn't easy, as Miriam Goldblum was the first to admit. She informed me, at one of the first rehearsals, that nothing in the theatre ever was. As she spoke, her large eyes seemed to lose their focus. She looked beyond me into a past that I took to be rich in curtain-call and gracefully cradled bouquets. She told me she had played Juliet, and that lying still as death in the tomb had been no piece of cake. "Timing is all," she said, and for a strange awkward moment I thought she was going to cry. But then she girded herself with her brave, red smile and carried on.

Miriam had decided that my hiding space would be small. Very small. Impossibly small. The scenery that hid me was, in fact, one of the several pieces of rubble that flanked the empty tomb Mary Magdalene found during the Easter presentation every spring. There were bigger pieces of the Easter set, including the five-foot-high boulder that had sealed the tomb of the crucified Christ. It was this large outcropping of papier mâché that had been used in past years to hide the shepherd boy. But Miriam had something else in mind.

She knew that if the rock was big and obvious, the congregation would assume there was a lost child behind it. As there always was. But that wasn't going to happen.

The revelation of my presence would only be effective if it seemed entirely impossible that anyone was there. "A *coup de théâtre,*" Miss Goldblum said, exuding an enthusiasm for French idiom that perfectly suited the cloud of perfume in which she was always enveloped.

And so, for ten minutes, or sometimes (depending on how many flubbed lines there were) closer to fifteen, I lay on my stomach every Thursday evening, stretched behind a piece of cardboard rubble that seemed too small to conceal anything. As a result, one of my clearest memories of *The Wayward Lamb* is cold marble. And my pressing oddly against its hard, sacramental smoothness.

Montrose had been completed toward the end of the 1920s. Marble was put to generous use. Such grand, solemn aspiration was the result of an upswing in the economy that, like all such robust, happy periods, was doomed to be replaced by something like its opposite. But by the Depression, Montrose's marble was firmly, unmovably in place. It was too heavy to have anything further to do with economic cycles. It looked like it had been there forever.

At the first rehearsal, Miriam Goldblum took my hand and led me to the hiding place she had chosen. She seemed, as she leaned over me, to fill not just my vision but the entire dark space of the church.

Miriam's dramatic inclination extended to her startling makeup. Her brows arched severely. Her nails were longer and a little more red than even her position as a woman of the theatre might have required. Her lips were wide and very red. Her black hair fell abundantly to the shoulders of her choir gown and its hem cascaded over the white stone steps. "You mustn't move," she instructed me. There was always mint on her heavy, sweet breath. "You must be as still as a statue."

Her long, flattened hand smoothed the place where she wanted me to lie. I did as I was told. And on that Thursday night, as at the rehearsals and the performance that followed, I became aware of something like discomfort, something like pleasure that was pushing against the stone. This hadn't happened before. And then the Angel spoke.

Angel: Wither goest thou on this poor . . .

Miriam Goldblum (*prompting*): "What do you seek?" Please, Mrs. Rymal. "What do you seek, poor shepherd, on this cold night?"

Angel: Sorry. What do you seek, poor shepherd, on this cold night?

I lay there, waiting, flushed, turning red in the face, hoping that no one would notice the front of my bathrobe when I had to stand to deliver my line.

Shepherd Father: Oh, strange visitor. I am seeking my son on this cold night. He is only young. And he went in search of a wayward lamb. And now the sky has grown dark. And there are wolves.

Sound Cue: *Wolves.*

Angel: Fear not. For this is a blessed night, as the prophets of old have foretold. And what was lost shall now be found.

Shepherd Father: I kneel to pray that this be true. (*He kneels.*)

Angel: Your faith is rewarded, old man. (*Exit Angel.*)

Shepherd Boy (*calling from concealment*): Here I am, Father.

"But don't rush your line, Oliver," Miriam said to me at the first rehearsal. "Allow a moment of silence to build after your father gets to his knees. A pause of expectation. A few beats for his prayers to rise to the heavens. Just as there are always a few long beats of nothing before Juliet awakens in her tomb. This is key. Do you see what I mean?"

I said I did.

"Timing is all," Miriam Goldblum said. "We must not hurry our moments." Her eyes were large. She reached to my forehead and began to smooth my hair dreamily. A shiver of fortitude ran through her, and her face became businesslike again.

Miriam stood—with a momentary wobble on her heels. But she smoothed the front of her skirt so briskly it seemed as if her unsteadiness never happened. She turned away from me, toward the white stage of the altar, in a swirl of perfume and choir gown.

"We shall be brilliant." Her voice called out to everyone. "I just know it. We shall devastate them all."

And so, it is here, at what I admit is a late stage of my letter writing, that things begin to circle back to where they began . . .

# CHAPTER THIRTY-FIVE

IT WAS THE LAST THING Michael Barton expected.

He was somewhere the hell in the rear of the advance. A dog-fuck. So said the Yanks.

This was the fucking northwest sector. This was fucking Italy. This was fucking August, in fucking 1944.

They were securing the dusty road to the south. This was the road that had been secured three days before. And two days before that. "The army secures roads the way it fills in forms," his C.O. muttered when detailing the orders. "In goddamn triplicate."

The road wasn't much more than a dusty brown line between the plane trees. There hadn't been anything German on it for more than a week.

The occasional crack of artillery echoed from the hills. The tanks were continuing north.

His position was just past the cemetery. He was in a marble

yard—one of several on the perimeter of the town. It was on the flats between the hills and the sea, backing onto railroad tracks that had been bombed to uselessness months before. The yard was a shipping area for blocks of stone, crusted brown on their outside but white with grey veins on their cuts. They were on wooden skids, lined in rows.

He was thinking that they looked like giant iceboxes, a thought that led him to a momentary daydream of cold beer. Then he heard the transport.

It was the only time in his life he could say, with perfect accuracy, that he couldn't believe his eyes. He stared blankly for almost five seconds, not entirely acknowledging what was there.

What could have been more unlikely than a German supply truck coming around the burnt-out farmhouse? What could have been more improbable than a Jerry flatbed bouncing over the potholes toward him?

There was nothing cautious about the attitude of the soldiers who were in it. What led them to think that they could drive straight up the ass-end of the Allied advance, he couldn't imagine. Then he heard their singing.

Christ, he thought. They're pissed.

He could not clearly see the driver, nor the man seated beside him. But three others were perfectly visible standing on the back. They were holding on to a rail behind the cab of the truck. Michael felt a smile crease the dust that covered his face.

There was something about the angle of the light that brought the transport into precise focus. The leader—at least the leader of the singing—had the happy, wide-open face of a young man who enjoyed his friends as much as he enjoyed anything. His free hand swung like a bandleader's baton. Except for their helmets and their grey uniforms, they could have been students hitching a ride home from a good party.

It wasn't that Michael Barton tried to miss. But there was something about the innocence of their approach that was unsettling. He was a good shot. But he allowed his aim to be careless.

He reasoned that their coming under fire when they so obviously anticipated nothing of the sort would alert them to their error. They might turn around before they reached the bridge. Instantly sober, they might just get the fuck off the road. Michael Barton's wasn't the most rigorous of military disciplines.

"A bit of a good-time Charlie, I see," Brigadier Todd had said, looking up from his desk in the red-brick Cathcart Armoury. A few trophies were listed on the form in front of him. "A yachtsman?"

"Speedboats, sir," Michael replied. It was a correction he'd made to people more than once.

Todd was even less impressed than he would have been with sloops. Anyone with the money to buy a powerboat could race one, presumably. "The newspaper Bartons, is it?"

"My father, sir," Michael said.

"But my understanding is that you are not seeking a commission."

"No, sir," Michael said. "I am not. The ranks are my preference."

"I see," Todd said. He considered the slender young man in front of him. His tan and his sun-lightened hair were the result, it seemed obvious, of an uninterrupted summer vacation. Todd guessed that the life of an enlisted man would not be a preference for very long.

Michael Barton should have just cut the three soldiers in half. Then he should have picked off the two others when they jumped from the cab of the truck. But he didn't.

He was pretty much sick of all of it by then.

He preferred, that afternoon, in that softly exact light, to be inexact. He preferred to imagine these jokers telling the same kind of story that he would enjoy telling: About how they found an abandoned farmhouse somewhere north of Lucca with a cellar full of wine, and how they holed up there for who knows how long. The Italian campaign had passed them by. They were so tired they probably could have passed out for a week. They were all pretty much sick of it by then, too.

And then, can you believe it, they almost drove, singing, straight into a town occupied by Allied command.

He squeezed the trigger. And it was the last thing Michael Barton expected.

The explosion hit him like a cuffed hand. The ball of orange obliterated the truck and the men. The smoke was like a dark fist, clenching and unclenching as it grew bigger. Michael never heard out of his right ear again.

He had no idea what they were carrying. He never did figure it out. He guessed that his first burst of gunfire sparked off the truck's chassis. It must have ignited whatever was under the roped canvas on the flatbed.

There was some wind coming in from the sea. The smoke thinned.

Their clothing was mostly gone. As was their hair. As was their skin. Their eyes were crazy with pain, and the holes of their mouths gaped with the howls they could not make. Their slow, sprawled movements on the ground were like the scattered legs of an insect torn away from its body.

As Michael stepped through shards of tire and metal he could see that one of them had spotted him and was struggling to reach his service revolver. Both the belt and the gun were improbably intact: good brown leather, solid black handle.

He gently moved the soldier's fumbling hands away. The

wrists felt like gristle. There was a sweet smell that would, for the rest of his life, seep into his many nightmares.

It seemed important to Michael that he should explain. But all he could do was meet their eyes with what, from that day on, would be the terrible sadness of his own. Only when he was back in the marble yard, leaning against one of the slabs of stone, did he realize he still had the now-empty Luger in his hand.

# CHAPTER THIRTY-SIX

CHARLES DICKENS'S TRAVEL JOURNAL, *Pictures from Italy*, opens with a departure from Paris. The trip begins on a midsummer morning in 1846 when an English travelling-carriage clattered out the gate of the Hotel Meurice in the Rue de Rivoli. "Going through France" is the opening chapter of a book that eventually takes Dickens—someone who seemed surprised to be so delighted by Italy—to Genoa, Bologna, Ferrara, Venice, and Rome, but also to the marble quarries of Carrara.

One of the two Parisian landmarks Dickens mentioned, as he passed out of the city on that midsummer morning, was a curious one: "the dismal morgue." It seems strange for him to pick this from amid so much else that the rattling English travelling-coach must have passed on that Sunday morning. And Oliver always wondered if it was in retrospect that the idea of using the morgue as a symbol had come to Dickens. He wondered if it was after Dickens had experienced the warmth of the Mediterranean that he thought of Paris as something that stood in sepulchral contrast to what he called "the bright remembrance" of "cheerful Tuscany."

Because it had been the same for him. Paris looked grey and dismal early one spring morning in 1968. The sun was not yet up. The pale old city was already busy bracing itself for upheaval when Oliver Hughson started south.

# CHAPTER THIRTY-SEVEN

Angel was a stone cold beauty. She was the kind of dame a man would kill for.

When Anna told the story there was always a gun on the kitchen table. It never did anything. Chekhov notwithstanding. It never went off. But she always included it in her description. It was a reminder that things are bound to go wrong.

The car was from the days when sedans were as big as boxcars. Its headlights were slashing through the shadows of the drive.

It was an old house in the country outside a town near the border. Everything gleamed, the way the nighttime does in black and white movies. This was the world Anna thought Oliver came from. It wasn't surprising, really. She'd never learned much more about America.

It wouldn't have been all that difficult—through veterans' associations and army records—for Anna to have tracked down the G.I.s who'd made their way up from the ruins of the villa, through the outcropping of rock, to the village of Castello in the aftermath of the massacre. But Anna only ever said that she was saved by the Yanks. And left it at that.

It was difficult to tell whether she viewed it as a good thing or just the best that could have been hoped for under the screwed-up circumstances of Europe in August 1944. "We were all saved," she said, "by Betty Grable and Lucky Strike and Hollywood." She shrugged. "What can you do?"

Angel moves to the window. She watches the car coming through the darkness. The light through the venetian blinds makes her smooth fall of hair look almost white. It is parted on her left, and its wave almost covers her right eye.

Good, she thinks. That bastard Johnny's here.

They move the heroin across the border near Niagara in statues: in the antiques and memorials and ornamental statuary that Angel guides through customs with her fur coats and her great legs and her enthusiasm for fine Italian sculpture that the guards always so enjoy.

She has a killer figure. She has a winning smile. She has a good prep school accent. For a hustler.

The junk is out of Indochina. By way of a lab in Marseilles and the manager of a marble exporter in Italy. That's where Johnny comes in. He works in a marble workshop on the Canadian side—about sixty miles away. He knocked up some girl there. He delivers every few months.

There isn't much that can surprise Angel. She's been around the block once or twice. But the news Johnny brings raises an eyebrow. Her left, to be precise.

She holds the cigarette in a V of elegant fingers. The smoke drifts across her face.

"Say that again," she says quietly.

"She's dead," Johnny repeats.

"I see."

"I didn't mean to. The baby was crying. She was shouting. So I smacked her."

Again, the left eyebrow. Angel is familiar with the way men smack.

Another drift of smoke.

"Okay. So a couple of times. So I smacked her a couple of times. But the thing was she fell. She just tripped over her own fucking feet. She was holding the baby. So she couldn't, you know, stop herself. She just fell. And she cracked her head against the corner of the bed frame. Right here."

He points to his right temple, as if with the barrel of a pistol.

"And that was it. Kapow. Just like that."

"Just like that," Angel says. She speaks slowly and with more skepticism than she feels.

"Whaddya think? That I wanted to kill her?"

"So you brought her here?"

"What else am I going to do with her? You got fields. You got woods."

"And the baby?"

"What am I going to do with two kilos of yellow powder, a dead body, and a baby? Call Children's Aid?"

"So what did you do with the baby?"

"I left it. Lino will take care of the baby. There's no goddamn problem there. But what I gotta do is disappear. Fast. Can you get me across?"

"I thought you said the old man was sick."

"He's not so old. He just looks it. And he's not that sick. He had a stroke. Not so sick that he won't hear a baby crying."

Angel considers all this.

One less border is always a good thing. And anyway, she'd

been thinking recently that the city was one big headache. This hood's turf. That hood's turf. She'd get in trouble sooner or later. That was for sure. And that's why she'd been thinking maybe the future isn't a big city. Maybe it's near the border. Maybe it's between the driveways and the lawns of suburbs and towns. They have families. They have money. They have kids who will want to get high.

She stubs out her cigarette.

Johnny is sitting across from her, bent forward, his head in his hands. He has dark hair, broad shoulders, strong arms.

He isn't crying. She kind of wishes he was. But the plan that is beginning to take shape is worth the risk. She's thinking about a small ornamental stone and monument operation on the American side. She'd have to be careful of Johnny, that's all. He has a selfish streak she'd have to watch.

But she knows how to handle him.

"Come here, you big dope," she says. And she shimmies to one side of the armchair to give him room.

# CHAPTER THIRTY-EIGHT

LINO CAVATORE HAS BEEN LISTENING to the baby cry for more than an hour. It was late at night when it started. But it was not for him to interfere.

He looks ashen. He looks very tired. He has always looked older than he is. But now his appearance seems to him not to be misleading. He feels old.

He might recover. He might be able to move easily again. The doctors say there is hope at his age. They say this very sadly, though. And after more than three decades in Cathcart, Lino knows English well enough to understand what they mean. They are saying that with strokes like this there's always hope. Just not much.

When Lino learned his trade in the Morrow studio in Carrara he was thrilled with the process of carving stone. The *sbozzatore* first roughs out the block with his point chisel. This is the beginning. Then the more detailed carvers work the stone, first with flat and claw chisels, then with an ever-more-fine system of rasps. Then the polishing.

He has a skill. He doesn't think of it as a gift—even if everyone else does. It's luck more than anything. It's just a talent he has.

Lino has the ability to see the one thing that makes a good piece of sculpture good. And a great piece of sculpture great. And to copy that. The size is just a question of mathematics. Copies are Lino's bread and butter. Michelangelo is a specialty. Lino sees nothing cheap in this.

When he was learning his trade his copying was always faithful, precise, devotional. He is proud of this. And anyway, when Michelangelo was little more than a boy, it was the skill of his copying that first drew attention to his genius. Vasari reports that the young Michelangelo "used to tinge his copies and make them appear black with age by various means, including the use of smoke, so that they could not be told apart from the originals." As a teenager, Michelangelo carved a Cupid in white marble and then buried it for a time so that it could be convincingly passed off as an antique.

Lino uses the same technique. He buries his marble figures—after knocking off a nose or an arm with a crack of his point chisel. But he adds to Michelangelo's technique six months of a trick he learned from Julian Morrow.

Lino is not a big man, but he pisses like a horse. For six months his torrents rain down on the earthen courtyard outside his studio on the outskirts of Cathcart. As he pees he looks out at the hydro lines and strawberry fields past his workshop.

Making souvenirs is how he first learned his business. When he was an apprentice in Carrara, his sibyls cradled telephones. His Bacchus was a candelabra. His Davids and his *Pietà*s were sold in railway shops in Florence and Rome and Milan. He did cigarette lighters. He did fountains.

In the marble studios in Carrara where he had apprenticed—and from the time he stepped, in the early spring of 1932, from the last of the trains that had taken him from Halifax to Montreal, to Toronto, to Cathcart—Lino was proud of the tradition of which he was part.

He wore a blue stoneworker's jacket. It came almost to his knees. His smudged glasses, his impatience with what was often the less than satisfactory efforts of the crew he oversaw on the grounds of Barton House, and his frenetic energy gave him the aspect of a finicky maiden aunt. He wore dust hats made of folded newspaper.

Lino would eventually settle in Cathcart, establishing Cavatore Memorial and Ornamental Stone on an overgrown lot he found at the scruffy end of Locket Street. This was not part of anyone's original plan. Lino's goodbyes to his mother and to his brother had not been the farewells of someone who would never return to Italy.

It was Grace Barton's death that had inspired this unexpected idea. Lino noted how quickly money and resources were marshalled for the memorial. He was impressed by the sedan that had pulled into the gravel driveway where he had established his temporary workshop on the Barton property, and he was impressed with the neatly dressed, efficient young woman from the *Chronicle* offices who stepped from it. No one had prepared for this considerable expense. And yet, there was Argue Barton's secretary, in a crisp blouse and woollen suit, stepping through the unfinished statuary on the driveway, handing him a manila envelope containing reference photographs of Isabella of Aragon's tomb and a cheque, signed by Argue Barton, for this sad, additional assignment.

Lino was beginning to see the true affluence of the place where he had ended up—affluent, that is, compared to the place from which he'd come. And it was while he was working on Grace's tomb that Lino Cavatore began to ask himself a question he had never previously considered: What if he stayed?

Lino had always seemed to be more sinew than flesh, and well before he was thirty he had a wizened tightness that made him appear much older than he was. It was as if he were passing through time more quickly than other men did—a characteristic that accorded with his serious nature. It isn't very common to have a stroke in middle age, but when Lino collapsed in the workshop of Cavatore Memorial and Ornamental Stone in 1948, nobody was all that surprised.

His voice had always seemed taut and elderly. The resolute intensity with which Lino had always confronted the turns of his own destiny made him steadily predictable. He would always do good work. He would always provide for those who depended on him. But Julian Morrow had been surprised on that late autumn afternoon in 1932 when, standing at the window of his villa, overlooking his pool and garden, he had opened the carefully addressed envelope and learned that Lino wanted to stay in Cathcart.

In the letter—one it took Lino days to compose, revise, write, and rewrite—he told Morrow of his decision. He could see opportunity in a place that would always need bank foyers and bathroom counters and cemetery monuments but that had no local access to stone or the skills needed to work it. The deep sadness that was buried in Lino's decision—the sadness of his not returning to the green valleys and blue sky of the hills in which he had grown up—was not something he acknowledged.

The truth was Lino was a lonely man, but his loneliness was not something he ever regarded as anything other than an unchangeable fact. Like the weather in the quarries, it was just the way it was. Loneliness was something he expressed in his exacting standards and impatience with incompetence.

He didn't care much for where he'd ended up. Everything was ugly. Except for the strawberries in June and the tomatoes in the early fall, the food was awful. But loneliness here was the same as loneliness there. He had the same useless desires. He had the same burning dreams.

Morrow was irritated by the letter at first. Lino's was a rare talent, and Morrow was unhappy about losing it. But it did not take him long to reconsider. His own practical self-interest helped him to see when the self-interest of others could be used to advantage.

Morrow knew Lino's to be the determined logic of emigration—and no logic was more compelling. There was money in Cathcart. It was as simple as that. Lino Cavatore had a mother and a crippled brother to support.

Morrow answered promptly. He wrote to say he understood. About seeing opportunity. At a reasonable but by no means overly generous rate of interest, he made available the funds needed to purchase the Locket Street property and the faded frame cottage at its edge. And, of course, Morrow International would supply (at a deferred but mutually advantageous price) whatever stone the new business would require.

But the baby is still crying in the night. And this has gone on for more than an hour.

So Lino Cavatore makes his way, very slowly and with great difficulty, from the little frame house at the edge of the workshop's property. In the dark, he finds his way through panels of marble lined up like trays in the yard. The bigger blocks are like iceboxes. He is on his way to the apartment above the workshop where, over the years, the apprentices he brings out from Italy have stayed.

Gianni's car is gone. This is odd. At this hour.

He unlocks the studio. With only one arm that works properly this takes a few minutes. Twice, he drops the keys.

The wide-planked floors, deep sills, and high, raftered ceilings of the studio look as if they have been carved from a cliff of marble. The rough wooden shelves are white. The maquettes are white. The armatures are white. The calipers and files and claw chisels are white. Only the workbench has had the marble dust swept off.

It was the worst luck.

Not the stroke. That was bad luck enough. But it was the worst luck that of all the apprentices he has had over the years, it was this one—this handsome one, this useless one—who was there when Lino Cavatore was taken to the hospital and then, five weeks later, returned to the workshop and his home.

He couldn't speak. He could not move very well. And this one, the handsome one, the useless one, was up to no good, somehow. Lino could see that. He had been planning to send him home. He didn't trust him.

And then the girl moved into the rooms above the workshop.

And then there was the baby.

He's seen such things before—a girl so young and strong she could hide it almost until her time. He hadn't noticed himself for a long time.

But what are they thinking? Lino collapses for a moment in his chair, beside the stove where he heats the abrasives he uses on stone. He is amazed at how tired he is. He feels like he wants to sleep.

They are keeping the baby a secret. From her parents, he guesses. They are living in a hiding place.

They are children, he thinks. They are playing house.

The stairs to the apartment above the studio are steep and narrow and very difficult. It takes him forever.

He knows immediately that something is wrong. The baby is on the bed. Even before he sees the blood on the floor he knows something is wrong. He stands there, unmoving, for almost a minute.

His mind is still good. He sees things clearly. He knows what he is going to do.

He senses how much movement is still possible. He can feel it inside him. He knows his left arm is useless, but the right is not so bad. He shuffles stiffly and slowly. But he does shuffle. If he finds something he can carry with one hand it could work. There is a pail.

He moves slowly in the darkness. He finds the blanket in the dresser. The wool is soft, the colour of dusty rose. It was sent to him by an aunt a few years after he first moved to Cathcart—long before it became clear, even to his female relatives, that he had no interest in finding a wife.

He finds a cardboard box. Aylmer. Grade A.

He flattens the cardboard with his feet. Then he squeezes it as firmly as he can under his elbow. He tucks the baby boy into the blanket and then curls it, as if he were seated, into the pail.

The streets are empty. There are crickets in the hedges he passes and in the dewy, carefully tended lawns.

When, almost two hours later, he makes his way back down through the garden from the pool, he does not return to Cavatore Memorial and Ornamental Stone. He turns right, not left, at the corner of Hillside Avenue. He isn't sure why. He is too tired to think. He wants to sleep so badly he thinks he might be dreaming. He still has the pail. And he continues up, along the switchback trails, stones slipping underfoot, slowly, so slowly, up.

# CHAPTER THIRTY-NINE

TOWARD THE END OF HIS LIFE, the frail old man had taken to sitting on a white patio chair while he worked. Cleaning the pool was his job, and so long as the pool was open—so long as the old filter was humming in its shed and the water was not yet covered for the winter—the job never ended. The old man was always cleaning the pool.

He was slowly poling hand over hand, drawing the head of the vacuum across the bottom. He had mastered this long ago.

It was unexpected to find him cleaning the pool at night. But it wasn't the time that was surprising, even though vacuuming the pool in the dark was something he had never done before.

But in the dream—one that marked the only few seconds of actual sleep that Oliver had on his flight from Toronto to Milan—it was not clear what other reason there could be.

Archie Hughson always held the long handle of the vacuum with his fingertips as if he were playing a flute. "I first fell in love with his hands," Mrs. Hughson once said—a remark made to Oliver at the dinner table when he was ten.

The Hughsons were affectionate with one another but reserved, and it may have been the uncharacteristic intimacy of Mrs. Hughson's confession—made when her husband was not yet back from work, made over the tinned spaghetti and milk she served because Oliver liked that particular dinner so much and because he had an evening rehearsal at the church—that kept the comment in Oliver's memory.

He was floating. He was staying still in the water. He was watching Mr. Hughson's hands as he cleaned the pool. In the rising backwash of old age, Archie Hughson's elegant fingers were the last shoals of his physical grace.

The old man sat, bowed forward, his floppy sun hat almost joining the raised knees of his loose khaki slacks. His forearms, outstretched, were slender, almost youthful in form, but they were mottled and badly bruised. The summer before he died he said, "My skin is so thin now. Every time I bump into something I start to bleed."

The water was black. The deck was made of marble paving stones, worn with age. Around the periphery could be seen, even in the dark, hermits and saints, satyrs and maidens shielding their faces from the ages with their draped folds of stone. At the deep end, the graceful form of a female figure was pouring water from a jug into the pool. Two other maidens, in the distance, were approaching.

The hillside loomed. It was little more than a wooded ridge. But it was like a bank of cloud, and those rising trails led up, Oliver knew, not to street lights and garages and tracts of Cathcart's new suburbs but to the cobbled square and thick walls of an ancient town.

When Oliver found the old man in a white plastic patio

chair, in the middle of the night, the still, humid air was heavy as slumber. He wanted to speak to him, of course, but that was out of the question. He was working silently, unimpeachable, in a realm that could not be disrupted, and Oliver knew that any movement he made would be a mistake. It was as if, rising from a midnight pond, he had come across something magical on the shore.

Oliver floated in the shallow end, trying to slow his breathing, trying to shield the silent air from the loudness of his heart. He knew that the slightest commotion—say the swallow of some familiar sadness—would change everything. The islands of lilac and maple trees, mapped black against the violet sky, would erupt with the hard memorial wings of an even older dream, and everything would be gone.

*Epilogue*

# EMERY

*He went round and round the form until he had achieved a polished surface of such accomplishment and perfection that the beholder experiences an intense desire to savour this shape in an uninterrupted circuit.*

—Rudolf Wittkower, on Constantin Brancusi's *Bird*

CATHCART, ONTARIO. APRIL 2010.

However late it comes, this is not the ending I have in mind. Like everyone, I expect more to follow. Like everyone, I count on things continuing.

I am now sitting on a chaise at my old pool in Cathcartario. It's not so hot and bright anymore. It's only April. It's getting chilly. But I'll write a little longer.

The bare trees seem very still. The sky is more pewter in colour than grey. But the marble flagstones are still warm underfoot from when the sun was out.

I've had some difficulty with the pool's filter system recently. And the cover won't last another season. So perhaps it's just as well that I am leaving. Perhaps, after all, I'm right. For once. It's time for me to be unreasonable.

I'm not sure I've said this to you directly. But if I'm going to, I might as well say it now.

I think I only made one serious mistake in my life. Thousands of unserious ones, of course. But only one that was serious. Only one that was a very bad mistake to make.

Of course, I didn't know you existed—not until you appeared, striding so determinedly up through the garden almost a year ago. And even though it was my mistake that caused this ignorance, I can't blame myself for what I didn't know.

But what I can be blamed for is this: it is up to all of us to know what we most love. Youth is no excuse for turning away from it. Nor is responsibility. We cannot always be reasonable. Love isn't. We cannot always do what is expected of us. Your mother knew that better than most.

There is no one to guide us, no one to inform us, no one

to instruct us about love. We have to know it for ourselves—otherwise it is not love. The same is true of beauty. It comes too rarely to be mistaken for anything else. It comes too seldom for us to afford a mistake.

Once that summer—it must have been in mid-July—Anna and I climbed the trails behind her farmhouse, up to the town of Castello. Anna did not visit the place often, but not, I eventually realized, for the reasons one might expect. She was not very sentimental. She didn't go very often to Castello because, as a general rule, she had no need to. But that summer someone opened a small restaurant, with a patio that had a view from the Castello wall, up the dusky headlands toward Cinque Terre and out to the sea. One evening—when we both had a little money from modelling—we decided that we would go.

We'd made our decision a little later than was advisable for anyone climbing up toward Castello on the steep wooded trails in the evening. I remember being surprised by the sudden nighttime of temperature when we stepped from the open field. We had not thought to bring a flashlight. After our initial adjustment to the darkness, this turned out to be a good thing.

The lattice of black leaves and the long hollows through the trees of the path we were following proved to be like magic. Sometimes Anna led me. Sometimes I led her. And this was our upward climb, sometimes talking, sometimes laughing, sometimes stopping to kiss, but never, not once, letting go of one another's hand. This, so ordinary, is the greatest claim I have to ever being truly alive.

On the face of it, I suppose, when I come back to the place where I once spent a summer, there will be a much older woman than the one I remember. But Anna's a sculptor. She's not much interested in what's on the face of anything.

She will be carving stone under a green canopy of light beside an old farmhouse in the Tuscan hills. She won't look quite the way I remember her, of course. But that won't matter. I'll have another perspective now. That's what time is for.

Behind her, at the bottom of the garden, at a spot where once there had been an ancient spring, there will soon be a white figure. The sky will be the bluest of blue. The hills will be the greenest green.

# ABOUT THE AUTHOR

DAVID MACFARLANE has won numerous national magazine and national newspaper awards. His memoir of Newfoundland, *The Danger Tree*, won the Canadian Authors Association Award for Nonfiction, and his novel, *Summer Gone*, was a finalist for the Giller Prize and won the Chapters/Books in Canada First Novel Award. He writes a weekly column in the *Toronto Star*. Macfarlane lives in Toronto.